Arrant Press

Forever Human

Tom Conyers, an award-winning filmmaker (The Caretaker – 2012), is also a poet, playwright, painter, illustrator and photographer. To check out his other books, including *Morse Code for Cats, One Shot* and the poetry collection *The Crime of Rhyme,* please visit his website:

www.tomconyers.com

Copyright © 2014 Tom Conyers

ISBN: 0980587115
ISBN-13: 978-0980587111

PRAISE FOR TOM CONYERS' NOVEL
FOREVER HUMAN

'(E)very literature professor's wildest dream. The layers, the literary references to other authors and genres, the social commentary, the biblical references, the interplay of characters, the foundations of physics and how we view reality; I could easily see getting an entire semester's worth of course materials from this one book … (D)eserves 4 out of 4 stars. It is a sweeping, epic tale of true love, redemption, reality and free will and it literally blew me away.'

OnlineBookClub.org review by S. Blake

'Centres around a multi-lifetime, multi-dimensional love story between Henri (art) and Cassius (science) … The secondary characters really bring the story to life, fading in and out at random, believing the rest of the world to be mad when really it is they themselves who hold that distinction.

D.Z.C, author, People Like Us, Xanadu

'(A) mind bogglingly beautiful story … tales like this merit the thumb worn pages of all literary triumph. I'm a bit star-struck.'

Mark White, film producer, The Caretaker

FOREVER
HUMAN

TOM CONYERS

ARRANT
PRESS

FOREVER HUMAN

This is a work of imagination that riffs on certain
historical events and persons. A great deal of the plot,
and many of the characters, are fictitious.

**Edited by Judie Litchfield
& Bryony Sutherland
Cover Design & Interior Illustrations by BrightSpark**

Author's Preface

I have long-enjoyed sampling in music, whereby musicians reuse snatches of other people's work in their own to create something new and fresh. The technique has been a mainstay of rap and some electronic music (the most famous Australian proponent would probably be the band The Avalanches), but it is not without controversy and potential legal ramifications.

Critics argue that it shows a distinct lack of imagination; supporters, that it can help create original, transformative work.

I am in the latter camp, and have for some time been keen to try my hand at a literary mash-up. Whilst this was acceptable in the past (even Shakespeare recycled, often verbatim), it can get you into copyright trouble today.

In Forever Human, I have avoided the problem by 'sampling' only texts that are over a hundred years old — that is, assuredly out of copyright. You'll find here countless uncredited quotes and near quotes from both creative and historical writers, all rubbing shoulders with my own writing. My own writing, however, still constitutes the vast bulk of the book.

I hope you'll agree the resulting mix is an original work that captures the oxymoronic quality of all human history: same but different.

Tom Conyers, Melbourne 2014

History

When I was young,
I saw life as a puzzle just begun.
Soon I was told
It was a picture completed of old.

– Anonymous, Circa 1750

Chapter One

Don't Let Them Get You.

Sunday 10th July, Melbourne 2005.

It's two days since I called. Two. And now I'm at a disadvantage. If I rang again that would say I'm desperate. And I won't do that. I just won't. Oh, I wish I'd never rung! That happens. You ring and they never ring back, and then they've got that over you: that you rang and they ignored you; that you needed them but they didn't respond. What if I rang now? If they're out again, I'd have to leave a message, and that wouldn't be answered either. No, that prospect's too horrible. To have it happen twice — horrible! No, I've still got strength enough to resist that. Why'd I ever ring!

A day's delay is fine. Yes, I can handle that, but longer is uncaring. No two ways. Plain nasty. You have to get them the first time you ring or you're done for, because they never ring back and then they've got that over you.

But I can't ever catch them out. When you run into them later — it could be months — you'll say, 'Didn't you get my call?' and then you've shown you care.

And what do they say?

'Oh, sorry. So-and-so couldn't have passed on your message' or 'I was going to ring tonight.'

Well, it's hard to prove either way. Intentions are like that. You can intend a million things but they amount to nothing if you never carry out a single one. But they've still got you, of course. And you can't call them a liar, because that's hard to prove. But they won't get me and I won't ring again, and when I run into them and they apologise for not phoning back, I'll pretend I can't remember ever having rung.

This is what I'll do. When they say, 'Oh, sorry I didn't ring back' I'll go, 'When?'

'Oh, um, quite awhile ago now.'

'Really? Well, I can't think why I would've rung *you*.'

Yes, that'll get them! I'll have it over them then! Won't be much of a victory but something, at least. I'll retain a little pride.

They know, you know. They know I know their games, but I won't let on, and neither will they.

Neither party ever knows for certain that the other knows, and that's the worst of it – that neither party lets on.

I ring anyway. (Only in my head, of course, and it's charming.) 'Hello,' I say, and 'Hello' they say back. And then I say, 'Don't you wish we could all stop pretending?' and they agree and then the magic takes over. Then, after their every sentence, I enthuse, 'Yes, that's how I feel too.' And they do the same.

But no, that's defeatist. That's what they want – the make-believe, and if you go along with it you'll never be happy with real people. And then they've got you. The hard thing's accepting people as they are, and not letting on that you want anything more, that you dream of anything special. You've got to shrug, 'Either way, I'm easy.'

But it's hard. I'll give you that. I go on inventing, dreaming. Like, for instance, when I buy a lottery ticket. I go into the newsagent pretending I hadn't planned to (though I know damn well I have), and buy the thing. Oh, but let on to yourself even once that it's premeditated and the whole thing's ruined.

Sometimes I manage to buy the ticket without thinking about it, push my way through the plastic cat-o-nine-tails, shuffle across the floor, and rest my thick fingers on the chipboard counter. But then it happens. Invariably. I get to thinking about winning, and they've got me.

Nothing ever happens that you think will happen. So you let yourself go. Might as well. Then you win the money, buy everything you want. You're rich, with a mansion and wonderful parties and never short of a friend, people ring *you* and you never ring back. You only talk to the ones who catch you at home, so it's a lottery for them, if you'll be in or not. And then you've got them.

Obviously it's hopeless. You'll never win the lottery. Not now after all this daydreaming stuff. Still, sometimes you hold out till the numbers come up on the TV. And then, first roll of the ball, it happens: 'What if I win?'

So there – you've shown it mattered. The winning. And they've got that over you. If you ever show you care, they use it. Show them where it hurts, that's the spot they'll press. Same when you meet someone. You say, 'They're the one,' and then they can't be, of course. Not after that. Nothing ever happens the way you want, so you've got to *not* want things any particular way.

You meet someone, touch them up with a bit of make-up, but then it washes off and you're stuffed again. Happiness, you thought. The real thing. Joy at last. But you were wrong to think they were right. Well, you knew it was too soon anyway. The suffering had to get to such a pitch that when the right one comes you'll scream with ecstasy. But you were silly to expect it so soon. Maybe next year. Or the one after.

Of course they've still got you. Don't forget that. You showed you wanted it and now they know where to push.

They know! They know!

Another example: that party the other day. I suspect I wasn't meant to see the invite that went round at work. I walked in courageously enough, looking at everyone, and not one of them gave themselves away. Of course, they thought they had me, had me close to breaking point. Well, they didn't *know*, and I didn't know if they knew, but it was understood. They were winning.

'Please, please, please – please, God, let there be joy!'

No, that would have broadcast defeat. I had to show that if they didn't invite me, or didn't ring back straight away, or at all, it was nothing to me. Whatever; I'm easy.

At any rate they didn't know if I knew – only suspected.

'How are you?' one of them asked.

'Fine, just fine. And you?'

'Me? Fantastic. Didn't you hear? I've just won the lottery – last thing in the world I expected.'

They knew, they knew!

And oh, it hurt the worst it's hurt yet. But I won't let on. They won't have it over me. Doesn't matter to me. Either way, I'm easy. Win or lose, I don't care.

But I do, but I do!

'My congratulations.'

Monday 11th July.

Three days since I called. Three. And that means they'll not be ringing back. That means they've got me.

Of course I've been out, but if they were going to ring you'd think they'd do it at night, not in the middle of a Monday afternoon.

Perhaps I should get an answering machine – but I hate them, I just hate them.

Work today. And terrible it was too with everyone talking about their weekends. Pam, the boss's secretary, asked me about mine as I passed by.

'Get up to anything, Bertie?'

'Bertrand.'

'Bertrand, then?'

Yes, I'd added another line to my rail network. From the lounge room to the kitchen. But I didn't tell them that. They'd only laugh.

So I'll tell you about my job which some might think is not very important, but it is. It has a title so it must be, even if it is only in a chips factory. People don't see that someone needs to do these jobs. If we all just took the exciting ones, the country couldn't run. I'm a Production Assembler and I work with two other people, Ralph and Cynthia. They don't try too hard, but I do. We stand at a conveyor belt and these boxes come out. They're colour and number coded, so Green 925 is Salt and Vinegar, Red 67 is Barbecue and so on. So what you do is, you put them on their right palette and then the forky takes them away. (That's the forklift driver, Dennis. He doesn't talk much.)

It's cruel work, designed to get me down. I get so bored, I hate every minute of the day. The way they crawl by.

I have a game. You need a game, I think. Until nine, I don't look at my watch at all. Just think of the day as a hill. You've got to do that, to picture it somehow. Otherwise you'd be a robot, like the conveyor belt. So I picture the day as a hill, with twelve o'clock the crest. I've just got to roll the rock to twelve and then it's all downhill. The worst is when there's more time to go than you've already done. But after twelve, well, you're on a roll.

The week, too, I divide up as well. Wednesday's over halfway, which leaves you only Thursday and Friday before it's the weekend. Sunday afternoon and night are theirs because you know it's work tomorrow, but you've still got a day and a half. Two, almost, if you add Friday night. It's enough. You can get by.

It's a big warehouse – cold. We have to wear paper clothes and hairnets. No jewellery, watches or keys. Can't have anything falling into the food, even down the line, where we are. The bosses won't accept the risk. It just takes one toddler to bite down on a safety pin and they're sued for all they've got.

It's noisy, too. So noisy you have to yell. The machinery, forklifts, trucks – all noisy. You can wear earmuffs, but only Dennis does.

It's an ugly place, too, and so cold you feel like a stick of celery in the crisper – bend your back too far and you'll snap. They've got you all right, but it's work at least. You get paid.

Today was Cynthia's birthday. I always remember birthdays. I gave her some flowers.

'Oh Bertie,' she said, giving me a fat kiss. She always wears short sleeves – don't know how in the cold – and the flesh swings on her arms, back and forth, higher and higher, but never quite looping over.

'Yeah, nice,' she said. 'Lovely Agatha Panthers. Got a son-in-law who's autistic. Paints all these lovely flowers and woolsheds and things.'

Then the boxes started chugging along the belt and there we were, Ralph and me, putting them on their palettes. I wear gloves now. Ralph laughs at me but handling the boxes all day, your hands dry out.

Ralph's a big man. Big stomach, big features. Likes to talk.

'So Bertie, me main man,' he said today. 'Goin' out with the sheilas tonight? Reckon you're gonna score? I'll give you some advice. What you wanna do is, you wanna give Mrs Palm and her five fingers a work-over first. Then you'll only shoot her through with the lead once. Can't go knocking up these sheilas, son. You'll be in all sorts of trouble. Christ, I had to leave WA over something like that. Didn't even touch the slut, but a bloke threatened to drop a fridge on me, the mongrel. Fuck, reckoned she was his pride and joy. Dancing toy, more like. Town fucking bike. Made me sick. Wouldn't even touch her with a ten-foot fucking barge pole.'

So, one of the boxes got stuck in the taping machine. It's Cynthia's job to sit at it – she gets to sit – and make sure the boxes go in right. Basically, she's got to press down the flaps and then the machine tapes over the top. All she's got to do is change the tape when it runs out and make sure the boxes go in right.

Anyway, one got jammed.

Made me think of a truck I once saw that tried to go under a bridge, and the top peeled off like a sardine tin.

So all these boxes were piling up behind the one that was stuck. They just kept coming through this hole with its plastic slats at the far wall. They had nowhere to go and were all falling on the floor, spilling open because they hadn't been taped up yet. We had crisp packets crunching everywhere and Cynthia flailing her arms around: 'Do something, do something!'

So Ralph was pulling frantically at the stuck box. The brown paper ripped, revealing corrugated cardboard underneath.

'It's stuck tight as a nun's cunt,' yelled Ralph. 'And as dry as one, too!'

The situation was getting desperate. Any more boxes on the floor and we'd never catch up because you couldn't stop the production line further down, you just couldn't. It takes hours to shut these places down. Much cheaper to run them 24-7. You make a machine you can't kill, what else can you do? You have to keep feeding it.

Boxes, more boxes. Dennis yelling from his forklift. The guys in their trucks toey, wanting to beat the traffic.

Suddenly I knew what to do. I got down under the taping machine and reached around. I didn't know it would be there, but thought it had to be: the release lever on the tape bridle. I pulled it. The metal scaffold flew up and the stuck box flapped free. Ralph pulled out the bits of shredded cardboard and Cynthia jumped back in her seat. We had to deal with the boxes still coming, but the ones on the floor – we'd get to them later.

So there we were, working ten times as fast to clear the backlog, with Ralph and I running here, running there, filling palettes. Dennis went mad loading the trucks, almost running over Ralph's foot with the forklift, which would've been like a rolling pin on dough (Ralph wasn't wearing his steel caps). Cynthia was taping the boxes madly and, at any break, picking up the spilt ones on the floor.

And we won! We didn't let the pressure get to us and soon we were back on track with just the usual amount of boxes coming, and not the backlog.

We were having fun now.

We'd made it.

Back to normal pace, but still going at it, and saying to the straggling boxes: 'Come on, come on, show us what you've got!'

Ralph did matador moves with his shirt and every time he threw a box over, it'd be, 'Stuck tight as, eh, Bertie?'

'Tight as, Ralph.'

Tight as. That's all we'd have to say and we'd be laughing. It started to hurt.

Tight as.

Eventually Keith, Danny and Rose took over for the 5:00 to 11:30 shift. We could rest. We had won. We'd had a little victory.

Tuesday 12th July.

I rang again this morning. I shouldn't have, I know, but I was feeling all happy from the day before. When you're in a good mood, it's harder for them to get you.

MessageBank.

So I left a message, but halfway through I stuffed up. Had to repeat the first half then wanted to hang up, but knew that if I did, they'd know I couldn't even get past their machine.

No reply.

So it's now four days since I first called. Four, and that's plain wrong. No two ways. Pretty much means they won't ring back at all. Not now. I should never have rung in the first place, but I won't ring any more now. Not me, not with how busy I am.

Work again today. And what a day too.

I went in well enough and got changed into my paper clothes. Went up to the conveyor belt and there was this guy, a new guy, talking to Ralph. Short, stocky, black hair brushed back – greasy. And he's got this black goatee and sideburns shaved to a point. You can see all his chest hair under the paper shirt. Looks like he's sprinkled pepper all over himself.

'Hey, Bertie,' Ralph collars me, 'this is ...?' He turned to the bloke.

'Mephisto,' said the guy. He was foreign. French or something. His words weren't ordinary curls of butter, rather rolled from a fancy scalloped spoon.

'Yeah, that's it. Meffo … Metho!' Ralph exclaimed in triumph. 'Hey, how about that? Metho! That's a laugh.'

The foreigner examined his paper sleeves, pursed his lips into a thin smile and looked up.

'How about Memphis instead?' he suggested quietly. 'That will do. You know America, don't you? It's what you watch on TV.'

'America!' roared Ralph. 'Ever met a Yank that was a shrinking violet, Memphis? Have you? Fucking friendly bastards, the lot of 'em. Make good movies, though.'

We started on the boxes, me, Ralph and the new guy. He was pretty quick, I'll admit. Learnt the system in no time. Didn't look big, or strong, but he could sure throw those boxes around like they were empty.

'So, Memphis, bet you suck a few sheilas in with that foreign accent of yours,' said Ralph, stacking the last of the Barbecue 67 on its palette and whistling to Dennis.

'I can't think what you mean, Ralph,' steamed Memphis. His voice was food.

'You know, the sheilas. Bet you give 'em a bit of the one-two, don't ya? Hey? In, out. Leave 'em laid out and drooling? So, come on. Going out tonight?'

Memphis twitched his nose as he grabbed two boxes of Salt & Vinegar 925.

'In fact, yes,' he said.

Ralph waited, but then had to ask.

'We-ell, gonna score?'

'Pardon?'

'Gonna give it to her, are ya? Get her squealin'?' Ralph paused to catch his breath in his excitement. 'Well, are ya?'

Memphis twirled the end of his moustache before darting a quick look sideways.

'Why? Did you want to watch?'

Ralph said nothing. Silent, for once. Then he grinned. Then laughed.

'Memphis, ya bastard!' he yelled, throwing one of the smaller Onion Cream 46 boxes at the man. 'Ya got me with that one! "Wanna watch?" That's a classic. That's a beaut. Hear that, Bertie?'

Memphis leaned over the rattling conveyor belt. The boxes were starting to pile up.

'Well, do you?' he asked, seriously.

Ralph was astounded.

'Yeah ...?'

Memphis threw the Onion Cream 46 box back at Ralph. Then laughed.

'Gotcha,' he said, with that smooth voice of his.

Ralph squealed. He'd been had twice. That Memphis was a class act. He could get people. That was obvious. And looked like he couldn't be got.

Ralph and Memphis kept nattering away, but I couldn't hear what the foreigner said. Only Ralph. Well, you can't help but hear *him*. And whatever that Memphis guy said, Ralph would roar. A box came through, bunny hopping 'cause one corner had been crushed. It was Salt & Vinegar 925 and Ralph's palette of Salt & Vinegar 925 was nearly full, so I threw the crushed box to him.

'Ralph!'

He only just caught it.

'Bertie!' he bellowed, blowing on his fingers.

'Stuck tight as,' I yelled. I had to. Remember, factories are noisy.

Ralph cemented my box as the last brick in his block of Salt & Vinegar 925.

'*Ralph*,' I repeated. 'Stuck tight as.'

The boxes were piling up on the belt.

'Dennis!' shouted Ralph, and Dennis lifted the palette with his forklift to take it to the warehouse.

'That box was damaged,' I protested.

'What?'

'Stuck tight as.'

Ralph gave me the biggest blank-wall expression you ever saw, then finally, 'Oh … yeah.' And he went back to his conversation with Memphis.

I went home. I rang star-ten-hash. '*There are no unanswered calls registered for this number. You have not been charged for this –* '

I hung up. Four days. Four! They'd never ring back. They had me. *And* I'd rung twice. Call once and maybe they've just missed it. Twice: no way. I'd showed them I cared.

Wednesday 13th July.

I read in the paper about an old lady. Dead in her flat a month. A whole month. That's how long it took for anyone to notice. Oh, they noticed the smell eventually, and complained to the landlord. And when they found her, she was brown and furry and seeping away into the carpet.

I got out my answering machine (okay, I did have one) and plugged it in. I thought maybe I was being unfair. Maybe they'd tried to call.

Then I went off to work and was late because the bus drove past me at the stop. I couldn't believe it. Had to wait three-quarters of an hour for the next one. That's how it is with public transport in the outer suburbs. In the city, it's a tram every two minutes; here, a bus every forty, just to make you wait. Whether you get to places on time or not, it's nothing to them. So I read, mostly the papers, to show I was in no hurry.

Today, waiting for that second bus, I was watching a girl who'd had a hardware facial. Rings here, rings there. Then, when the 6:40 pulled up, she got on and the driver shut the door on me. I got jammed.

'Sorry, mate, sorry,' he kept saying.

He hadn't seen me there.

When I got to work, having run the last bit from the bus stop, I was sweaty and worried. All those boxes – how would they manage, just Ralph and Cynthia?

But when I went in, after I'd put on my paper clothes, Ralph and Memphis were working away and everything seemed fine except that they just looked at me vaguely, then laughed. Then Memphis threw a box that had gotten ahead of the pack to Ralph, who caught it and jammed it in as the last brick on his palette of Salt & Vinegar 925.

'You've stuck that tight as,' said Memphis.

Ralph laughed.

That got me red. Very red.

'What are you saying that for, Memphis?' I asked. 'You don't know about that day. You weren't there.'

Ralph was silent; Cynthia looking over from her seat at the tape bridle; Memphis twitching his nose. I realized I was yelling, yelling louder than I needed even with the background noise.

Then there was a pause in the production line. Some problem further up: no boxes for a good fifteen metres of belt.

And Ralph said, 'Of course he knows what it's about, Bertie. The thing is, mate, how would *you*?'

What? What was this?

Ralph continued, 'The other day – I don't know where you were – but a box got caught in the taping machine. Big fucking pileup and all. If it wasn't for Memphis, here, well …'

'Well? Well what?'

'Well – he saved the day.'

I turned to Memphis, who smiled a nasty 'I've got you smile' then took up the torment.

'That's when, Bertie,' he trickled between sharp teeth, 'I coined our little phrase "stuck tight as", which has sustained us so wonderfully with amusement and distraction these past days.'

I couldn't talk. I wanted to scream, to hit that pasty little man, but the boxes were coming again, thick and fast. We had to get back to work, and the moment passed.

An hour in, Memphis turned to me with the tiniest smile of warning and victory before throwing a box to Ralph and saying, 'Stuck tight as.'

Ralph laughed. He was about to throw the box on top of his palette when I screamed, 'Wait!'

Ralph looked at me. Cynthia looked over. Memphis smiled.

'Wait, Ralph,' I said. 'That was *me and you*. Not him!'

Ralph looked a fullstop at me.

'It was me – ME! I saved the day. Memphis wasn't even there!'

Ralph and Cynthia stared at me hard like they were trying to wake up. Memphis watched them first, before turning back to me, snapping the floor with his foot. Then it struck me; just the way he stood – it seemed like his bottom half was back to front. His legs bent the wrong way.

Ralph blinked before looking down as a lone box trundled past. 'I don't think so, mate. It was Memphis, here.'

And Memphis winked at me.

So what I thought was: at the end of the day I'd ask Cynthia. She wouldn't play their games, not her. I approached her at the caff.

'... and there he was, neck-brace one day, and claiming everything, then out with his brother-in-law the next, lifting boxes. Lifting heavy boxes. No neck brace or nothing. He got caught out.'

'Cynthia?'

And I asked her.

'Um,' she said. 'Yeah, that was Memphis.'

'What?'

'Look, Bernie – '

Bernie? She never got my name wrong before. Oh, the others had, to make fun of me, but not her. Never her.

'Memphis started that "stuck tight as" stuff,' she said, and I tore out of there fast as I could.

At the bus stop, I pushed my way into the queue. The guy in front and the girl behind stepped back like they'd been buffeted by wind, but I managed to get on the bus without the driver shutting the door on me. He wouldn't get me with that one again. It was the same driver, you see. That's too big a coincidence. To have the same driver twice – that's telling me for sure that they know I know they're trying to get me.

So I got home – just. At the zebra crossing on my street, the cars didn't stop and I nearly got swiped. I had to wait for a break and run across. They're big roads out where I live. Six lanes with big fenced-off areas of nothing happening. Sheds, factories, flats and houses.

I put my key in the lock of my front door and was about to turn it when I heard, 'Hey you!'

It was Mabel, my neighbour.

'Um, excuse me, Sweetie, but do you know Bertrand?'

Yes, yes, I wanted to scream. I know him very well!

'Just good to see Bertie has a friend, that's all, honey. Toodaloo.'

A friend? So everyone was in on it! At work. My neighbours. No one could be trusted from now on. Not a soul. Oh, it was the most elaborate plan yet, I'll give them that. I'll have to give them that. But they wouldn't get me with it. They sure as hell would not.

I checked my answering machine. No calls. I rang and left a message.

Thursday 14th July.

Cynthia always picks me up Thursday mornings after visiting her mum Wednesday nights. Her mum lives in my building, so it's easy. Today, I waited out the front. Waited and waited. In the end, I had to give up and run to the bus stop, but two went straight past. Then when I called a taxi, the driver circled slowly twice, and I had to walk out in front of him to get him to stop.

At work, Sue, the receptionist, looked at me as I came in and I nodded. I usually just nod. She always smiles. And she did today, only differently. And when I'd half passed her, she got up and stood between me and the entrance to the warehouse.

'Can I help you?' she asked.

I didn't know what to do. Can I help you? Very funny! I thought maybe she wanted to carry something, so I held up my lunchbox, which is pretty light, seeing as I don't eat much.

'Oh, you must be the new guy,' she said, relaxing. 'Go on through. Ask for Ralph.'

No, not funny. But I wouldn't let her get to me. I wouldn't give her and the others something to laugh at. So I said – they wouldn't get me with this one – I said, 'Ralph? I think I'll recognise *him*.'

Okay, the joke wasn't that good, but it showed I knew their game, that I could play along with it, that it was just a game to me, too. Whatever, I didn't care.

But it surprised me – scared me that Sue was in on it too. In on it along with the bus driver yesterday, and the taxi driver today who even pulled over to pick up another fare – I had to tap him to remind him I was there.

Well, I'd just be even more careful from now on. Whatever. It's nothing to me.

So I walked in and Ralph and Memphis were there.

'Ralph,' I said, and he looked up.

'Yep, that's me.' And he shook my hand. 'Over there's Cynthia' (Cynthia nodded) – 'and this guy's Bertie' (pointing to Memphis). 'A real character.'

Bertie? Did Ralph introduce Memphis with my name? Bertie? I couldn't have heard right. I couldn't!

But that horrible goatee guy stepped forward and took my hand, and somehow I couldn't pull it away. 'And you must be Memphis?' he said and twitched his lips.

Me? Me, him? Me with that stupid name? What was this?

'Mempfiz?' said Ralph.

'Try Metho. It's easier,' said the creature. And my mouth opened and closed ten times like an asphyxiating fish.

'Meffo! Ha!' roared Ralph.

'Or even Turps.'

'Turps. You're stuck with that one, mate,' said Ralph, patting me on the shoulder. 'Turps! Hear that, Cynthia?'

That creature, that rat, touched my arm. He leaned in, whispering with his Camembert breath.

'You don't mind, do you ... Turps? Only, Memphis doesn't flow too easily. It gets stuck between the teeth. One might almost say, "tight as a nun's cunt".'

Ralph and Memphis exploded with laughter while Cynthia waved her hand, muttering something about boys being boys. And this is what I heard that charlatan whisper – I didn't imagine it – just loud enough for me to hear: 'Oh you humans, you make it so easy for me.'

I froze. I coughed. I deep-freeze-dried inside. And that Memphis? I watched his irises become red wells and as quickly dry up. Then he went on with his work.

The rest of the morning was all 'tight as' and Ralph's roar.

At lunch, I went outside for a smoke. I don't normally smoke, so I had to rat one off Dennis. When I went to go back in, they wouldn't let me. They said – and I couldn't bear it: 'Employees only.'

I got home and didn't know what to do, so I decided to go to the park. I have a dog, a poodle, and we both like the park, though Winnie's shy and I have to pick him up when the big dogs are around. He's very small, too small perhaps, but I like his ears. Cotton wool, without that horrid feel.

I can't stand cotton wool. I simply hate the stuff though I don't know why. I just don't. Once I had a cast put on my arm with cotton wool poking out and I screamed all that night. But I don't do that kind of thing any more. You've got to cope. The worst crime in this world is not coping. You've got to show them you don't care. Cotton wool – it's nothing to you. Otherwise, they'll use it against you. 'See that man,' they'll say, 'he can't stand cotton wool.' Well, I won't let them say that. I won't let them get me. I just won't.

Anyway, at the park I picked up Winnie. It's automatic now – the other dogs come along, and he jumps straight into my arms. A lady once said I should let him play with the other dogs, but I won't do that. He'd get mauled. He's not a strong dog, Winnie.

We like to watch the other dogs, Winnie and I. He kind of yaps but knows they're too big for him. Too rough, and – what's the word? – ready. The other owners chat and I like watching them. I needed to, today, so I wouldn't think about that Memphis, that thing pretending to be me.

They're a funny lot in the park – a very funny lot – but I've come to know them. Well, not personally, but I've watched them and listened to them. All of them. And I know they're not really there to walk their dogs.

There's this one fellow – an old codger – who talks to all the girls. He wears shorts all year round – khaki, like his shirts – so I call him The Colonel. He's got very brown arms and legs, and his nose has a funny black streak that's sleek and translucent. It's the black of

24

spoilt bananas. He owns a black kelpie that chases the cars, and Winnie, too, if he can.

I try to listen to what The Colonel says. He seems to know everyone who walks a dog, and he's always down there, in the park. There's this schoolgirl, very pretty, and he calls her his girlfriend.

'And how's my little girlfriend today?' he'll say. (I've heard this walking past them.) 'Still teasing all the boys?'

I see her looking behind her, at her watch, everywhere but at his nose. Once I've passed, I pretend to do up my shoelace or something, and then they walk past me. They don't nod any more. And they certainly don't say hello, but I'm used to that. Makes me happy, in a way. It shows I've succeeded, that I can listen in so well that they don't even notice me doing it, that they don't know I'm there. They can't touch me.

And so I build up a picture – slowly – in these fragments of conversation. I bet they think I'm mysterious. A stranger. I can see that they're curious about me. They want to know who I am. There I go, walking straight ahead. I don't need anybody and I don't let on. I'm a mystery. An enigma. Someone who doesn't care.

One time, though – I don't really like to mention it – I came upon The Colonel with Blue Rinse. That's the name I give to this lady with a funny dog. She always wears her best clothes, even though the dogs jump all over her. Whenever one comes running, she does this little scream, and it's a great joke between her and the other dog owners. They all reckon she has a curse. She said to me once that mine was the only dog that didn't jump on her. And then she said, holding her red cardigan sleeve up to her mouth — she'd stretched it over her hand — 'No, it jumps on you instead!' And she laughed this odd little laugh.

(I can't stand the way people stretch their sleeves. No one thinks about the work that goes into them. The craftsman out there. Everything, even the small things you throw away, like chip packets, are made by someone.)

They were standing next to the bottlebrush bush, Blue Rinse and The Colonel, and I don't think they'd seen me.

'We're having a Christmas party, Pam. Right here, under this tree,' said the Colonel. 'Friends of the Park.'

'Oh, lovely. Dogs included?

'Oh yes, Pam, can't do without the dogs.'

Blue Rinse — or Pam — looked down at her blue dress.

'Imagine the madness! I think it will be the only party this Christmas that I'll be attending in my old clothes.'

The two laughed. Pam stopped.

'Oh, are you putting up a notice?'

'No, just word of mouth.'

'Good thinking, because there's that Bertie, the Womble, with his rat-dog to think of.'

Then they said some more things I didn't quite hear. Their dogs had located another hound through a fence and their barks echoed back and forth. Pam and The Colonel called to them, then parted ways, but Pam stopped a few metres up the path and turned around.

'You know, Julian,' she said, 'I bet he doesn't even feature in his own dreams!' Then she saw me and stopped, her mouth still open, so The Colonel followed her gaze. Both had obviously been about to laugh but now almost choked instead.

I don't know why I did what I did next. I made it easy for them. But I couldn't let them think they had one over me. That I cared. So I said, I said – this is what I said to them, 'I'm going away this Christmas. With my family.'

Of course I had to stay inside all the next week. Just until the festive season was over.

I don't enjoy the park so much these days. It doesn't feel so sociable any more. I feel sorry for Winnie, though. That people should talk that way about him. I see that he'd like to play with the other dogs but they're so big and so dirty. They're not right for him. I had him spayed and I tie a little ribbon in his hair now. A white one. I run a blade of my scissors over the ends so that they curl up in a tizz. It's very pretty. I can see he's the envy of the other owners. Always so clean and white.

But today I had nowhere to go except the park and I couldn't stay inside. I couldn't bear to think about him – about that Memphis pretending to be me.

For the first time since I was a kid I am scared of the dark.

Friday 15th July.

Nothing, not a thing. I rang again this morning. I had to because something terrible happened last night, the worst thing yet. I hardly made it home and then turned on every light I could. I even pulled out the fan-lid so the oven light would come on.

Last night, the park was empty. No people. No dogs. So I thought I'd let Winnie have a run off-leash. I'm always holding him now, so I thought he'd like it, the change, and he did. He picked up a stick and kept throwing it down, then running off a bit and barking. Then I'd throw it, and he'd get it. He was yapping, having fun, and was the liveliest I'd ever seen him. But I wasn't paying attention and we'd strayed too close to the road. I threw the stick. Let go too soon. It hit the bitumen. A car was coming. Winnie ran out and … and …

The driver didn't even stop.

I wrapped the pieces of Winnie in my coat. I thought if I got them home, I might be able to piece them – him – together. I made it home, just, and that's when I went a bit mad.

Monday 18th July.

I tried ringing again. Pressed redial all last night. Nothing. I had to do something. I had to keep busy. So I tried to go to work. I thought – what I'd do was – I said to myself – I'll push my way in if I have to.

But I didn't get far. I couldn't even find the bus stop. It seemed to be ... missing. I tried to hail taxis but they kept nearly running me down, so I thought I'd walk to the city. A long way but worth a go. Then the walk sign just never turned green. I was imprisoned by a wall of traffic. I turned around. Walked home and only just found my flat.

Tuesday 19th July.

I'm running out of food. My throat is sore, my muscles ache. I've been slipping in and out of sleep – one minute hot; next minute cold.

I had this dream. Awful. It showed they've nearly got me. If they can get you even while you're asleep, that's the end. That shows nowhere's safe.

I was standing at the conveyor belt, alone. The boxes were trundling along like traffic on a highway, but I was keeping up, I was okay. Tired and thirsty, but okay. Then I wanted a break and needed someone to relieve me. I kept calling out, 'Hey, please, I want to wake up! Can someone take over so I can wake up for a minute?'

No one came. I couldn't leave the line. It would be a disaster, a mess. The boxes started spilling over. I couldn't keep up. I needed someone to relieve me. I had to wake up. I screamed ...

When I sat up, my room was deadly dark. I fumbled for the phone, and rang that same number. And ... for the first time ... someone answered! Not just a recorded voice, but an actual person. A girl! It was the secretary. I'd made the first step.

'Sorry, but we can't put you through,' she said.

'What – what about my messages?'

'What messages?'

'From me: Mr. Pale.'

'Pale?'

I could hardly talk, my throat was so sore, and she was making me repeat myself.

'Yes, Bertrand M. Pale,' I rasped.

'What?'

'Bertrand Pale!' I shouted, and my throat ripped.

I heard the distinct sound of paperwork being shuffled. So, so obvious.

'I'm sorry but there is no one on our files under that name.'

'What? What?' I was furious.

'Can I take a message? Get Him to call you back?'

'No, no ... yes. Yes, just tell God this. Tell Him I'm done with him. For good.'

And with that, dear Reader, we leave poor Bertrand M. Pale after his desperate attempt to get through to God. Bertrand does come back into our story at its beginning (yes, what you have read is its middle), but we have many more characters whose diaries, letters, transcripts and even thoughts – yes, even those – we must compile before we have this tale in its entirety.

'Why, who am I,' you ask, 'that I am able to gather, collate and organise the writings and even thoughts of people across society and time?'

'What was that? Across time also?' you persist, mouth agape.

Yes, even across time.

But every revelation has its place.

For the moment, we must travel out of Bertrand's apartment, across the atrium, and into the mind of a certain Miss Mabel Pinkerton ...

Chapter Two

What Could I Do Without?

Friday 8th July, Melbourne 2005.

La-di-da, Friday night, here I am, getting videos. I have no life. It's tragic, I know. But I don't really have time right now. I've got so much on this weekend! Not social stuff, just ... Oh, listen to me nattering on. If I wasn't so damned cute I wouldn't get away with it!

Have I got something on my face? Where's my pocket mirror ...? Oh no, that man was staring at me, that's all ... Yes, him, the video store clerk. So cute! But he's definitely too young. Doesn't stop you looking, does it, though actually I'm not. When you're not looking, that's when it will happen.

He's talking to that girl now. Look at her! Makes me realise *I* know how to dress. That sounds vain, doesn't it, but I'm really not. If I had *her* figure, I could look so-o-o good. I wouldn't be tarty. I would dress well. I'd be amazing. But a see-through top at a video store – whatever next?

You can see he doesn't treat her that well, can't you? She's got to come in practically naked to get noticed. Wait … didn't she used to come in with that tall guy? Don't see him with her now. Some people have got to ricochet from relationship to relationship. I'd rather be alone.

I went for a two-hour walk this morning. Another one tonight, if you count the stroll to the video store. Tell me if I'm talking too much.

Am I talking too much? Tell me if I am, won't you? I get so hyper. Too much caffeine!

Oh look, they've got posters.

'Can I have that one, please?'

The video guy points at the poster behind him.

'No, sweetie,' I say, 'not *Vertigo*. Oooh, I'd love to get *Vertigo*, but not right now. Just *The Third Man* for the moment, thanks sweetie. You look tired.'

'Long shift.'

Poor guy. See those hangdog eyes – so cute!

'Can I get you something at the 7-11? I'm just going over. It's no trouble.'

'Nah, it's cool.'

'All right, sweetie. Here, let me put away those videos.'

'Oh, no, look – '

'Now, now, I know where they go. I'm off to the Horror section anyway.'

So cute!

Do you think he's watching me walking to the back? La-di-da, just be natural. *An American Werewolf in London* – such a good film! *The Wicker Man* too! Who hired these out? Maybe the video guy himself. It's *too* good to be true: he's smart *too*!

Uh oh, *Braindead* next to *Carrie*. Who stacked this shelf? 'B' comes before 'C', duh! If I wasn't here to save the day! Oh, I'd love to work at a video store. Sitting round, watching moo-vies all day. It'd be so much fun. I could get these videos in better order, though. That sounds vain. I'm not vain.

I should pick my videos. I've been here half an hour already. So tragic! Okay, why not get *An American Werewolf* and *The Wicker Man*. But I can't get both, that's *too* tragic. Which one haven't I seen *as* much? They're both so good! All right, *An American Werewolf In London*. That guy in it is so much cuter than Edward Woodward!

La-di-da, there I go, another horror film. What must that cutesie think of me?

Hang on, why's he staring at me? Have I got something on my face? Uh, I know, my name! He needs to know my name to call up my details on the computer.

'Mabel Pinkerton, Flat number – '

'Yeah, I know.'

He knows my name! Can you believe he knows my name? Look at those fingers as he scans my videos through … I really notice fingers. They say a lot. I have to imagine myself being with a guy. If I can't, he can be as cute as all hell, but it's just no good.

What's he got playing on the television? Oh, *Collateral Damage.* He must *have* to play that. I'm sure he's got good tastes. Why's he staring at me again?

'Hey, I put your vid' the other side of the beeper.'

What's he saying to me? Wake up, Mabel.

'Sorry, sweetie?'

'It's right there. You can take it.'

'Uh oh, silly me. La-di-da, who's asleep? You have a good night, darling. See you next time.'

Out in the cold again.

Walking, walking, walking. So good for me. It's such a good thing the video store is so close. (About the only thing that *is* close around here.)

Uh oh, there I go complaining. What have *I* got to complain about?

Maybe I should have gotten *The Wicker Man*.

Why did I have to think that? Choices!

I'm always thinking about what I could go without. If I had to lose something, what would it be? Like, of the five senses – although I believe there's a sixth (*The Sixth Sense*, another good film; maybe I should've gotten that?) – which one could I go without? Taste, touch, sight, hearing or smell?

Give me a minute ...

Um ...

Smell.

No, taste!

But I don't need to taste food, do I ...? Half the taste of food is its smell anyway. So I *could* go without taste. But I definitely could *not* go without smell. Smell brings back memories! I'm always smelling something that brings back a good time. Some herbs do that for me – like rosemary reminds me of my mother. She used to put it in everything because we had a rosemary bush. She didn't really know how to cook, my Mum.

Walking, walking, walking. So good for me! I don't need a car at all.

Imagine if all your memories came back at once? All the ones you thought you'd forgotten? There are so many things we forget. So many we *need* to forget. A good thing we don't keep them with us. Uh oh, I'm going to have to remember something I *wanted* to forget now. Quick, quick, decide which memory. If I've got to recall something unpleasant, which memory does it have to be?

Primary school, Grade Five, asking Eleni, 'Where do *you* come from, Eleni?'

'Greece.'

Then Yasser.

'Palestine.'

And lastly Lisa, the Aboriginal girl.

'Here.'

'Yes, but where do your *parents* come from?'

'Here, Australia.'

'Yes, but before that?'

I kept pestering her. She started crying but I thought she was just being difficult.

Uh oh, why did I have to remember that? Is that how it really happened? 'Cause our memory of the past is different to our *actual* past. I don't know that that really happened. I mean, was it Lisa who started carrying a butter knife to school? Was school that bad? Don't go there, Mabel …

Wednesday 13th July.

Videos on a Wednesday night, not so tragic. Walking, walking, not much further. Good to be nearly home. Walking up the landing. Who's that? Someone going into Bertie's place. Bertrand M. Pale. Very quiet, hard to talk to. Has a lovely white dog though, Winnie. I should ask what this stranger's up to, nosing about Bertie's place. You've got to look out for your neighbours. But, whoever he is, he *does* have a key – so he must *know* Bertie if he has a key.

Funnily enough, he even looks like Bertie.

'Hello, sweetie, I'm Mabel. I live over there.'

'What?' he stammers. 'I know you.'

He knows me! That's strange. Bertie must've talked about *me* to *him*. I didn't think I figured in Bertie's life enough for him to do that. Have *I* talked about Bertie to anyone else? N-n-no. Who do I know I'd hate to think had never mentioned me to someone else? Oh, that's too horrible a choice. I wish I hadn't asked myself that one. But I've got to decide now ...

'Um, excuse me, sweetie, but do you know Bertrand?'

Oh no, look at him! He's practically combusting.

'You won't get me with *that* one!' he yells.

'*Get* you, sweetie?' I ask.

Uh oh, better backtrack outta here, and fast.

'Just good to see Bertie has a friend, that's all, honey. Toodaloo.'

Phew!

Walking, walking, walking, nearly there. Reaching in my purse for my keys.

He was an odd one.

Ooh, something going on next door!

Someone moving about ...? Of course! The flat must've been taken. Mmm, hello, he looks cute. I hope he's not just the removal guy. Nope, looks like he's the tenant. Yum.

'Can I give you a hand, honey?'

'That's it, thanks, I travel light.'

Uh-oh, hear that voice, would you! So deep! Voices really do it for me. A guy can be the cutest guy in the world, but if his voice is mismatching there's *no* hope!

'The name's Henri.'

On-ree, that's how he pronounces it.

'It's French.'

He takes my hand. See those fingers – *feel* those fingers! So long and strong. Have I told you hands really do it for me?

He doesn't have a French accent. In fact, it's hard to place. Got to get him talking more.

'I should finish tidying my things,' he says. Oh those lips – so full!

'Okay, honey, if you want a welcome coffee, just knock.'

'Maybe another time.'

'All right, cutie, you sleep well.

'Actually, I'm just on my way out.'

'Ooh, you're going out on the town? Hoping to pick up? I would've thought you'd have a girlfriend.'

He laughs, and the sound comes from somewhere deep in his chest. So manly.

'I don't *have* girlfriends,' he says.

'What, you're ...? You're gay?

He smiles.

'Damn it! All the best ones are gay. Wish *I* was a guy.'

He laughs again. Such a rumbling laugh.

'Uh, sorry, I'm usually not so flirty,' I tell him. 'Can I get you something? Do you want a *Red Bull*?'

'No, I need to shower, spruce up.'

'A *Red Bull* keeps *me* going all night, sweetie. Are you sure you don't want one? It's no trouble. I'm getting one myself. No, don't be silly. My treat.'

Quick, inside Mabel, get the man that *Red Bull*. I know it's your last one, but *you* don't need any more caffeine.

What's that? He's asking me something and I'm halfway through the door. Pirouette left.

'Sorry, what was that, sweetie?'

'Is there somewhere to eat round here?'

'No, we're pretty isolated.'

'I'm trying to recall Melbourne's geography,' he says.

'You been away?'

'Europe.'

'Europe! I so-o-o want to travel! How nice would it be to travel? You're so lucky. That's why you're single. No, before you ask, I'm not ready yet. It will happen when it's meant to. I've just had too many scary coincidences in my life *not* to believe.'

'Believe in ...?'

'Coincidences. We're alone because we're special, sweetie. It's just not meant to happen right now, that's all. You're not ready for it. It will happen when it's meant to. The video guy flirts with me. He's *such* a sweetie! I posted him this big cutout of Pamela Anderson. He says he *loves* Pamela Anderson. Didn't say "thank you" for it though. Oh well. Cost a fortune.

Can't say much for his tastes. *Barbwire* wasn't a great film. I'm not talking too fast, am I?'

He laughs again.

'Good. Tell me if I'm talking too fast, won't you, sweetie?'

'I really should be getting ready.'

'La-di-da, silly me. You have a good night, honey.'

Quick, Mabel, get inside. Shut your door. Now wait till *he* shuts his. Click. That's it. Okay, Mabel, duck outside again. He's not there. Phew. Quick, down the stairs. Walking, walking, walking, must get there and back before he leaves.

Why did he have to be gay? If only *I* could find Mr Right, I could go without anything! Let's see, what could I lose? Arm or leg? Leg – no, arm! Oh, that's a terrible one. I wish I hadn't asked that. Choosing taste was *so* easy. But I can't let it go. Now I've asked it, I've *got* to decide.

Who would I hate to think had never mentioned me to anybody else …?

'That's enough!'

Oops, did I say that out loud? Mabel, did I? Caught talking to myself, when I'm not really there. What am I saying? Of course I'm really there. But is there just the one of me? There's got to be at least the *one* of him. He's out there somewhere, I know it! How will we find each other? If only I knew what he looked like. Or, even better, his name. Now a name would be helpful.

I mean the name of *the one* of course. He doesn't have to be perfect. In fact, I don't want him to be perfect. There *can* be something wrong with him, something missing. Uh oh, now I've thought that, I've got to decide what it is. Now what's the one thing in a man I could go without …?

Walking, walking, walking. Round trip completed. Knock on Henri's door. A bit of noise within. Great, he hasn't gone yet. Door opens. Standing in a towel. Yum! This is too much! All that chest hair …

'Ah, hello,' he says.

'Hey, sweetie, I went to the pizza place and they'd accidentally made two. Here, I got you a Coke to go with it. No, don't be silly. Take it. It didn't cost me anything. They made two.'

'Two Cokes as well?'

'The Coke? Um, er, the Coke comes with it.'

'I can't accept – '

'Look, you can buy *me* a Coke sometime, honey.'

'Really, I can't – '

'It's a gift!'

Silence. He's staring at me. Quick, Mabel, save the situation. Speak!

'No, no, no, I'm so sorry, sweetie. I didn't mean that to sound rude. I didn't mean you *have* to buy *me* a Coke. Only if you want to. Let me pay, please. It's *my* shout. Neighbours should make each other feel welcome, don't you think, sweetie? Most people don't even know their neighbours any more.'

He's just smiling at me. If only that towel could get caught on the door handle when he tries to close it … I know what *he* could go without. Uh, enough of that, Mabel. Turn around, walk away.

'La-di-da, don't mind me.'

Wait, what's he saying to me? Just listen. Hear it now but digest it inside. Good, he's done. Now he's gone inside and shut the door. Towel stayed on. Okay, into your flat. Take a seat before you think about it. Ahhh, that's better.

Now, what was that thing he said? He said he wanted to share my day one day. Said he wanted to follow me round all day – he wouldn't say a word – he just wanted to see 'how you live'.

He's so funny! Did he mean how *I* live, or just how *to* live? He's such a cutie. I said okay.

What a funny day.

Glad to get off my feet. This is a great couch, though, isn't it? I've got good taste. If I brought someone back here, he would see I've got great taste …

La-di-da.

Clock ticking …

Don't remember it being so loud.

La-di-da …

You know, I'm a bit worried about that guy at Bertie's door. But he had a key, so it must be okay. He *must* be a friend of Bertie's. Or maybe his brother? He looked like he could be Bertie's brother. You should look out for your neighbours. I'd hope my neighbours would look out for me if someone was going into *my* flat. Not much danger of that!

Oh, listen to me, I'm such a dag!

Now what could I go without ...?

If only our dear Miss Mabel Pinkerton were alone in asking that question. Yet, just one door to the left of her but four flights down on the ground floor, a Mrs Ellen Barkly is having her own qualms about what she could, or could not, do without ...

Where Are The Monsters?

Wednesday 13th July, Melbourne 2005

Today I have been busy packing tired, old things away in boxes. It is my dolls that I am least willing to consign to stale cupboards, moths and silverfish. I suppose they should be left to decay like all things and humans. Once they were fabulous, exotic creatures, all captive radiance, and the victims of my jealousy. Yes, peculiarly, my jealousy. As a little girl,

44

each night, in bed, I would place them in a circle about my head, each one a petal and I ...

Yes, I ...?

'Tell me what you did today, Jezebel?' I would ask. Jezebel was pale porcelain – my own dear, my favourite.

My voice, sultry even then, could lower or heighten in pitch to speak as hers or mine.

'Under the Surly-Tree with leaves of Jade, we sat and, in song, the birds we bade *adieu*.'

How beauteous! How redolent of charm and colour.

Of course my dolls were bored with what *I*, little Elly, had to tell them of *my* day at school. Nonetheless, I would talk to them about it for hours.

Or so it seemed.

Dad would knock on my door.

'Where are the monsters, Elly?'

That was our game.

'There, Daddy, there.'

And he would answer: 'Where, Elly, where?'

'See my skirt, Daddy? The way it's all crumpled up on the floor? Why, the pleats are teeth.'

And Father, the beloved, would hang it up, till the creases fell out and the monster was now gummy, now gone, and finally a harmless skirt once more.

'You can sleep now, Elly.'

'I don't want to, Daddy.'

'I bet Jezebel's tired,' he would say, tucking Jezebel in beside me. Then, leaning his ear to her lips, he would add: 'Yes, Jezebel's saying to me, "*Can't* we go to sleep now, Elly? I'm beastly tired." '

'*I* can't hear her, Daddy.'

'You're just not listening hard enough.'

And he would kiss me on the forehead before rising and walking away. Then, with the light leaving the room, I would turn to Jezebel's bright, white face before it became a pasty black and ask her why, when she was so free with Daddy, could she not even mumble a syllable to me.

Jezebel would say nothing.

I would cast her from the bed.

Things became tense between us, and finally impossible.

Day after day, I beat my dolls senseless, demanding they speak. I invented traps. Casually, having left my room, I would swing my door open and expect to see my dolls in motion, preparing for the day's picnic, the adventure they never invited me on. I never once caught them out.

Undeterred, I devised tortures to make them talk. Needles, flames, the fear of being left in the kennel of our dog, Barney.

But they never broke down and vomited up their secret.

That is until, on a winter's day, dark and moody, Jezebel, torn by tooth of dog, spewed foamy entrails and I laughed.

Yes, today I have been busy packing tired, old things away in boxes. My husband has looked on the whole time, wondering, and I can see he wants to take the air. I suggest a walk but I hate them now.

Must people stare?

The children, I can understand – even forgive – but the grown adults, open-mouthed, pointing? They, I will never excuse. And when they see him limp this time, they will even add comment to the glares.

'You should walk him more,' Pam will say, looking at his stomach.

But I can't walk him more, not with his leg the way it is.

'You should walk him less,' Julian will say, looking at his limp.

But I can't walk him less. That way he really will get overweight.

Everyone's an expert! A complete (well, if not a complete then a relative) stranger knows better than I do. Ha!

And yet *he* still makes friends with them, as though *I* were the cruel one, the one without *his* interests closest to my heart. I can see them summing up a situation they have no way of properly gauging. She keeps him in all day, she lets his health deteriorate, she's controlling. She is really quite, quite in …

But wait.

What's that?

A sound outside. Leave the boxes, Elly. Open the curtains. Take a look. In the neighbouring yard (which is empty except for a pile where a house once stood and the first palette of bricks ready for building another) are two men. One is tall, jowly; the other's short, with sideburns and goatee.

They are stealing the bricks.

We now venture out of the block, rise into the air, and float to another location close by. There, we descend through the roof of the local police station to hear certain admissions of one Mr Tony Havelock.

How I've Gotten Where I've Gotten To.

Wednesday 13th July Melbourne 2005.

Describe my whole day? From the start? What is this? Look, I wouldn't mind waiting for my lawyer … Off the record …? Yeah, sure. (I know you bastards …) All right, all right then, coppers! Look, I know you're just doing your job but don't do a job on me.

Right, the facts.

I'd seen this pile of bricks every day as I was driving back from the factory. I live in Toorak and the chips factory's in Whoop-Whoop. You probably know where I live 'cause I reckon you guys have the place bugged ...

Nah, I'm not registering a complaint. Just aggravating you. Getting a rise.

Okay, this pile of bricks. Thing is, I like a bargain. That's how I've gotten where I've gotten to. I *could* buy them new, but I hate to pay a cent more than I've got to, and when I don't have to pay a cent at all, that suits me down to the bone. The current wife's on at me about this path, right, that I said I'd put in from her front gate to her steps, *then* she'll leave me alone. She's gone and gotten quotes and everything. But *I* said, we're not using diamond bricks, 'cause that's how expensive her quote was. Who's the brickie, I asked her. Fabio? So I wanted to do it myself and I know she's away at the moment. The Whitsundays.

Look, some tosser knocked down this house, got the first palette of bricks in, and hasn't had the cash or capital to build anything since. So the site's an eyesore. If it'd been me, you'd have had the whole works by now, dual occupancy, multi-storey, up and occupied, tax-indexed back to my third wife's earnings and paying for itself already. But some people are suckers. They take an opportunity, but can't see it through. Which is where I'm different.

But you guys don't wanna go for the losers, do you? You target the doers. The guys actually building infrastructure in this country.

Okay, I'll tone down the party political. I donate a good deal of money to the Lib minister's campaign and he still raises tax on big business. Well, that's where this Memphis guy comes in … No, I don't know his last name. I didn't ask and he's new to the factory, but somehow we got talking at tea break. Don't normally talk to the workers … Well, you know, footy's their language. But this guy's smart. Obviously wants to get up, and he offers me a hand picking them up, the bricks no one wants. I tell him it's illegal, but he says he'd sort it out. His idea, see. Look, I'll pay for them now if that will help … Too late? It's never too late. How about five thou'? Could make out the cheque now …

What? … No, never. Look, forget it. Don't try and stitch me up. Is this a stitch-up job? … Good, 'cause I won't say anything more till I've got my lawyer.

No, I *am* calm.

Anyway, we're in the car, I'm driving.

When we get to the spot, he says … Oh, it's not relevant … What, you want it anyway?

He said this was where one of my workers lived. Bert … Bertrand … something like that, and why didn't I give him a lift to work each morning? It's on my way. This Bertrand can't drive, apparently. Hardly my problem … Look, I don't know *all* my staff. Some managers say you have to, but hey, with the numbers I employ that's just not feasible.

Okay, so we're driving along, and I'm telling him about the business, inside out, 'cause he seems to want to know, and I don't mind helping people so long as they don't try to cut under me with my own knowledge, but this guy just seemed eager, though he did say one thing I didn't quite get. He said, 'The only thing worse than people is their absence.'

Look, I don't know. He's foreign. I wasn't taking much notice ... No, it didn't strike me as odd at the time. Hell, some of these foreign guys even kiss. Yeah, on the lips. But look, I wanted help. They work better, right? Out here, starting off. Not like these lazy homegrown sods. Got it too easy. Want full pay, all the benefits. Holidays. Sick leave. Anything they can do to kill an honest businessman trying to build his business.

And here's this guy, this Memphis, helping his boss, and out of hours at that. That's the sign of a smart cookie. Someone who wants to get up in the world. Not afraid to put in some unpaid time for his future. Been one of our own guys, the bastard would've stuck me with an invoice afterwards. But shit, hey, that's not a bad one, is it?

But the point is, I actually wanted to help *him* out. In return, like.

'Look, Memphis,' I said to him, 'I could probably do you a deal. I'll let you in on something. I'm not just in the chips game. Entertainment. That's where it's at. That's my main thing.'

'Television is a sedative, Tony,' he said, 'and I've always preferred stimulants.'

Okay, that was an odd thing to say. That was probably the first time I really sized him up. Something about him was actually pretty familiar.

'Have we met before?' I asked him.

He put a hand to his chest, pretty affected-like.

'Why, I'm touched you remember, Tony. Yes, as a matter of fact, in France during the Fifteenth Century. Your hair still has a bluish tinge.'

Well, I'm a bit touchy about that. Even dye it. He must've seen down to the roots. But the *Fifteenth Century*? I asked the guy what the hell he was on about.

'Tony, to sloppily quote Nietzsche, some people are dead before their time; others are born posthumously. But us? We have been born and died many times. Therefore, we are of *all* time.'

'Yeah ... sure ... right.'

'You don't believe in reincarnation?' he laughed.

'Can't say I do, mate.'

To be honest, by now he was starting to unnerve me. I put my foot down a bit more on the pedal but you have to allow more time to brake at the lights with the trailer on. He leaned over, flicking my key ring – it's a James Dean one – with his squat fingers.

'But Tony,' he said, 'just look at immortality for your movie actors: I mean, they die and come back as merchandise!'

With that, he laughed the queerest laugh you ever heard. It started deep in his chest but ended up like a cat squealing. Nearly ran me off the road. The guy was too smart to be packing boxes.

'What did you do back where you came from, Memphis?'

'Are you implying, Tony, that I haven't mastered the accent?'

'The accent?'

'Please, assure me, my friend – still my questing heart! – but is this not Melbourne, Australia, circa 2000?'

'Er ... sure. 2005 to be exact.'

He smiled, then put his feet on the dashboard. Pretty damned rude, I thought. Most outlandish shoes, though. Even had mock spurs on them.

'May I be so importunate as to inquire, Tony, but have you ever read a book?'

And yeah, I've read a book. Cover to cover. So I say to him, 'Yeah, know what it was, Memphis?'

'Tell me anyway.'

'*Penthouse*.'

Ha! *Penthouse*. Not bad, right? But this Memphis just looks at me.

'No, truly,' I tell him. 'Good articles.'

'Probably best that you don't read, Tony,' laughed Memphis. 'Books don't alleviate; they exacerbate. Let me give you a little history lesson, Tony. Just as astronomy arose out of astrology, and chemistry out of alchemy, so from the occult world came the mental sciences. And to know how the mind works, we must recognise when it doesn't. Don't you agree?'

I'm not even sure I've got it right now. Can't say I understood it to agree or disagree.

Well, he dumbed things down a bit for me. Seemed really keen on my entertainment line, too. Reckoned it would make his 'job' faster, whatever his job was. Yep, entertainment was the go. Obviously had it all worked out in his own head. To tell the truth, by this time I was starting to wonder if he wasn't a nutter, but sometimes nutters have the best ideas anyway.

We were almost at the vacant lot by this time, so I asked him if he was sure it was okay with the bricks and he said he'd squared it with the owner.

No, honest, he said he had. Ask him … My office girl says, but there's no Memphis on the payroll? Look, that's not my problem. You guys couldn't find your own way to your arses except you've got your sniffer dogs to guide you. Much higher IQs.

Okay, okay, fair go, that was a bit raw, but you ask the blokes who were on the factory floor with him today. They'll know him … Which ones …? Their names? Um, Ray? R-something …? Look, I manage from the top down. I can't know every nut and bolt at the bottom. You boys will just have to do your homework.

But what if *they* don't know *me*? Of course they bloody will. I'm their *boss*.

Look, the point was, I told him, 'We're at our capacity now. With this plant and the other, we're supplying much of Australia. We'd have to go offshore, but well, what's your hobby?'

'Humans.'

If you ask me, he's one of those boat people. Memphis probably isn't even his real name. Why don't you check that detention centre up in Timbuktu and ask if they're got some Mr Curry Chicken or Monsieur Peking Duck who hasn't come back from laundry duties? Do your work. I tell you, the guy exists.

What happened next? I said to him, 'Say, I reckon you talk better'n most. That's why I could do with you in the selling area. Might be able to take us upmarket.'

'Thank you, Tony, I would very much like to master the intricacies of this bestial tongue.'

See, he was a plant, a terrorist. Taking over. And you've got *me* in here. Me, a fucking patriot!

What did I say next?

'Sure, er, look, mate. I might get you in on the ground floor later in marketing and targeting. Can't promise anything. At the moment, I can't afford to do anything they can stitch me up for.'

'You mean the police?' he asked.

And at that point we pulled up at the spot and both jumped out. I put my gloves on, but he didn't want any. I tell you, for someone his size, I've never seen a guy move so fast. We had the trailer nearly loaded in minutes.

Halfway through he muttered something else pretty strange. 'Oh you humans,' he said. 'If it isn't boxes you're stacking, or bricks you're piling, it's rocks that you're rolling uphill.'

Then this woman sticks her maw over the fence. What ...? Yeah, okay, I know she's got a name. You blokes have already told me it's Ellen Barkly or something. That better, Miss ...? Ms. Whatever! Letting sheilas in the force. You put up with this, Constable ...? Sorry, Sarge.

Yep, yep, yep, I'm trying. Okay, so this Ms Ellen Barkly puts her head over the fence.

'What are you doing?' she screeches. Off her nonce.

'Calm down, calm down,' I say.

And that's where this refugee steps in. He's all smooth with her. Tells her the story. And, lo and behold, she gets to agreeing with him. The bricks are a bit of an eyesore, after all. She's wanted them moved for a year, and something – 'something!' – built on this rubble. Her words.

If you ask me, if a guy gets on with a girl, really gets on, he must be a poof.

But I'll give this Turk his due. Turns the woman right round, and now she's telling us to come for a beer when we're finished ... What? Nah, look, I only had one, right. Just one. I'm off my P-plates now – for the *second* time. That crash was two years ago. And *that* was a stitch up. Just 'cause I burnt off an unmarked police car at the lights ... Yep, your mate, Damo. It wasn't that that shitted him so much. More the fact that *he* braked. The cunt couldn't outrun me.

Yeah, well, just don't try to trump up a drink-driving charge, too, 'cause, as you'll remember, I never got back in my car and trailer with those bricks, did I?

Well, okay, afterwards we go round the front of her flat and knock. The bricks are loaded in the trailer and, if you want it from me, we've done that street a favour, but, well, okay, we go in. Nice place. Too many things about. Cluttered up like my wife's. The third one's. I mean, what is all that porcelain shit, anyway?

She didn't have too bad beer, though, and it *was* beer. I'm getting to like this imported stuff. Not so harsh as your VB or Fosters. Less indigestion. Hey, you wouldn't have any Quick-Eze, on you, would you ...? Nah, sorry, I forget you coppers have no guts. Too busy picking on the easy targets to go after those foreigners coming in illegally. Like this Arab who got me. Memphis. Or Italian. Hell, I don't know. You don't need to, living in Australia. At least, you didn't once.

What? What are you saying …? Officer Ko … Kosoumis could tighten those cuffs for me? Yeah, okay. Give a guy a break. A woman copper and an I-ti … Okay, Greek … Yeah, sorry, luv … Okay, okay, Officer.

So, we're just sitting there, right, talking shit, drinking beer, Memphis is getting along well and all, and since I only know one kind of language to talk with a lady, and that's dirty, I let him go on.

And that's when it happened …

Yeah, when *it* happened.

I shit you not.

This dog walks out, I'm not kidding, this seven-foot tall dog, walking on its back legs. So up I jump. Course I do. Well, this woman doesn't bat an eyelid. This Memphis bloke doesn't either. Reckon they were both in on it. Just goes to prove, doesn't it? But I sure as hell shitted *my*self.

'What the … what the fuck?' I spluttered.

'Oh, I'm sorry,' says the woman, 'how rude of me.'

And she goes on to apologise for not introducing the dog to us.

'This is my husband.'

Yeah, you heard; her husband.

He even had a name. Can you guess?

Barney.

Her fuckin' 'husband' was called Barney.

Memphis puts his hand forward like it was the most natural thing in the world to have a seven-foot tall dog for a husband, and shakes hands with this cow-sized mutt. Sorry, shakes its *paw*. The damn thing even tipped its shaggy head at him.

So then the three of them sit down again, the dog taking up a couch just like you or I, and they go straight into the weather or some shit, and I'm just standing there, gaping, going, oh no, no, no, this isn't right. It was sending me mad.

'Listen, Lady, and you, Memphis, you can't just fob this off like it's okay, like this is the most ordinary bloody thing you ever saw, tea at the fuckin' races. *That's* a great big bloody seven-foot tall mutt there carrying on like Lord Bloody Muck, and *she* says it's her husband.'

I was probably red from the screaming, but what does that woman reply?

'I understand people will be at first curious and ask questions, but any inquiry beyond that surpasses the merely interested and verges on the rude.'

'Verges on the rude! ? Lady, this isn't right.'

At about that point, there was another knock at the door. She goes to answer, and that's when Memphis and the dog left ... No I didn't see them go... Yeah, I know I was in the room with them ... No, not more than a metre or so away from either of them ... Look, I wasn't really thinking about them, then, was I? I was wondering who was at that door ...

No, I've got no idea where they went.

And that's all I'm saying till I get my lawyer …

The ending? You know the ending …

All right, all right. She walked back in and said: 'That's the police at the door. Apparently some neighbour saw you stealing the bricks and loading them into your trailer, and alerted the police. They want you to accompany them.'

And the final sentence, the clincher.

'People will make a fuss about the most trivial things, won't they?'

Leaving Tony where he most definitely belongs, let us now rise up out of the building I alluded to so mysteriously but which you will now understand was not so mysteriously a police station, jump forward three days, and waft through the fourth floor window of Henri's apartment, into the very mind of the man himself …

I've Got a Lot of Love.

Saturday 16th July Melbourne 2005.

Oh well, back in Melbourne. Can't say I'm happy about it. One can't travel forever, I suppose. Guess I *should* 'grow up,' whatever that means. People are always trying to grow up, not getting in touch with their inner child.

Imagine having children, though. I've got about ten lesbian couples all wanting me to sire their progeny, but it would be *such* a responsibility. Don't know if I could do it. I mean, how would I explain school to a kid? 'Look, Kid, it's horrible. *I* didn't like going, but I'm making you go anyway 'cause that's how it is.' It'd be liking bringing a friend to a party you knew was going to be crap, just so you wouldn't be standing around on your own.

Lesbians! Now they don't want men, but they *do* want a man in the picture. They say, 'We only want you to visit the kiddies when *you* want to, say every second weekend.' But I know what would happen next: they'd be hitting me for child support.

Big city, Melbourne.

It's actually as big as, or bigger than, many European capitals. Did you know that?

Look, Melbourne's okay, very cosmopolitan and all, but it's like this little piece of Europe, without the location.

Even more so, once you're away from the centre of Melbourne, as I am. Where I've landed is an out-of-the-way place that's pretty much a self-contained village made of nougat concrete. Cheapest thing I could get.

And as usual it's just me and my beloved backpack. That's really all I've needed for the past ten years. We have an understanding, my backpack and I. You know, the way a shell has an understanding with a crab? Well, my backpack says, 'Grow any bigger, Buddy, and we're parting ways.'

So I don't accumulate. Things *or* people.

How do breeders do it? *I* couldn't imagine being stuck in the one neighbourhood all my life, in a shell you can't take with you. I tried to go up to the roof of my flat the day I moved in. Thought I'd check out the chance of some all-over tanning once the weather warms up, and I can tell you it's got a depressing view. I even saw a guy down below – at least I think it was just the one – stealing bricks from the vacant lot next door. Called the police on my mobile – my good deed for the day. No, I think I'll count it for the week, especially as it looks as if it's put a stop to me going up on the roof. Yesterday when I tried again, the building manager was busy putting a great big bloody padlock on the door. Isn't that just so petty?

It's definitely not much of a place to live, though I've got quite a sweet neighbour, I must admit. A little dumpling called Mabel Pinkerton. Will have to watch her, though.

'Hello, Henri, can I get you something, anything?' she asked me this afternoon.

The balcony partitions are too low, but mine gets the afternoon sun. In fact, that's about the only thing that clinched it for me when choosing this abode: the balcony would be a good place to lie naked.

'Oops, sorry, youch!' screamed Mabel. 'I've got my hands over my eyes, sweetie. I didn't see anything. Tell me when to turn around again.'

I pulled a towel over my groin, and chuckled. You need to *hear* my chuckle to know what it's like. People even *call* me Chuckles. It's just one of my names.

'It's safe to look now.'

She put her head back over the tin partition.

'How was last night, sweetie?'

'I was feeling a little naughty,' I told her, 'so I went to the beat.'

Her jaw dislocated. I love ruffling breeders. But this one had her mouth rewired in a second.

'Okidoki. So how did it go, honey?'

'Well …' I was a bit ruffled myself, 'I picked up this little woggy boy, postcard perfect, fluffy chest, tight buns but, just between you and me, he wouldn't have killed a chicken.'

'Wouldn't have killed a …?'

Her hand flew to her mouth to stop her laughter.

'You're terrible!'

Didn't stop her from quizzing me about it, did it? Beats have their own rules. It's about eye contact. You're not really meant to talk. If the other person does, that's okay. You've got to judge it. I've had some really amazing moments at beats with guys I've hardly said a word to, haven't seen again, and don't expect to. Okay, sometimes you *can* crawl home feeling like a cockroach (you've got to be careful), but mostly it's okay. I mean, *I* never have trouble – just drop my trousers and they're lining up.

'How do you know when …?' stuttered Mabel.

I sat up proper, keeping the towel positioned like a napkin. I have impeccable manners.

'It's in the look.' I gave her a demo. 'But I'm always the one making the first move. It's so easy for me to do it, unless I'm smitten, which is nearly never.'

'But isn't casual sex a wank by another name?' she asked.

I nearly lost my towel altogether at that. I'd have to watch this one!

'That beat stuff is,' I chuckled, 'but a pickup doesn't have to be. Should maybe have gotten the guy's number. He did have a certain something.'

'You're such a honey,' giggled Mabel, her pink digits gripping the tin partition. 'Sending you the biggest hug! Someone new will come along soon, sweetie. Plenty of fish in the sea, especially when you're as damn cute as you!'

See, she's quite special, isn't she? Can't say the same for the only other resident I've spoken to. Actually, I'm still not feeling too good about *that* one. I told Mabel about it, and she said it must've been Bertrand M. Pale. I bumped into him on the landing when I was going out last night. He had his coat wrapped tight around something. Kept crying out,

'Winnie, Winnie, my poor Winnie.' I didn't know what to do.

I felt bad about it afterwards, because I think he wanted help. But what could *I* do? Mabel told me which flat was his.

'Before I head out tonight, I'll see if I can do anything.'

'You're going out again tonight?' she whooped.

'I need some fresh meat.'

'I couldn't do that,' she said, doing some sort of impromptu exercise on the partition. 'I really have to love a guy. But I get all the freaks! Like that John Dewgrass in Number 42. Met him?'

I was pretty sure whom she meant. 'Hair: short, back and sides. Suit: black. Briefcase: old-fashioned, tanned. That him?'

'Yup, dat's da one, sweetheart. Believe it or not, he's our landlord. He's proposed to me every day for the last year.'

This Mabel seems to have more men lusting after her than I do!

Anyway, no, I hadn't actually spoken to this John Dewgrass, but I confided a suspicion I had about him to Mabel.

'Do you know, when I came home on the train this afternoon, I think our Mr Dewgrass actually raced me from the station?'

'You're so cute to think that!' laughed Mabel.

'No, I mean it. Does he race *you*?'

'You're legs are ten times longer than mine, honey. I'd say you were more of a challenge.'

Funny kind of challenge, but I'm *sure* he was racing me. And it got funnier still when someone else gave him a good run for his money: this short guy with black hair, goatee, sideburns, and these funky, pointed shoes. I did laugh when he overtook me and then hurried on after our Johnny boy.

But do you know the really odd thing? After the goatee guy had gotten ahead of me a couple of metres, he turned around and gave me this conspiratorial 'I'll get him' wink before disappearing up the street after Mr John Dewgrass.

The Situation Is Perfect.

John Dewgrass' recollections of Friday 15th July 2005.

Dear, dear Audience, hear me out and do not interrupt, please. To enliven my existence and indulge my desire to excel at something (I was never good at any conventional profession) I, John Dewgrass, have fostered in myself an addiction to an absurd act.

'Absurd act?' you ask. You will laugh, no doubt, for it is simply this: each day, returning home after work, I depart the train station along with the other passengers and race them.

I have invented the rules, so I am never frustrated, and never lose. There is no opposition or large erroneous foundation to be razed before I can perform, for, by my willing it and providing its purpose, the situation is perfect.

'How do you transcend from the observable phenomenon of people walking from the train station in their journey home to whole event *being* a race?' you object. Dear Audience, it is the idea of it which charms! The mind is warped with many strange notions from birth. A time there was when women wore corsets, gloves, and dresses which hid their ankles (good heavens!) in reverence of their womanhood. What of it today and mini-skirts? Yet the idea was real and unrelenting as a rock to those in deference to it.

My effort was the unison of two states, dream and reality: a surrealist exercise. And please do not say of me that I am a fool as you have all no doubt behaved similarly. For instance, when walking on a concrete path with your easy steps, have you never avoided the lines? You have done this, but why? And have you never played the game whose purpose is to avoid stepping on other people's shadows?

Is all that any sillier than plush carpets and dining with Pam and Julian on Wednesday nights?

Philosophy majors, Brad and Scooter, were walking not five metres behind Mr Dewgrass, engaged in their own commentary.

BRAD Surrealism is wishing for something other than what is – a respite from interminable reality. The rock's 'heartbeat' is not the rock's heart beating but the rain's pounding on it. 'If it's flaming giraffes and lobsters in odd places you want,' I said, 'Why not, then, inclusively get stoned, pissed, legless – it's effortless!'

SCOOTER Scooter, did you know I was an artist? No? If you did, you wouldn't say this. I'm no good, really I'm not. I don't want to etch where every line is only a line and nothing underneath.

BRAD Never mind, dear chap. Let us drink this Shiraz '85.

SCOOTER Oh, Brad, it's a remarkably full, huge, rich, dense, solid, vigorous, high-coloured, voluminous nose, strong flavoured, long-in-the-mouth, soft, lingering, dry red!

But enough!

It was on a certain evening that a most calamitous event in my life unfolded. I shuffled from the train, as usual, was herded with the other passengers who filtered through the station's exit gate in an hour-glass shape, and began the race for home.

SCOOTER Well, he's off – Mr Dewgrass the walking champion. He has competed in this race 635 times now and is undefeated.

BRAD Yes, Brad, as always, he made it out of the start-gate with alacrity and speed, and is moving into the lead now ...

SCOOTER ... overtaking a schoolboy and a lady with shopping bags. Only three more people to pass now; and the race has just begun.

BRAD Yes, Scooter, it looks as if it will be an easy win once again for the reigning champ, Mr Dewgrass. But I have heard his briefcase is especially heavy this evening with paperwork. It could be quite some handicap.

SCOOTER Well, if it is an impediment, Brad, it's not slowing him down. I'd say he has conceived this race well and his triumph is secured. Certainly he has differentiated himself from the world of objects (animals, trees, rocks) and become a self-determining agent for choice, a substantive existent.

BRAD Would you believe, Scooter, yesterday some existentialist guy talked of having developed the criteria for an authentic existence; said how it separated him from the herd: he felt more keenly, more deeply than the ordinary man; said how *man is an abyss*; and how he could map his own authenticity on an exponential growth curve that never touches the Y-axis – he just keeps on getting authentic!

SCOOTER I think *man is a machine* and my etchings are merely metal plates with a layer of bitumen on each, corroded in parts and busied with lines. They simply *are* ...

BRAD Sip that *Shiraz*. But what of Mr Dewgrass?

SCOOTER Right now, he is wandering up Longevity Street tapping each parking meter with his foot. Oh, but he misses one and, knowing it is unlikely he will come this way again – at least till Monday – and also that he is unlikely to remember which one it is (unless he counts them which he can't – he hasn't the time), he wanders back and drums it with his foot.

BRAD And discerning that the moment is precipitous, pausing at the cast iron gate with its forks, he shields his eyes, having imagined himself tripping.

SCOOTER Yes, and his eyes being gouged out. But wait! Mr Dewgrass has purposely stopped! And now Memphis is ahead and, by a factor of two, multiplies his lead on Mr Dewgrass ...

It was absurd. I was testing myself to see if it were possible to allow this man before me to win. It was, after all, a game — a mere frivolity. We were some twenty metres from my door and I knew the man ahead lived several doors further on. I saw him glance at his watch and, noting the time, find it necessary to hasten his walk. I held back a moment and realised then his verisimilitude. His seemingly casual steps were a pretty artifice with which to conceal his fierce intent — his wish to beat me.

BRAD Oh, this is unexpected! Mr Dewgrass is deliberately holding back while Memphis is walking speedily onwards.

SCOOTER No, Mr Dewgrass is off again and furiously pursuing Memphis. He must've had a change of mind. It's going to be a close finish!

BRAD Mr Dewgrass is two lengths behind, with his house just five metres away. Mr Dewgrass is on the inside. He's moved onto the verge. The grass is slowing him down, causing friction. Mr Dewgrass is half a length behind Memphis. Memphis is just half a metre from Mr Dewgrass' letterbox. Mr Dewgrass is level with Memphis. It looks as if he'll win — HE'S FALLEN! Mr Dewgrass has fallen! Memphis has won the race! This is unpre-e-e-cedented, ladies and gentlemen!

Oh what false charge is this that I am marked with the losing place? The villain ran, and running is cheating! I thrashed the rapscallion for his own good and still he maintained his deceit, pretending – if you can believe it – that he knew not of the race or that he was a contestant! The police were mistaken in arresting me! Am I always to be subjugated to the will of other people?

SCOOTER I am concerned with the nature of mind and matter, perception, self, free will, causation, time and space, and ethics. I must know this to be at home in the world.

BRAD Are such philosophical excursions conducive to happiness?

SCOOTER Scarcely so. In fact, NO!

Perhaps you are now seeing that time is not necessarily continuous. Sometimes I wake and it's yesterday. Please don't touch my aura; let us just press on as we again return to Henri and his communications with Mabel.

Chapter Three

It Will Happen When It's Meant To.

Monday 18th July, Melbourne 2005.

Today, instead of conversing with Mabel over the balcony partition, I invited her in. Couldn't have the dear standing on her balcony furniture all evening, gripping that tin partition with those chubby fingers. We really should have gone to her place, since I have not a single item of furniture except a temporarily acquired bed.

'Did you knock on Bertie's door on your way out last night, honey, and see what the matter was?'

Yes, before heading to town (Sunday at the *Laird*), I'd seen Bertrand standing at the bottom of the metal staircase, wearing his long duffel coat, his hands hanging by his sides. I shouted hello and waved but got no response, even though he was staring right at me. I mean, it was plain rude. Suffice to say, I went on my way.

'Oh well, honey, can't have been too bad if he's up and about.'

Mabel edged the conversation towards my last night's exploits.

'La-di-da, I'm terrible,' she apologised. 'I have no life, I know, but I can live through you, can't I, sweetie?'

'Mabel, I met this very special man last night. Tall, well built. Dark eyes – almost black. I was very impressed. I smiled at him across the bar but *he* came over to *me*. *That's* taking the initiative. He's quite scruffy. Not one of these Prahran Lab mice, all hairless and toned. And like all Melbourne people, he was in black, as though the weather isn't dark enough as it is.'

The funny thing was, he knew my name. Straightaway.

'Henri? By God, it's you!' he shouted across the pub.

I asked him if maybe we'd met during the 'Foam Party' at the *Peel*, but he said he didn't know what that was.

He said his name was Cassius (such a strong Roman name!) and I said, 'Well, Cassius, if you don't know the *Peel*, then I'm revoking your gay citizenship. You do know how the gay summer goes, don't you: *Midsumma*, then *Gras* (that's *Mardi Gras*, of course), then *Chillout* at Daylesford? You know Daylesford? Little country town, big name on the map.'

I must say he got a bit cross at that.

'Of course I damn well know it, my flighty friend. But is it only our sexuality that unites us, Henri? Straight people don't congregate at "straight functions". They get together because they like speedboat racing or betting on the dogs, or something equally meaningless.'

'Oh, get off your soapbox, please. What do you think a pub is, if not a straight venue? And if you really believed life was meaningless, you'd be dead. You would have killed yourself.'

'Henri, if I thought death was the end of everything, then yes, I would have killed myself. Life is a terrible thing to live with, my friend, and I'm not so fond or foolish as to overprize what I had no part in the getting. Now, I ask you, Henri; do I not agitate *any* part of your remembrance? At least when we first met in Pompeii, circa first century AD?'

I chuckled.

'That's got to be the most original pickup line I've heard. "Hey, babe, haven't we met in a former life?"'

'*Lives*, Henri. Plural. Would that we had just the one, but the cycle is as endless as Sisyphus' labour. You, my friend, are the unstressed syllable to my accented beat. No verse of yours ends with the termination of a line. It is but the enjambment poetry

I carry over into my next flourish. We two *were*, *are*, and *will be* again.'

A complete nutter, of course – but *such* wog boy looks! Have I told you about that weakness of mine? He had orbs so black you'd need a torch to see into them. Stature: 'shambolic' (the word he used), fortress eyebrows, battlement cheeks.

I went home with him (as you've probably guessed) and he had such a strange house. Had photos lined up from one end to the other, and this coffin with thumbtack pictures. Kinky stuff.

'But it was nice, Mabel, and I can tell what that look means. You wanna know, "Did we?" Actually, yes, and it was much better than the previous night's effort. I think I was a little smitten. The way he had actually dared to make the first move with *me*. It made him so vulnerable and of course if you don't feel vulnerable, then you can't really be intimate.'

Mabel rocked on her backside, feet pulled tight in, lotus-style.

'I'm waiting for the one,' she whispered. 'I know he's out there.'

'Oh, now you're sounding as fanciful as Cassius,' I chuckled. 'Don't tell me you believe in past lives as well?'

She believes.

Dear Mabel! But now Cassius (who certainly knows a thing or two about past lives) takes up the tale.

Is Nothing Remembered For Good?

Monday 18th July, Melbourne 2005.

That confounded stripling, Henri! I thought I would never find him in this lifetime and yet here he is, still unaware. Must *I* sometimes remember whilst he *always* forgets? I met him last night, at the *Laird*. Never one to suffer gladly the contrivance of social gatherings, I was nonetheless taken by a whim for human company, and it was a whim, for once, I was glad I acted on. As I was sitting one side of the main bar, near the pinball machines, a few men tried to engage me in conversation, but I am not much suited to the pettiness of small talk. It was at that moment, through bar staff and beer haze, that I saw him.

'Henri?' I cried. 'By God, it's you!'

The recognition was not mutual. I went over and, characteristically, Henri inquired if I might not know him through some preposterous queer event.

When I answered no, he prattled on in that charming, but completely fatuous, way of his, till I pleaded with him to listen.

He maddened me some more till at length he asked, with that customary forthrightness of the

77

shameless, 'Well, dear, aren't you going to invite me back to your place? Mine's a mess.'

Is it weakness to say I submitted to the proposal? And yet what a feast! I awoke to his body as I have never quite awoken to anyone else's, and mortally sorry was I for the intervening lifetimes. I was forbearing of his miserable, degraded character at the bar, but relieved when the slough of custom fell with his clothes upon the floor, and the real Henri emerged. Truly, the undegraded acquiesced to the purer, untrammelled communion of soul with soul, as translated through the language of body. We made and unmade each other many times, lost count of limbs, forgot ownership of parts, and were unmoored in number and selves. Brought back were all my long-suppressed yearnings for a unique passion, the desire to be held and understood.

But eagles must rest on the same rooftops as pigeons, and so we swooped down to perch snugly in sleep, cooing into each other's breasts.

When we awoke this morning, he rolled from my arms and sat up, easing himself to the back of the headrest.

'Who's the painter?' he asked, nodding to the prize I keep above my dresser.

'Why, you!' I shouted. 'Painted in the time of the High Renaissance, under tutelage from none other than Titian. Had you lived beyond your teens, you would have surpassed even that master.'

'Dear, I've never picked up a paintbrush in my life. A toothbrush, yes, but that's it.'

I sat up against the headrest with him.

'What? You don't paint? Henri, in Pompeii people would endeavour to pick the very grapes you daubed on our garden walls. Must everything be learnt again?'

I wanted to tell him: Henri, you and I *are* the congregation of art and science, the rational and intuitive combined. We are the only hope and agency against all that is corrupted.

But too much too soon would only send Henri scuttling from me.

Yet again.

It was but a year after my father, Cassius the Elder, had brought him from Gaul that Henri painted a spider on our portico wall. It was a spider so real that boys and girls alike would not suffer to touch it, Sextus the brave among them who was never again the brave after that. Yet *I* put my face against the spider, even as I shuddered within. Henri took up his brush and painted a fouler thing and I pressed myself against *that*. And when an even fouler creation followed, still I forced my flesh against it. Then, huffing, Henri sketched himself. The master's haughty pride over his slave is a terrible thing, and so I would not condescend to press my body against *that*, though every pore in my skin ached to imprint itself on the stunning likeness.

All the memories, each so unforgettable. Yet here was Henri today, chuckling as he unfolded himself from my bed and strolled down the hallway, surveying my photos while I hastily donned my diamond-patterned dressing gown. I threw another gown over Henri's shoulders but of course, in his love of nudity, he soon let it slip.

A questioning finger hovered over a photo.

'Why ...?'

The walls of my house hold a long line of photographs, beginning with the first my current parents ever took of me and ending now with my Polaroid of Henri from last night. It's a pictorial timeline of my present life, originating at the front door, circling the whole house, and then spiralling up the walls, each complete circuit representing a year. At present, the photos reach to Henri's and my height, which are very nearly the same. Not surprisingly, I have chosen to reside under the high-ceilings of a Victorian home.

I cooked Henri some toast, and spread it liberally with butter and jam in obeisance to his gluttony.

When I returned to the hallway and gave it to him, he ate absentmindedly, staring at one particular photograph. I noted he still talked with his mouth full.

'Hmm, who's this girl? I love those heart-shaped patterns on women's grey tops after jogging.'

'She is a complete stranger to me,' I answered.

He stopped eating to regard me and, immediately, I was at pains to explain.

'Henri, our lives are not just compounded of the momentous but aggregates of momentous and trivial both. In death, our lives are reconstituted, much as a dream rebuilds the preceding day.'

He crunched on his toast again, which I interpreted as encouragement to continue.

'Entertain for a moment a fantastic conceit: if someone dies in surroundings to which he is deeply attached, then his spirit will not instantly fly into the body of a newborn, immediately forgetting its past life, but will cling, in a kind of limbo, to the environment it holds dear. Thus these very walls you see about you, lined with snapshots of the most intimate as well as the most trivial moments in my life, serve much the same purpose as did the hieroglyphics in the tombs of Pharaohs. Both are a reminder to the dead of their lives.'

I hastened to the study, Henri following dumbly.

'Mark this sarcophagus.'

'You have a sarcophagus?' he choked.

'I commissioned a carpenter to construct it; he was most obliging. Here, let me remove the lid. Now, as you can see, the inside is lined with thumbtack-sized copies of all the photos on the walls, arranged in the same sequence. Thus, after my death, the slow corporeal decomposition of both my body and its permeable housing will facilitate a *gentle* passing into my next life without me forgetting this one. I've learned to do something similar in each of my lives with whatever materials and technology are available. And that, my friend, is why I know you from past lives. Only *you* always forget, whereas *I* remember.'

Henri placed his cold toast sticky side down on my sarcophagus lid. His eyes danced with an inscrutable light. Would he, at last, *believe*? Barely could I wait to know. Finally, he responded.

'Well, dear, you're certainly not standard-issue gay. Past lives, pictorial histories, Roman heritage – sure beats Marlene Dietrich records and glam pics of Liza Minnelli. Can we sit in the sun?'

Only by drawing on my deepest reserves of restraint, could I conduct Henri with anything approaching civility to the backyard, and thus into the light he so desired. He insisted I ferret out a blanket for us to sit on. My hands could barely resist balling themselves into fists. When I grimly suggested fetching dining chairs instead, he huffed, but draped himself indulgently on the ground, and my hands were soon stroking him, despite my pique.

They were laughed off in a second.

'I just can't get over it: photos of strangers on your walls! Baby, let me tell you about *my* favourite stranger. He's the serious-looking guy alone on the train (a bit like you, maybe), wearing some out-dated business suit and staring nowhere. Then, quite suddenly, he's all smiles and everyone wonders why. He doesn't really know why himself, but no matter how hard he tries, he can't stop till it's all laughed up.

Sound familiar?'

My compressed lips relaxed a few millimetres.

'There!' chuckled Henri, pulling at my cheeks, 'a smile!

'Blast you, Henri!' I shrugged him off. 'You're still adorable.'

'Let's leave off the *still,* shall we? Unless you mean in comparison to last night?'

'The matter of our past lives is no jest, my friend. Henri, no one dies forever who once lived. Each person – '

'Hey!' he interrupted.

'Yes?'

'Can we drop it?'

The sun passed irretrievably behind greying clouds, and we sought warmth indoors, Henri insisting on turning my heater to maximum. After a session of lovemaking in an atmosphere too overheated in the surroundings to be worked up to any great energy in the performance, my arms once more pulled him close, as we lay spooning on the floor. But it was not to last; Henri eased away, and sat up.

'I'm sorry,' he whispered, pinching my nose. 'I'm a different person after I've come.'

I answered with feeling: 'With you, I'm the same.'

Henri's eyes sailed the skirting board till they beached on the hearth at the base of the heater.

'Look at that cat – such a slut!' My tabby, Pandora, was practically lying on the heater. 'Hmm, is that fur I smell burning? Now she's toasting the other side. Could you have your legs any wider apart, Puss? I might come and join you for the warmth. Think she'd move over for me, Cassius?'

'What, and leave me that old recourse of hot-water bottle or current-sozzled blanket?'

'Lucky water-bottle.'

He had by this time stood up, and was swaying languidly by the window. I rose to join him, and lifted the blind.

'Cloud's clearing,' I said. 'And I confess a drive down the coast would redeem my spirits. Would you consider joining me for the intake of air and scenery?'

'Spend the rest of the day with you? Nuh-uh. Listening to your madness would send me sane. I'm about due for some *me* time.'

'Apologies for making claims on your prized hours,' I retorted. 'At least submit to relinquishing me your number.'

'Sure, but don't go texting me, will you? Guys do that to me all the time, just so the sole responsibility isn't on them to ring. No guts.'

'I won't be texting you, Henri; *I* will call.'

'Are you as good on the phone? Oops, now I've got you blushing, red as that cat's belly. Isn't she

84

gorgeous? Going to let me pat you goodbye? Ready for that number?'

For a moment, I thought he was still conducting a conversation with the cat.

'Yes, Henri, I am.'

I keyed the number into my phone and saved it. Henri swaggered to the front door but, instead of opening it, turned back to me. Was he going to stay?

'Aren't you going to repeat it back?' he asked. 'All the guys repeat my number. They couldn't bear the misery of writing it down wrong, and getting some granny on the line.'

Had he forgotten even my facility for numbers? I rattled it off, then thrust my mobile in his face as a double proof of my capability. Without flinching, he read and nodded, then pulled me in close to plant a hasty kiss. Before I could respond with greater passion, he slid backward through the doorway, like a magician's stooge through the false bottom of a conjuring box, and was gone.

The remembered tumult of all our lives together made me slow. I doubt Henri heard my belated shout: 'Why, if you aren't even more foppish and conceited than in former incarnations!'

Blasted idiot.

And so, dear Reader, let us journey together into the mind of Cassius the Elder.

What Of News From Rome?

Pompeii, 89 AD.

I have put off youth as one discards a toga for sleeping, and my bones are draped in sallow hide. I hurry home to him (my son, Cassius – how old now?) and his mother (my wife, Calpurnia), and already my farmstead peeps round the pine. Spur on the steed, old man, though your sinewed hands stiffen on the rein. For too long now you've been gone.

Closer still, and softly there, my horse. Would we have them warned of our arrival? Is that Fabulus with wood for the family hearth? Look how he struggles to enter at the door with it. Have I caught him in age at last? No, *he* is the more wizened.

Whoa at last, and let me alight. Tether you there. Let me thrust open the door and enter: Hie, for I am come home! And lo, such shock and consternation! Uncork a full of Alban wine, my wife, and set me a banquet while I see to the present I have brought in this sack for our son. Where indeed is our son? Aha! Can he have grown so? Come closer, Cassius, look at my gift for you. Don't trust the lamplight too much, but I'm sure you'll find he's just as fair in full sun. *He?* Why yes, your gift is a boy. Calpurnia, a boy for our boy! What is this shyness, Cassius? Sooner a dog turn its back on a hare, than my son shun a slave boy. Come now, take a closer look at him. Hold up that candle so. Not on a slant! The flame gutters. Look piercingly. What say you?

Is he not indeed a good gift?

Ever you stroked hair more flaxen, or touched skin more soft? He is my gift to you, and a gift … relatively untouched. Look you so, Calpurnia? Do I lie? Cassius, Son, I *swear* this boy is a virgin…

By what do I swear, Calpurnia?

Why, by my truncheon!

Ha, please! My sides laugh along till they would cough up my innards. 'I swear by my truncheon' – that is a good one.

What say you, Calpurnia? Why call you for your maid? To have the boy bathed and washed? How you dote. You are no Spartan.

Finally the fire roars. We will have some heat and, with it, light. Aye, that is better; I see you now and yet …

Well, well, my dear, I'm away a year and what do I find? Look you, Fabulus, at Calpurnia, her complexion still as fine as the pinkest rose. And those ringlets that flounce on her shoulders. Woman, you will find plenty of ivy from my garden (if you have tended it well) to bind back those curls. Fabulus, do you believe I was the first to aim his shaft from Calpurnia's bow, as I was the first with this boy?

There, there, lad, don't whimper so. You are my son's gift. Smile lightly on him.

What say you, Calpurnia …? That Troy was besieged more than once? Ha! Triple-tongued Cerberus has not more lip.

And lo, who parts the curtain? Is this the new servant girl, Minia, of whom you wrote? Very pretty, and a gentle expression. She returns my smiles and glances – but what is it I read in them? Don't look so, my girl; dissemble a little. Such transient fruit must needs be plucked before it perishes. Fear I see, at least – to me, a bigger draw than her figure. Indeed, despite it torturing her features, how fresh she looks, and you, too, my wife. Never before wore you such short dresses, always keeping those beautiful legs hidden.

But is this room not blistering, or is the heat all my own? To have this slave-girl, Minia, at my bidding, along with my wife in such a state of undress, is akin to striking tinder on kindling. Fetch more water to dilute this wine, my man; I sweat intemperance.

Yes, your countenance can mean only one thing, Calpurnia. So, you have taken a lover, my love? Serve me right, Minia, for trumpeting her beauty. I've pimped her charms and news travels, even to these reaches. But, by Jove, she's mine alone! I don't ask that you be faithful, Calpurnia – you're far too attractive. But keep your misconduct for bed. And tidy your hair! That degree of dishevelment takes more than a bad night's sleep.

Fabulus, the lady is fatigued. Plump out a cushion for her, do. Fan her face, slip a little footstool under her dainty feet.

But what of news from Rome? Caesar extends his Empire. Barbarian lands fall at the mighty onslaught. And fair-haired whelps such as these are the ancillary prizes ...

Now where *is* that little Gaul? He told me his name, the only sense to be had from him. What was it ...? Henri! That's it. And there he is, roistering with my son.

How the two wrestle! Does Henri overpower you, Cassius? Dare you blub like a babe? Mark you well, my son: even bulls can be broken to plough, or spirited horses subdued with bridle and bit. Let your bowshot skewer his breast. The worse the wound, the deeper the branding. Sear your name in his eye. Already he looks upon you as Pandora upon Hope.

But never look upon *him* with anything like longing. He is your hobbyhorse only. You will have your sixteen-hands-high steed soon enough.

What is that, Calpurnia ...? Our son is too young for bareback? Though of green years, what are calendars to you, my Cassius? A mere babe was Hercules when he strangled the hydra. And this Gallic boy has only the *one* neck.

But what of news from Rome?

Let me tell you of the sanded arena where Caesar staged a mock battle between the Persians and

Greeks. I was there and, I tell you, if blood and entrails could clean, I was bathed then. This boy's family played the part of the Persians. Is it too little to say they lost?

In time, Cassius, you will fight such a battle – a real one in some foreign land.

What is that, my wife?

Cassius is more fit for the arts? Already a budding orator? A marvel in math and rhetoric, Pliny says.

Bah! Pliny is a milksop! No, this son of ours will be brought up for battle. Cassius, your righteous javelin shall more than match the enemy's treacherous arrows. Justice and right shall march before your banner. Conquered nations shall know Roman civility, as shall this whelp Henri know obedience by your hand. That's it, strike him, my boy. Bite back. I hope one day to sing of your valour, and that you will do honour to your father and your father's name.

Calpurnia, what is that glance you give Minia? Your *maid,* Minia, I do add. So you choose to cuckold your man? At least cuckold him *with* a man!

But no matter, wife. Two can play at mischief. I will have this maid of yours whipped! By Jove, slave girl, with lightning I will –

How now, Calpurnia? You dare stay my hand? Why, what issues from your orbs, my darling? Are they tears? Truly, can women *love* women?

No, this is too much. Apollo laughs along with me ...

Fie, your wailing proves it so.

Well, well, it seems I must congratulate, not castigate, fair Minia. Young girl, you've played your fish on the hook that's taken, made a servant of a mistress!

Go to, Minia, serve the sweetmeats now, but it is you I shall bed tonight.

Dismissed!

Now, where is that slave boy crawling? Fabulus, take you this Gaul to the barn. Make sure he is fettered. What's the use of liming a bird's wings if it escapes?

And give me not such long looks, my son. You will have plenty of time to play with Henri tomorrow.

Come, sit on my knee. Nay, on my knee. Look you so at your father? Has your mother armed you with false notions against me? I am no tyrant. Climb up. That's better.

Cassius, did I tell you of my battles with the Germans? But wait, my throat is parched.

Pass me that wine, Calpurnia. And yet … should I drink more, and risk cooling my inflamed loins? A small wind will fan the fire, a gale put it out … Ha, no doubt Minia hopes I will drink a skinful. And yet, Cassius, this is not a tornado easily untwined. A snake teased will bite.

Retire you to bed, Calpurnia. How your face is as pale as the Gaul's. Be gone; I would be alone with my son.

Now what more of Rome?

Cassius, my cherished, after long absence of fighting, with my men I rode into the colonnade on snow-white steeds, preceded by the fettered captives of our campaign, the fair-headed Henri among them. Is he not indeed a good gift?

We now turn to Minia herself, some fifteen years on, for the tale of those years and of how Cassius and Henri first parted. (You will note that Henri's character and voice are quite different to his present, more vacuous, incarnation. What circumstance and education can do to mould a man! Do you think you would still be you if you had been born elsewhere and in a different time? As for me … Well, it takes real force of personality to remain timeless!)

Handsome Henri.

Pompeii, 79 AD.

I remember well the day Henri came into our household. So unexpected, the master's return after seven years away, and such a surprise when the bundle he set on the table turned out to be a child! A 'Gallic rascal' to help about the house, said the master.

Henri was certainly the scruffiest thing you can imagine, but with such fair features and eyes! As soon as I could, I gave succour to him, and it was a wondrous thing to have a child of my own, for that is how I regarded him – foolish woman that I am. Me, a slave! Still, it was something to hold him. And, though treated ill, he soon grew quick and strong.

The master's coming home put paid to the passion the mistress and I had enjoyed, but while our hearts grew wan, the same could not be said for the boys, who were soon fast friends. Inseparable. Only the wood nymphs could hear what they talked about late into the evenings – children have more to say than adults, I'm sure. And yet their friendship was not without imperfection. Cassius' father would often warn his son against becoming enamoured of a slave boy, but more and more Cassius burned with love for handsome Henri – and who could blame him! Oh, don't mind me.

Ahem. Ah yes … Cassius tried to hide the flame in his dark looks, but he could not hide it from *my* eye. I'm very smart, you see. No, I'm not vain, merely too honest to be humble. *I* knew why Cassius was always slinking into the beech plantation where, alone with his futile passion, he would lament to wood and hill.

In time, Henri's limbs grew long and lithe from labouring, Cassius' hard and sinewy in the swordplay his father required of him. Poor Cassius! So gifted in math and rhetoric, but honour-bound to follow in his father's warmongering footsteps. Thus the day arrived when young Cassius was called away to Rome, a captive to war, at risk of perishing, unpitied, in an alien land.

For the two boys, it was a sullen parting on both sides, neither admitting the essential blow, corn-blonde in Henri and bear-black in Cassius. Who valued more the middle way: Henri, standing glum by the narrow riverhead, or Cassius borne onward astride his sunny steed?

In the years that followed, beauty, freshness, and youth receded from me, but were met in amorous unfolding in Henri, whom I urged to forbear inquiring of distant lands, or beating his breast about his tethered-state. Rather, I would counsel, he should focus on his modest needs. Poor dear, he was naturally jealous of Cassius' adventurings.

Upon that subject, I should say that we received many letters from Cassius, while Henri was ever lax and limpid in his correspondence.

'Dear Henri,' Cassius would write. 'Life in Rome is full of unimportant rituals and of everyday matters.'

And Henri would not write back, or would write precious little, or sometimes get me to quill a note.

'Write this to him, Minia ...' he would begin.

'I can't write *that*,' I would interrupt now and then. '*Or* that!'

He had grown into a very tall and handsome man. Still that flaxen hair – and such hands! (Have I told you how hands affect me?) Henri was rumoured to be quite vivacious and easy with the farm boys.

Anyway, time marched on, and Cassius wrote from Jerusalem, complaining of a troublesome sect.

'Minia, you ask how I am faring, and since the letter speaks only in your tongue and not that other, it is to you I shall address my words.'

I nudged Henri meaningfully.

'I am proconsul in Jerusalem, employed in the services of Trajan and dealing with a degenerate cult carried to extravagant lengths. Its members call themselves Christians and I have informants who give me the names of suspects. These, I have brought before me that I may put them to the test. This I do by requiring them to recite an invocation to the gods, make offerings of wine and incense to our emperor's statue, and revile the name of their Christ. It is a wearisome task and many times I have had to extract the truth by torture.'

'What is their crime?' asked Henri, leaning lazily on my shoulder, the two of us stealing some rest in the field.

'They believe in the One God,' I answered.

'That seems economical,' he yawned.

I tried to point out the error in such thinking. 'Imagine having just the one god for love, for war, for messages. It would be a very busy god. Busier even than I am with domestic chores.'

Henri grinned sideways at me.

I read a little more to him of Cassius' correspondence.

'I believe my time would be better spent in study, in improvement, roads, sanitation, mathematics. Above all, mathematics.'

Mad Cassius, and madder Henri.

'Oh what fun to worship the *many* gods,' I shouted, 'paying special tribute to the Corn-goddess.'

Henri placed a wreath of oaks leaves on my head, lifted me up, and we danced an impromptu jig.

'Ah no, I am too old, Henri.'

We fell on the cheerful grass.

Yes, we were very happy that day, because that morning our master had died and Cassius was to come home to take his place.

When Cassius arrived on his steed, there came with him the queerest personage. Cassius introduced him as Memphis, and when this Memphis alighted from his horse, I had the fleeting but alarming spectre of a satyr before me – one who smiled at my unease as if to say, 'You got me!'

That night, they sat at table without Henri who, after all, was a slave. To me, Cassius' listlessness at dinner proved him still in love and though mute to begin with, much injudicious wine soon elicited his secret thoughts, which were all of the same theme. And that clearly was one he ached for Memphis to play, as on a harp.

'He prides himself that his tenderness surpasses any girl,' I heard Cassius say. Then, when asked if the absence from home had dimmed his ardour, it very quickly became clear that neither time nor any number of sleek boys or tender girls could redirect his passion. Though he had tried to copy the Stoics' indifference to reversals in fortune, he still remained a master in bondage to his slave.

'I am Pegasus anchored by terrestrial Bellerophon,' he sighed between sips of Alban wine.

Memphis merely grinned.

On the morn, Cassius ventured out with the excuse of surveying his newly inherited establishment, and I insisted on going with him.

By the pine grove, we saw Henri, reed pipe in hand.

'Here I loll, serenading the woodland spirit beneath a spread of sheltering beech!' he smirked.

'You should be about your work,' barked Cassius.

Clearly, if Cassius was in love with Henri, it was a decidedly reluctant love.

'I *am* working,' said Henri, pointing. 'I drive your goats. This one drops her twin kids (the hope of your flock) in a hazel thicket.'

'But she must leave them on bare flint,' scolded Cassius.

Henri chuckled, and lifted one of the kids to his chest.

Cassius stared hard at the tiny thing's unmarred whiteness.

'What do you see?' asked Henri, perplexed by the strange squint in Cassius' eye.

'I see a little goat,' replied Cassius, 'forehead bumpy with budding horns. And I see that one day it will be slain and its blood will dye the block with prognostications of love and war.'

Henri chuckled again, letting the goat go with a slap on the rump. Bleating in protest, it retreated to the thicket.

'What did you see in Rome, Cassius?'

'You received my news?'

'But not from your lips.'

'One time I saw bones snatched from a starving bitch by beggars; another, an old crone in an alleyway looking for one last lover. How I've longed to live the simple life of the farmer, here in the fields so dear to me, studying nature and its workings, with Pan my guide and confidant.'

'Let your apple crop go hang.'

'And my vines untended?'

'These very orchards are crying for you,' sighed Henri. 'But not for me do they sing. What am I to do, Cassius? There is no way out from my slavery. I made my petition to your father, but he did not grant it. Ah, fortunate you are. Here, among hallowed springs and familiar streams, you'll enjoy the longed-for shade. It is your rich inheritance, Cassius. You own this, all this, and ...'

And we all three knew what else.

Henri roused himself, and stood, surveying the hill, his momentary distress but a flimsy cloud veiling an inextinguishable sun.

'Look how rich is the fallow ground,' he murmured.

'I see only roaming flocks and oxen fatigued by the ploughshare,' contradicted Cassius.

'You are in a dark mood today, Cassius,' I made bold to remark.

The two blinked at me, and then Memphis appeared, unnervingly, like one who had always been there but only now made his presence known.

'Tell me of your travels, Cassius,' repeated Henri, but Cassius did not respond.

'Your friend Cassius was a soldier,' laughed Memphis. 'You think that sheen on his sword is rust?'

Henri stared at Cassius' sword, as did I.

'Rust indeed!' snorted Memphis. 'Why, no, his sword still smarts with blood so thick upon the blade that he, in scraping off a layer, keeps finding older coats beneath!'

And Memphis regaled us with the tale of how he and Cassius fought the Parthagians in a prolonged battle. After one skirmish, Cassius returned from the field, his muscled body alloyed in blood. Memphis looked long in delighted horror, and shouted for the priests, but Cassius merely regarded his blood-soaked trunk, then turned to Memphis. At length, he said of all that crimson: 'My friend, it is not mine.'

'"My friend, it is not *mine!*"' Memphis squealed with glee.

'Memphis!' Henri's enthusiasm was palpable. 'That is what *I* long for! To leave here and go adventuring to Scythia, bone-dry Africa, the chalky spate of Oxus, even to Britain, that place at the very world's end. Ah, and my native land. When shall I see again the turf-dressed roof of my parents' simple cottage? Or, wandering, whisper to the ears of corn that were all *my* kingdom?'

Cassius was clearly puzzled. 'Why hanker for countries scorched by an alien sun?'

'*This* is the alien sun for me,' Henri countered. 'I was snatched from family. I am a Gallic ruffian.'

'Must you harp on that? This is your home now. The grafted stock adopts alien bounty.'

'This root has not taken.'

Memphis snorted with laughter.

'I never felt I have quite owned him, Minia,' Cassius confided to me several days later. 'Even since my father's death, he is no more mine than before. And my swarthiness is nothing against his dazzling fairness.'

Memphis was silent in the corner where he sat, but I rushed to reply: 'Remember, the pale privet blossom falls no less than the dark-toned hyacinth.'

'Minia, *he* looks down on *me*! He never considers what I am: my station in life; the respect owing to me. Rather, he is proud simply because my maddening mother gave him a single acre.'

I fell at Cassius' feet, gripping his hands in mine.

'Master, grant Henri full Roman citizenship!' I pleaded.

'You overstep your place, Minia,' said Cassius, his anger rising in his throat. 'I really don't ...'

Without warning, the walls shook and a vase toppled from a shelf, clattering to the floor, where its shards rolled apologetically. We ran to the window in search of explanation, but could see nothing to explain the interruption; only Mount Vesuvius looming with hunched shoulders against the sky.

In the following days, Cassius became very solicitous of his time, and I know he was working on his theories and theorems. I heard him argue with Pliny and later say to Memphis: 'Pliny's a fool. He accumulates facts, but what are they without a tablature for their use? I must look to the example of Pythagoras. As there are general rules for the properties of squares and triangles, so too must there be for thoughts, feelings and events!'

Cassius hinted at financial woes; his father had managed the land as well as his temper; Memphis offered to buy Henri from Cassius and it was with the keenest disappointment that I marked the lack of response from Cassius. He was actually considering it.

That night, I encountered Memphis when I was fetching wood for the hungry fire, and his sudden emergence from the dark so frightened me, I dropped all I had gathered.

'Dear, Minia, allow me.'

As he gathered the wood, I made bold to touch on a topic that was troubling me. Memphis encouraged me to speak freely.

'Cassius risks himself as Prometheus did, in bringing knowledge to humans,' I said, the words tumbling out. 'With knowledge comes grief.'

'Minia,' laughed Memphis, 'why, I can see you are an observer. There is, however, something more pressing you wish to ask me, is there not?'

'Since you ask, yes: why do you play them off against each other?'

'How?'

'Offering to buy Henri!'

Memphis did not answer – merely waved a finger at me, smiling. But the next day, when Cassius sold Henri to him, Memphis granted Henri full Roman citizenship on the spot! The look on Cassius' face could not have been more indignant, especially when Memphis further added insult to injury by also giving Henri money.

Cassius and Henri were soon neighbouring landholders. No longer slave and slave owner but equals! They met at their adjoining fence and I stood back, listening to their talk, which was at first cordial, then heated, until Cassius stormed off in my direction.

'Minia, this is the limit! Well, Henri, I say, graft your pears, set your vines in rows, move onward like a little she-goat! Browse all you like on bitter willow and clover flower!'

A twig snapped. Henri was behind us.

'Cassius, it is bitter only to you, and not these little goats,' he said, feeding a bouquet of clover to the goats flanking him on either side. 'Why not rest with me tonight, and sleep on a bed of green leaves?'

Cassius' dark eyes flicked momentarily to the green.

'You're welcome to taste *my* mellow apples, *my* floury chestnuts, *my* ample stock of cheese,' said Henri. 'Look over there – smoke rises readily from the rooftops and longer fall the shadows cast by the mountain heights.'

Suddenly, a rumble similar to the one we had heard several weeks before, saw us stagger on the ground like it was the heaving deck of a ship. To my horror, a dark seep of blood issued from Mount Vesuvius.

Cassius and Memphis were evidently made of sterner stuff and could make light of it.

'Vulcan smelts his iron,' said Cassius.

'Jupiter farts,' laughed Memphis.

Memphis gifted Henri yet more money.

'Just look at him!' Cassius would say to me. 'Strolling around, puffed up with wealth, but fortune does not change a slave. As he perambulates in his toga of twice three yards, the faces of passers-by, this side and that, express the most patent indignation. Do you remember when my father brought him to us? His flanks were calloused from Spanish bonds and his shanks from hard shackles.'

'And I remember your look too, for you had a mate and a new plaything.'

Cassius said nothing.

Cassius fell more and more into his sums and figures. I, with others of the household, was left to attend to matters alone, just as we had towards the end of Cassius' father's reign.

Our Cassius was particularly enchanted with Plato. 'Minia,' he said one day. 'Plato was inspired by the gods with his ideas on forms. Is the form of beauty beautiful? We have all betrayed in thought if not in deed; and *been* betrayed. We have all known terror as well as enchantment.'

With Vesuvius rumbling on, Cassius was of the opinion, shared by many, that the dark reverberations we were all hearing was merely a type of earthy indigestion. To flee would be as childish and cowardly as to run from thunder or lightning. Henri believed otherwise, and was planning to leave. He and Cassius met once more and I accompanied them a little way on the hills. I sensed in both a certain detachment which both seemed eager to remedy, so I let them get ahead of me, but after a few brief words, they parted in anger. Later that same day, Henri left Pompeii, along with more of the remaining townsfolk.

The mountain was now continually arguing with the sky, dyeing it black even in sunlight.

Cassius stayed and, despite my mounting terror, I was to remain with him. But that night I too fled, having to climb through the window to do so, such was the level of the ash that had built up against the door. Coughing, I made my way to the harbour and spent the rest of the night there. Next day, I chanced upon Henri, who was selling his goats, and as we talked, the mountain erupted in earnest, smothering Pompeii in ash. We stood with Pliny's son at Mycenae as the last flotilla of boats was readied, all of us in awe of the giant cloud over Vesuvius. Pliny described it to me very memorably as being 'like an umbrella pine, for it rises to a great height on a trunk and then splits off into branches.'

When I turned to relay the description to Henri, he was gone and one of the ships was already out to sea.

And Cassius? He was entombed in ash and pumice.

With the insight of Minia's reminiscences, perhaps you can now appreciate that the relationship between Cassius and Henri was hampered by a 'history' far exceeding the troubles attendant upon the average couple. And to make matters worse, one party (Henri) could not recall the shared past, while the other (Cassius) was all too burdened by it.

I should also mention here that when Henri left Cassius' house some two millennia after leaving him in Pompeii, the immediate reaction of the two was just as you might expect. Cassius, keenly stung, settled in his study to work on formulating an equation for describing the mistakes of history and by extension a formula for avoiding their repetition. By contrast, Henri, as you already know, made his way to that eponymous block of flats and revealed, to the nearest person available (Mabel Pinkerton), his impressions of his strange 'one-night' stand, and in the day that followed, continued to confide his innermost thoughts to his willing listener.

You know What I've Been Thinking.

Tuesday 19th July, Melbourne 2005.

'Mabel, I nattered on too much at poor Cassius, I know! I must've sounded so up myself. I even teased him over how many days it would take him to ring – the next if he was super-keen, or the standard three if he was being cool.'

'How long's it been, honey?'

'Well ... two.'

'You stayed at his house, didn't you? Can't you find your way back?'

'You don't wanna know my sense of direction and my mind was in such a whirl. I know I travel endlessly but that's because I don't know where I'm going ... I said some stupid things.'

'You were nervous, sweetie.'

'Me, nervous? Never!'

Good ol' Mabel. I'd invited her in again after she'd pointedly turned on every appliance in her flat to announce her presence. When I eventually knocked on the wall, she rushed straight round. That started a dangerous precedent and one I'll probably live to regret, though an ameliorating factor was, the dear brought two pots of crème caramel. Mass produced, but still tasty.

Mabel dug out her last spoonful.

'Hey, honey, you're probably gonna think me stupid, but ...'

'Ask it.'

'If I was to meet a guy I liked at a nightclub, that doesn't mean I have to go home with him, does it?'

'Ha! No, course not.'

'Not everyone's there to pick up that night, are they? I mean, I could give him my number.'

'And make sure you get *his*,' I added with meaning.

'I could ring in the next few days, couldn't I? I mean, I've decided I'm gonna be a bit more forward like you from now on, because you're obviously never short of a guy. I don't have to sleep with them.'

'Girls decide when they're gonna fuck a guy, anyway.'

'How would *you* know?'

'I've been there, Sista!'

'So, honey, that means I'm in with a chance?'

She really is special.

'Mabel, you're insatiable!' I chided her. 'Remember, *you* can decide. A guy with another guy, there's no contest. We both know we're easy. But you can have those straight boys eating out of your lap in no time.'

'You're so cute. Think I'm gonna ask that video store guy out. I'm sure he likes me. Will you come with me just to get things started? But if I pick up, you're dumped!'

'No, Mabel,' I chuckled, 'you've gotta do it on your own ...'

While Mabel hurries to the video outlet, the store clerk – not the one she fancied when hiring The Wicker Man, *but another (shorter, still lean, but with tuba-like fingers and a high, jockey voice) – is filing videos in their places. He reaches on tiptoe to put* Down & Out *to the right of* Everlasting *(not quite alphabetically but what does it matter when the customers will replace out of order anyway?) and hears the door open. When he turns, he's pleased to see the cute, dumpy girl he's been noticing rather a lot lately. She must be a good ten years older than him but age when it equates to experience is often a good thing, a sad affair when it does not. The clerk eagerly trots towards Mabel Pinkerton.*

Will You Go Out With Me?

Tuesday 19th July, Melbourne 2005.

'Hey, Mabel, I've been thinking: superheroes are just giants who've shrunk. No, I'm serious. It actually makes sense when you think about it. Listen, superheroes can pick up cars and throw them around, right, the way a kid can pick up a matchbox car and throw *it* around, yeah? Well, a superhero can do that because he's actually a giant who's been shrunk. So a car to him is just like a toy car to a kid. It just *looks* impossible to us – the way he can throw it around – but not when you remember the superhero is actually a giant shrunk to our size. See, he still has the strength of a giant. You can't shrink that.

'Me, I'm a miniature person who's been enlarged to normal size. No, it makes sense. All right, an under-average sized person, but the way I can pick up and throw a toy matchbox car around is incredible. And the way I can pick up these returned videos and stack them back on the shelf is downright miraculous. It's like *you* picking up a beachside house and relocating it to an inland cliff. You see, I can do feats that would be normal to other people, but they're superhuman to me because I've still got the strength of a miniature guy. That doesn't grow when *I* grow, just like a giant's strength doesn't shrink when *he* shrinks. So I'm a superhero. Make sense?'

'Oh, sweetie, whatever you say.'

'No, I'm right, Mabel. I'm a superhero. Would you go out with a superhero?'

'I don't believe you're asking!'

'That would be pretty cool, hey, telling your girlfriends you had a superhero for a boyfriend. Look, I like you. Your eyes are the right space apart.'

'Oh my god, are you really saying this?'

'No, listen, it's a compliment. I reckon my eyes are too widely spaced. See how you can't look me in the eyes? You have to look me in the *eye*. You've got to decide which one.'

'Your eyes aren't too widely spaced, sweetie.'

'You're just saying that to be nice. But it's okay, I can take it; I'm a superhero.'

'So am *I* a superhero?'

'No, you're a normal person.'

'Shucks. I wanted to be special.'

'Sorry, but *you* haven't been shrunk *or* enlarged. It's we superheroes who have been changed in size, though never in strength. And we can't fly, either.'

'Aww, what do you mean superheroes can't fly? Superman can.'

'No, it *looks* like he can fly, but that's just him taking really large steps as a giant. Since he looks normal-sized *to* normal-sized people, his walking looks like flying, but no one can actually fly. I mean, that's fantasy.'

'Okay, honey, I believe you. Whatever you say.'

'And when *I* walk, now that I've been enlarged, it looks to my miniature friends like I'm flying, whereas to you it's just normal steps.'

'So do you see these miniature people the same time you can see us normal-sized people?'

'Yes, of course. I'd introduce them to you but your eyes are too narrow to see them.'

'Narrow! Now I thought you said I had nice eyes?'

'You do.'

'Now you've gone and confused me, sweetie. Anyone ever said you were – you know – a little bid odd?'

'Never. No one has ever said that.'

'Oh …? Uh … Yes, sorry, honey, must just be me.'

'So will you go out with me?'

'Um … No.'

'Why not?'

'Just … because!'

'Come on, you like me.'

'No.'

'I can tell you like me.'

'No!'

'I bet no one's ever complimented you on your eyes before.'

'I can assure you they have, honey, but not to say they were the right space apart or too narrow or whatever!'

'Then they're not true connoisseurs, are they? How could you put up with people who don't fully appreciate you? Phrenology is an art unfairly dismissed.'

'Have you escaped from anywhere recently?'

'I'm from Lilliput.'

'Lilliput!'

'You've read *Gulliver's Travels*.'

'I've seen the movie.'

'They always stack the *book* on the fiction shelves at bookshops, which is really annoying because it's memoir not fiction. It's Lemuel Gulliver's real-life account of his travels. Lemuel certainly isn't fiction; he really existed. And he visited the land where I'm from (Lilliput, home of the miniature people) way,

way back in my great-great-great-grandfather's time and the story has been handed down. He's a bit of a legend, Lemuel. We've got his journal in our library but of course *we* have it in the biography section. They called him the Man Mountain.'

As Mabel prepares to make a swift exit from the video store, another customer, who had been exceedingly quiet in the foreign section (French films), comes to life. His name is Edgar Bumpton, a name so perfectly suited it is as if a tailor has seen to the fitting. Let's hear him now.

Chapter Four

Oh My, Oh My.

Tuesday 19th July, Melbourne 2005.

Pardon me? Did I hear right? Oh my, oh my! Does that solve the very problem that has been perplexing me these countless years?

Lemuel Gulliver was *real*? Of course! So silly of me, and here I've been trying to find *mathematicians* with the corresponding initials, not a character from a book!

Whoops, perhaps I should explain myself. I am the owner of a special item – a very special item indeed! – bought from a myopic street-seller in Cairo. Cruelly, the poor man didn't know the fortune that was briefly his. Excuse my *bon mot*. I have a terrible predilection to humour.

The object in question is most extraordinary, cuboid in shape, and is called a supersolid. I wear it round my neck since it has a silver chain connected to one of its faces. On the opposite face are engraved the initials L.G. Now can you see the reason for my excitement? I have always wondered who was the original owner, and now I know!

Who would think it? I have visited the most abundant libraries and trawled even further with the advance of the internet, yet here I have the mystery solved at my local video store. And all from a conversation between the young man behind the counter (a Lilliputian no less!) and the girl trying to seduce him. My, my!

'Thank you, Sir, so very much, but no video for me tonight. You cannot know how inestimably helpful you have been. You, too, madam. Thank you again.'

What stares they confer upon me! Edgar Bumpton, no time for explanations. You have a mission, my man.

No time to pass the time. Oh, that's rather nifty.

Back to my flat.

Home.

Perhaps I should explain what is so remarkable about this supersolid, and why Lemuel Gulliver – that supposedly fictional character – makes sense as its original owner.

William P. Love, a mathematician at the University of North Carolina, thought he had invented the 'concept' of the supersolid, but he didn't. It's not hypothetical but real.

In length, it is one centimetre along each side so it has nominally a finite volume of one centimetre cubed, and a surface area of six centimetres squared. In one half of one face are two cylindrical holes, each with a radius of a quarter centimetre. In half of the remaining half are four cylindrical holes, each with a radius of 1/8 of a centimetre. In half of what remains, are eight more cylindrical holes, each with a radius of 1/16 of a centimetre, and so on *ad infinitum*. The holes penetrate the cube from one side to the other, thus producing two identical, Swiss cheese faces.

Even though the surface area of the cube is reduced by the area of both circular ends of the cylindrical holes, the surface area of the cube as a whole is increased by the inside surfaces of each cylinder. Thus the area gained is greater than the area lost, so that even though the cube should have a finite volume, it boasts an infinite surface area.

Neat, don't you think?

And yet the initials L. G. always puzzled me.

'L. G. … who could he or she be?'

Lemuel Gulliver!

And yet is it possible? Could it be true that the trinket once belonged to the fictitious protagonist of Jonathon Swift's masterful satire? Certainly the supersolid should not exist at all in our world; its actual presence is impossible according to earth-space physics. So perhaps it did belong to the similarly unreal Lemuel Gulliver, and should have resided elsewhere with him, in the imagination of Swift's readers.

Now let me formulate an hypothesis from this first premise.

If Lemuel Gulliver was a real person then ...

'Oh!'

I've just bumped into a gentleman on the steps to my flat.

'Dear me, a million pardons, sir, I was deep in thought.'

My new neighbour. Can't think of his name. French-sounding, but never mind.

Let us, for the moment, leave Edgar Bumpton to organise his thoughts and return to Henri, whose mind is on matters of its own.

Human Tolerance Threshold Anyone?

Thursday 21st July, Melbourne 2005.

I'm about to go mad in Melbourne. Tried having a little bake on the balcony – I do love to, even in the winter sun. And when Mabel popped her head over, I didn't even try to hide my dangly bits.

'Mind if I come over, sweetie?' she gasped, though

didn't bother waiting for a yes before dashing from her pad to mine.

Luckily my front door was unlocked so I wasn't required to get up for her, and I was glad to see she'd caught on that my joint was BYO; she'd brought Chi tea. Even went to the kitchen and made us both a cup while I got dressed.

'Mmm,' I groaned, sitting up and taking a sip. 'Delish.'

I didn't know how to tell the dear that my human tolerance threshold had been reached and breached for the week so I sat back and mostly let her prattle about some jerk in the video store.

'Might as well get out there, luv,' I told her. 'Saving yourself is like not drinking the milk in your fridge – it still goes off.'

Her brow knitted together

'Cassius was a treat,' I said quickly.

Her face ignited.

'I hope this works out for you, sweetie. But you're not to ignore me if it does. I've had other friends go into honeymoon hibernation. If you call me up in six months, I won't know you. And I need someone to talk to, with all the odd things happening round here. Sweetie, have you noticed anything yet?'

I sat up, squinting into the sun. 'Like what?'

'Well, Edgar Bumpton.'

And yes, he's certainly an odd one. He flew out of his door this morning, saw me across the atrium (his door is directly across from mine) and hurried over. His forehead is the first and last thing you notice about him. So steep and wax-like with exactly three hairs pasted over the crown like charcoal marks on char-grilled chicken. His eyes: pale fish behind glass. And such an odd way of talking:

'Young man, I have a favour to ask of you. Now, now, it is not a great one, or even very taxing. I tried to ask Mr Bertrand M. Pale, but he completely ignored me. Completely! How long can that man stand at the steps? I went the long way round by the fire escape just now to avoid him.'

Can't say I liked the reminder of poor old Bertie.

Anyway, I told Mabel what Bumpton had said, that he was planning a couple of weeks' sojourn in Tasmania and wanted me to watch his place while he was away. Mabel didn't look too happy when I told her how he leaned in and whispered dramatically: 'I'm on a mission.' He's mad, of course, but other than that, I could see no reason for Mabel to be fussing about Edgar Bumpton.

'Okay, sweetie, but *something's* going on,' she said. 'Our landlord, Memphis, says he's been concerned too and has already started to tighten security. Says he's organised to get bars on the windows. And June Pratchet in number nineteen is organising a committee. Just wondering, cutie, if I could nominate you for president?'

'Ha! No thankyou, dear. I'm not a committeeman.

Actually, don't know if I'll be here much longer. My feet still haven't been emptied of ammunition.'

Mabel's cute little mouth collapsed from a supernova to a black hole.

'What would I do without you?'

'What you've been doing up till now.'

Poor old Mabel hurried home to grab pen and papers. Seems she's to be the secretary for this committee, since she's good at shorthand and can type sixty words a minute. Boy, I've never really stayed in any one place for long, but I think this might be a record short stay.

Meanwhile, Edgar Bumpton is very much on the move.

Swift The Lauded Satirist.

Saturday 23rd July, Bass Strait 2005.

Oh my, a mere five days since I postulated my premise. So good to be under way, adventuring. My good neighbour Henri will watch my flat.

My premise is becoming certainty: Lemuel Gulliver is real. In that case, Jonathon Swift either chanced upon or deliberately sought Gulliver's journal, perhaps having heard of it from sailors to whom Gulliver had spoken.

Now, does this make Swift – the lauded satirist – a mere plagiarist? But then, which artist has *not* borrowed that which ends up in his work from some place, situation or person? Indeed, which artist has invented something entirely original? Especially when one considers that, of life and art, the latter distils from the former its essence, after the dross, the tedium and the irrelevancy have been siphoned away. Think of Descartes describing the things that appear in our sleep as being 'like painted representations, which cannot have been formed except in the likeness of real objects'. And elsewhere saying of painters that, even when they create the most extraordinary creatures, they 'cannot give them wholly new natures, but only mix up the limbs of different animals'. As with artists, so with authors.

I gave these thoughts a few hours' percolation. Then, as they became stale, I brewed yet more, arising from the repetition of that statement: 'As with artists, so with authors ...' Oh my, it is obvious. Swift was the first true surrealist!

Yes, it can truly be said that Swift was something of an early Marcel Duchamp, since he did very little 'mixing of limbs' with regard to Gulliver's journal – he simply found it 'readymade.'

And why that parallel? Well, Duchamp's once-notorious readymade sculpture (*Fountain*, of 1917) is but a urinal to which Duchamp had changed very little. He merely removed it from its usual place, denied it its usual function, signed it with 'R. Mutt' and exhibited it as art. Hence the description for this vein of artwork: readymade. Yet who would suggest that the engineer who designed the urinal or the workers who produced it should have a claim to the brilliance of *Fountain* or to the sagacity of its adoptive father, Duchamp? No one. And so, too, with the canny Swift, who took Gulliver's journal and presented it to the public as fiction, knowing discerning readers at least (those aware of his reputation as a satirist) would see in it a contrived piece of lampoonery.

And just as Duchamp had done with the urinal, so had Swift slightly modified Gulliver's journal to extricate it from its context – its grounding in fact. For instance, Gulliver's possession of the supersolid evidently allowed him to travel through 'gates' into the worlds of the Lilliputians, the Brobdingnags and the Houyhnhnms, but Swift suppressed this and other details. No doubt, he deemed them irrelevant to the work's new thrust, which was satiric.

And now to the clincher of my argument: the video store clerk saying he was a Lilliputian? Well, it matches the theory, which constitutes an hypothesis, which tallies with the fact of the supersolid.

The tiny supersolid provides a simile that helps describe the nature of infinite parallel universes. However, mark you that similes are clumsy. While it may seem interesting or witty likening one thing to another, a simile is never as good as a reference to the thing itself. However, a simile can achieve economy of language when innumerable words might otherwise be needed. So let us compare the case of infinite parallel universes with the supersolid. The infinite universes are not precisely cylindrical, and do not nestle side by side; rather, they inhabit the same space. Communication between these universes can be accessed through gates and keys, the model supersolids.

In the country of giants, Gulliver can 'appear as inconsiderable ... as one single Lilliputian would be among us' while Lilliput (again the simile) compares to a smaller cylinder than ours. In the case of the Houyhnhnms (of like size to our terrestrial horses) and the Yahoos (of similar size and make-up to humans) they must live in a cylindrical universe next to and of the same size as ours. Any claim that the Struldbrugs or the place of Laputa or of Luggnag are to be found on earth is a bogey undoubtable inserted into Gulliver's account by Swift. Instead, what can be found on earth are gates to these people and places.

According to Gulliver, the gate to Lilliput is northwest of Van Diemen's Land (Tasmania now) at latitude 30 degrees 2 minutes south. Assuming Swift didn't alter Gulliver's co-ordinates, all I need do, I realised, was reach that spot and then sail through the Lilliputian gate.

My mind perfectly clear, I immediately bought passage on the ferry that crosses regularly from Melbourne to Tasmania and made arrangements to charter a boat there. That same day, I went to see my sister.

'Listen, Biddy,' I said to her in the second-hand bookshop at Monash University, Clayton, where she works. 'I've got here a folder filled with certain things – letters, photos, funeral arrangements etc. – which I'd like you to look after and open only in the event of my death.'

Biddy looked worried, as I knew she would on hearing such talk. 'Don't worry,' I said. 'It's just that I've had a delicious idea for my funeral, however far off that might be. Some stuff to do with a countdown from ten, a plunger and dynamite in my coffin.'

I'm glad to say Biddy accepted the folder. I then went home, organised my needs and travelled the next day to Tasmania. From there, I set sail for the gate to Lilliput.

I voyaged to the very location where Gulliver recorded the co-ordinates of the gate to Lilliput. Of course, in the story Gulliver floats a whole half-hour beyond his recorded co-ordinates before arriving in that land, so I had a substantial area to search.

I began by examining the supersolid. I thought – nay, hoped – that it might indicate my proximity to the gate by warming up or beeping, but it did neither.

It was, however, glowing, so I sailed in the direction in which it glowed brightest. As I sailed, it glowed brighter still until it reached its ultimate brilliance. And lo – I, and it, fell through the gate.

As Edgar Bumpton enters his gate, a certain Rena Dinati is leaving hers. How and why she relates to our narrative is not yet clear, so we must listen to what she has to say …

Tell Me About It.

Saturday 23rd July, Melbourne 2005.

How's it going, darl? Not too good? Tell me about it. At least you look like you're getting some. It's been so long since my last root they're making me resit the exam. Know what it's like to go for your Ls when you're in your thirties? Pretty damn embarrassing.

'Rena,' Nonna used to say, 'you make me so ashamed. When you gonna find a man?'

Don't even wanna think about the last guy I dated. Talk about a crap kisser. Kept having to wipe my face with my sleeve. Back to puppy love. Still, give the poor dear marks for trying. I *swear* he gave it his best with my little man in the boat.

Ever had one of those moments where you've just given up and said, 'Here, darl, let me take over'? Well, it was kind of like that except I couldn't take over.

Tell me about it. Dogs have got it over us.

Lord knows I've tried. Last time I went to yoga, I spent the next week on my back. Yeah, and not in a good way, either.

Do you have friends who say to you, 'Darl, you're trying too hard. You've got to stop looking. When you're not looking, that's when it will happen'? Yeah? Well, fuuuck them! Like staying home's the answer. Unless some pretty goddamn hunky Jehovah's Witness comes knocking on my door, I'm sorry, sweetheart, but it just ain't gonna happen.

Cock update.

None.

Seriously, why bother?

They always come with baggage. And always, 'Do you love me?'

Do I love *you*? Hell no. Do I love *me*? Hell yes. Listen baby, you weren't always there for me. *I* was.

Honestly, sometimes …

Most men … I can't even begin.

I mean, it's like working with gifted sheep.

It's not even like all men are sex mad. And that's all they're meant to think about, supposedly. It's the only possible reason that could justify why they haven't got much else goin' on in their brains. If you take sex out of the equation, what are you left with? Not bloody much. You ask some of them how many times a day they self-medicate – that's my term for it, darling, because it *is* life-saving – and you'd be surprised the number who say once a week. Once! I feel like shouting, 'Honey, if you can't be bothered showing yourself a good time, you're not going to be much bloody good in a relationship!'

My boredom levels were so high at work the other day I almost self-medicated. Right there, in the ladies.

Actually, I did get started on the finger-popping. Bloody Sally Newton had to spoil things. If ever a mop bred with a bucket, she's the outcome. Kept knocking on the toilet door asking if I was all right. I'm pretty loud. Even *with* another person. Someone's got to be enjoying it, right? I'm like that at films too, or plays (sorry, *theatre*, darling) — always the one laughing loudest.

I mean, what is it with guys not making noise during sex? Is it because they can only think about one thing at a time, and if they make a noise they'll get confused and lose wood? Multi-tasking ...? Never heard of it, love.

Don't you hate the ones who say afterwards that it was nice? That was nice! Honey, either tell me it was worse than crap or it blew your socks off, but don't tell me it was nice. They're the boys I usually have to ride anyway. More control. And if I'm really lucky, I can pretend I'm a girl again and on my pony, *Stallion*. Don't ask.

Why are bad boys better roots?

What is that?

Yet crap at relationships?

I mostly get the nice boys, anyway. The Wet Ones. That's my term for them. I had this Wet One I was dating for a week who kept cooing into my ear, 'Oh, Rena, you're so nice and normal.' I felt like saying,

'Honey, I wouldn't even wanna hear that coming from my mum.'

Nice?

Normal?

When's a guy gonna tell me, 'Rena, you're the whore I adore, the ho I know, the slut to rut, and the scrag to shag'?

'And will you marry me?'

Never.

Does he exist? Think not.

The kinky ones are a bit better. Not much, but a bit. I call them the KYs and that's not even an acronym. Went out with this one particular KY who looked like an arsehole on stilts. Picture that. It was fun for a while. But you don't really feel clean after a golden shower.

Oh, and then there was the forty-year-old pre-schooler. What a dick. Used to eat his greens first so the meat would be saved till the end. Wish I could say the same for our sex life. I sure gave that dick the arse.

Yeah, no, not like that, thank you very much.

I think guys are scared of me. Any woman with a decent brain between her legs, that's gotta be confronting.

Now you reckon if you paid for sex you'd get the goods (yes, I've been there) but think again, honey. When I give a guy dosh to fuck me, I don't wanna hear his shit. It's bad enough when you're dating.

I have a problem with guys because of my upbringing. Well, that's my excuse, Toots, and I'm sticking to it.

But seriously, parents have a lot to answer for. You know how every parent's meant to think their child's a genius and all? Not mine. Try this for familial support: I wanted to be a ballerina, right? Yeah, hard to credit now, but *as* a girl. Anyhow, when I told my parents I had some talent in me, they replied that I was full of it.

Tell me about it.

Even Mum says I intimidate the guys. 'Ah, Rena, you shoulda close your legs more often.'

She means my mouth.

When we were going to school, my sis' and I, she'd tell her neighbours, 'I'm-a so worried. My bubbas are goin' to bisexual school.'

It was co-ed.

Couldn't get anything right, according to my mother. If I stayed around the house, I was a 'homophobe.'

She meant stay-at-home.

And if I went out all the time, she'd say I was a 'slut'.

She meant slut.

Dating?

I was worse than crap at it.

Had more luck double dating as a duo with my sister.

'Hey, Rena, Liz,' the fellers would say, 'you girls are real funny. Like, you two should do a double act.'

'Funny,' I'd say, 'guys are asking us to do that all the time.'

Not bad, my sis'. Guess we got along 'cause we both *didn't* get along with Nonna and Poppa. Can't stand her now they're dead.

Which brings me to my friend Henri, who isn't. Dead, that is. God knows he should be. A complete whore-bag. Can you tell I'm jealous? I whore myself, too, at times, but I keep making the one fatal mistake: falling in love. Hard to credit with a guy, I know. Wish I could be a lesbian. But *I* don't even turn me on.

Tell me about it.

Our 'complete whore-bag' Henri picks up the tale.

Time To Get Away.

Saturday 23rd July, Melbourne 2005.

Oh, the boredom of living. Already, I'm feeling totally trapped and wanting to get away, though there's a dog here that seems to have decided I'm never meant to leave the building. Name's Barney, Mabel says. Rang my old friend Rena yesterday to see if she wanted to rescue me, but my mobile's playing up, so it looks as if the only way I'm going to travel again is if I make some money. And that means an actual job because dole and rent assistance hardly add up to much.

I confess I looked at my mobile just then. Confess? That's just the sort of phrase Cassius would use. Okay, I have been thinking about him a *bit*. It's five days now since I stayed over and not a word. Five! That's not fair. That's unreasonable. That's just plain rude! Now, now, remember to breathe (some say I'm a natural).

Maybe I should have gotten his number ... but I *never* get the other guy's number!

Maybe it's good to make exceptions.

Noises from next door. Not Mabel's side but the other. Eardrum walls! Don't know the guy's name, but imagine a lock of auburn hair from a brumby – that's his ponytail. Haven't really met him yet. I've more heard him. Must have just come home. Certainly making a racket. Uh oh, TV. I can't stand people who, first thing they do when they get home, is turn on that horrible box. It's a war, and I've never forgiven them. To this day I still won't allow a TV in the house.

I don't remember one in Cassius' sweet abode ... There *was* a heater. Getting fed up with this cold. The only time I can stand the cold is when I'm skiing. I love criss-crossing the slope, making my large scale abstract paintings, white on white ...

Oh no, what's that they've got playing? Cricket. It's not even in season here so they must have cable. Shouting now? Please.

Mabel would say another odd thing to add to her list. I'm really not too sure what she was on about, but the sooner I make some money, or enough for a plane ticket, the quicker I can get out of here. Now where's somewhere hot?

Oh, that screaming! I hate getting involved in people's domestics, but ... saved by the mobile.

'Hello, hello ... Cassius ...? No ...? Rena?' I tried not to sound disappointed. 'Just a minute, will you, luv, I have to get outside my pad. Reception's bad. I think this whole apartment block's a communications black hole ... Yes, that's what my living arrangements have come to. Hey, it's pretty cold; think I could come over? Actually, think you could pick me up?'

If I can get past the dog.

Back to Rena. So many existences we each have! In our own and others' thoughts ...

Even *I* Don't Turn Me On.

Saturday 23rd July, Melbourne 2005.

First met Henri at a nightclub. I was the act. I'm a stand-up comedian. You couldn't tell? Anyway, God knows what Henri was doing at a straight venue.

Supporting a friend, he reckons. I walked up to him and tried what I thought was one of my better lines.

'I've never been with an animal, so how about it, Tiger?'

He chuckled. You've got to *hear* his chuckle to believe it. Almost makes me wish I had balls.

'Well,' he considers, 'a hole's a goal.'

All charm, isn't he?

But enough faffing about. Reason I mention Henri is that I caught up with him today. Yes, the man's in Melbourne. Talk about a meteorite that comes past every couple of years only the tail gets longer. He met me out the front of his place. I was waiting when he jumped over the wall. Said he had to bypass a dog. Left some meat for it. Yeah, right. I bet he was avoiding someone he wanted to give the flick. And the other bit Henri said – just as hard to credit – was that he's been seeing a guy called (get the name, would you) Cassius. The unbelievable part is that Henri is hankering for a second date.

Trust a ho to get hitched.

I know, tell me about it. I'm the one lusting for love and he's the one who finds it, even if *he's* still faffing over it.

'Honey,' I said to Henri, 'the guy's got a dick you can feel, private income, his own house and car – for crying out loud, what else do you want? So-o-o, he believes in past lives; we've all got histories. If you ask me, he's heaven-sent. Most guys have barely enough to talk about from their present life; this guy's chalked up two millennia. Handcuff the babe to your bed before *I* do.'

We were still standing outside his place deciding what to do. His apartment was hardly near any place you'd associate with culture. Could he have picked a more out-of-the-way location? Well, yeah, I guess: Europe, though Henri would turn that around. He'd say Australia's out of the way. But they've got all the world maps upside down. Australia's on top, thank you very much, and Tassie's its little halo. And above even that, the white bit, Antarctica? That's the cloudy sky on a bright blue day.

Since we were so far out to begin with, we went to a national park. Henri needed to see bush.

'Right here, honey.'

But he wasn't looking. He meant the floral kind. So we wandered the national park – me in my Gucci shoes, he in his scuffs, while I tested my latest material on him. He said I was great.

'Don't I know it, darl'. Everything I say is great. It's like flying at 6,000 feet. Constantly. Occasionally, I wish I could crop-dust. I've got routines going back two decades that still haven't seen the light of day and will probably be another two decades before they do. Why's that? Why, I'm twenty years ahead of my time.'

Henri – just trying to be helpful – suggested maybe I write something that people will get today. In that case, it would have to be over twenty years out-of-date. And not even the first things I wrote are contemporary yet.

We drove to my place. Made ourselves comfortable, Henri leaning back on my non-existent headrest (i.e. the wall), me propped up on pillows. Yes, we were in bed. My bed. But in the boring way.

Henri looked over the top of his oversized mug of coffee.

'Hmm, I think you're right about Cassius, Rena; he *is* special. I've still got my bruises.'

'Honey, please!' I exclaimed, 'you're making me jealous. Let's have a look. That one's still blue.'

'It's not really love if you don't get hurt,' he whispered.

But by the look of those shiners, he was onto the real thing. Wish I could remember the last guy who made me gasp instead of yawn. I pulled his sleeve back down over his wrist. Couldn't bear to look at the fun he'd had.

'You know I'm not going to have an iota of sympathy for you if you let this one go,' I told him sternly.

'I know,' said Henri.

But did he?'

And so to Mabel Pinkerton …

Whatever You Say, Honey.

Saturday 23rd July, Melbourne 2005.

La di da, here I am, talking, talking, talking. Talking to myself. Don't mind me. Mabel Pinkerton – you're such a chatterbox! Knocked on Henri's door this morning. No one answered. Knocked on it this evening. He's back. Said he'd been out. Like tell me something I don't know, stupid.

Haven't heard from that video clerk. Guess *he* hasn't heard from *me*. I guess there are always two ways of looking at things – more! We'd have to have compound eyes like flies to see all angles. That's what I reckon. Uh oh, glad no one's hearing this. What would they think!

La di da, don't mind me.

Henri went out today. Oh, I've told you that. But did I say it was with *another* friend? *Her* name's Rena. 'That's it, sweetie,' I told him. 'Seeing other women – it's over!'

Henri chuckled.

They went to a national park together. Not a road in. Completely surrounded by private property. Imagine that: a public park surrounded by private property. Er, stupid. Like someone in Parks and Whatsit get a brain, why don't you?

People are so dumb. I mean, *so* dumb!

Uh oh, Mabel, off in the clouds again. Good thing we can't hear each other's thoughts. That would be terrible, wouldn't it! Or *would* it? We wouldn't have any secrets then. But that would mean nothing private. You'd be a public park surrounded by public property.

'Don't want to be a public park surrounded by public property, do you, sweetie?'

'What?' says Henri, turning from the window and looking at me funny. 'A public property?' he asks.

Oops, Mabel, you don't have to broadcast every great revelation, you know. A public property, surrounded by private property, but with a public road in. I'd tell Henri that, but he's eyeing up all the bars on the windows below. Brad and Scooter's work. They've done up to the third floor so we're next.

'That's what they've got planned tomorrow, sweetie.'

'I thought I was mad, but maybe the world is,' he sighs. 'When I came home today, I found the main entrance welded shut, so now we have to go through the garage door to get in. And even if it's only some temporary thing, I mean crossing the green to the stairwell with Barney there? That's like running the gauntlet.'

'Ha! *I tort I taw a puddy tat.*'

No chuckle from Henri about any of it.

'Okay, sweetie, I'll talk to June tomorrow.'

He yawned.

I jumped up. 'It's okay, I get the hint. I was going to get more videos but with the lifts no longer working ...'

Remarking that the failure of the lifts was more inconvenient than strange, he showed me to the front door. Click. Cold night air. Into your apartment, Mabel. Turn on the lights. Sit at the table. Write this down: Tomorrow, Henri, June, Barney. Can't have Henri leaving just because of a dog ... and a few bars, and some welding and a big, fat padlock and ... hmmm. Yes, I'll call a meeting with that June Pratchett.

I've taken to feeding him. Barney, I'm talking about now. Once a day. Okay, twice. I don't think that's too much. Don't think J.D. and Cooder like it, though. Okay, some people! But what can you do? They look so funny when they're sitting together, J.D., like a sickly porcelain doll in black leather and, Cooder, like a stick insect with no flair for blending in. They're in the two flats opposite mine and one floor down.

Cooder thinks everything that ever happens to him is weird, but I've had heaps weirder stuff happen to me. Like, just last week I went looking at houses. Okay, Henri's not the only one thinking about moving.

I'll talk to June Pratchett tomorrow. Maybe she can talk to Memphis about closing off somewhere for the dog, leaving a path where we can still get in and out. And maybe she can get him to see he's going too far with all this security. I mean, electrified wires on the surrounding wall – can't see how that can even be legal!

If Henri left, who would I talk to? Uh oh, another horrible thought. Mabel Pinkerton, no sleep for you tonight! Worry, worry, worry, that's all you do!

I'll talk to June Pratchet – argh, like that will be fun! I don't hate her. I don't hate anyone. That's giving people you hate too much of your time. But she's hard work.

June Pratchett. You have to *hear* her speak to believe it. I don't, and I've heard it.

As Mabel attests, one has to hear *June Pratchett speak to believe it, and hear her you shall now as she picks up our Chaucerian comedy*

Chapter Five

The Need, The Necessity For A Meeting.

June Pratchett's reminiscences of June/July 2005.

I, June Pratchett, set forth our grievances and their sorry end. At first Memphis came on foot, next in train, and lastly in limousine, the black-tinted windows reflecting our fortress and the fortress walls of adjoining high-rises. Did any of us complain when he began what has culminated in our impossible situation? Ashamedly, only Henri carped about his freedom to 'come and go' as Barney (whose purpose it was to guard the walled surroundings of our complex much as a serpent patrols a castle moat) became all too effective. Soon, no outsider could easily enter without being bailed up against a wall, but nor could anyone leave without being leapt upon. And to be leapt upon by Barney is to be laid flat.

Suffice to say, in very short time he stopped all traffic. He is, after all, a mutt the size of a bull.

On the morning of the last visitation by Memphis, Mabel again embarked on her accepted duty of feeding the dog, which I was alerted to by her habit of putting on her rabbit-hair, red-flecked jumper just prior. From my barred window, I saw Barney waiting for her beside the briar bush as usual, but this time he rose sluggishly, one paw in the air. Mabel, instead of locking the door as was the agreed protocol, left it ajar in her haste to attend to his apparent injury, and the moment she was upon him, Barney leapt up, the ruse revealed. Mabel, realising it too late, could not prevent the mutt from charging through the doorway (though it barely admitted of his bulk) and making good the opportunity to get inside.

I hurried downstairs, passing through the fur-tooth maw of an entrance. Barney was not in sight, having no doubt already made it to the inner atrium or beyond. Mabel offered her bowed head to my remonstrance in an odd recognition of my superior position as president of the flats committee, and yet how thoroughly she sided with the dog, much as a rueful teacher might with an impish student against the principal.

No amount of entreaty or proffered tidbits could persuade Barney to resign his new land claim, and decamp to the outdoors. We had lost ground.

Cooder and J.D. complained at supper. How would

we get the dog back outside?

I did not wish to harp too minutely upon Mabel's lapse. Besides, since it was Memphis who owned the dog, we all reached agreement that we had merely to wait for him to come the next day, but he came not at all, necessitating that I call him. Unfortunately, I had never *gotten* his number.

In any event, I had a graver problem: I discovered the phone line into the building was severed, rendering all our landlines useless. So too was the one mobile amongst us (Mabel's) as the always patchy network access from our building had eventually become non-existent. Moreover, it was discovered that a truck was parked against our exit to the outside world, all others having been welded shut by Memphis' men.

I figured to myself what might portentously be with us all being so confined, and Barney too being unable to leave. And where, indeed, *was* he?

I went that night to the last place I had seen him, and with the floodlights making the courtyard penetrable to its extremities, I discovered Barney at the farthest end. He had made the inner courtyard. Some object, black and white in shape, was held lightly betwixt his jaws, reminding me of a statue outside a Chinese temple – they are lions, I believe – with a granite sphere between its teeth. Barney lumbered towards me and I own I screamed. He loosed the object, which bounced at my feet. I kicked the soccer ball to distract him while I made my way indoors.

The next morning, the truck was still blocking the entrance (the door opened less than a degree of its natural arc) and still we saw and heard nothing of Memphis or any other source of help.

Shut off thus from the world and shut in with a dog whose size and bulk more than matched the heftiest bull, we were looking at a none too pretty situation, made the more absurd by the rag-tag make-up of our party. Nonetheless, we gathered together in conference – Mabel, Cooder, J.D and I. Mrs Barkly had not surfaced in days and Bertrand M. Pale remained, as he had done now for a whole long week – immovable at the top of the landing. We six were the sole remaining residents of the building (seven, if you counted Henri who had not answered frequent knocks at his door). As president of the flats committee, it was incumbent upon me to make an address, which I did, and I was quite magnificent in my articulation of the facts. All the same, I carefully avoided overstressing the more forbidding aspects of our imprisonment. We were alone in a building to all intents inoperable. The windows barred. No phone line to the outside world. No visitors expected by any of us. On this common point, we each equally started in our seats. Who, from the outside world, would raise the alarm?

Mabel had the first sensible suggestion: hanging a

banner from the top windows to flag our predicament in the belief that construction workers atop the high-rise opposite might see it.

'Sweet,' said Cooder, 'me and J.D. can do it tomorra.'

'Tomorrow?' cried Mabel in disbelief.

'I've decided tomorra,' reiterated Cooder, leaning back, duffel-coat arms folded.

Consequently, the making and hanging of the banner was postponed for twenty-four hours.

The next day, we duly gathered together in a common area we now called 'the conference room'. Then, for two hours or more, Mabel and I were continually fetching, after long searches and grave, the items (or near enough approximations of these) which J.D. and Cooder requested: rope, scissors, tape, Blu Tack, tea and (while it lasted) beer.

What the banner came to in truth was a poor mock-up of an S.O.S, a compilation of efforts I hoped were not all of a type with vain desires and imaginings. At any rate, it produced no immediate result: the construction workers on the building opposite seemed never even to glance our way.

Dinner was made, as to be expected, by Mabel and myself in a markedly scrounging manner, the contents of our collective pantries not coming together too well in any cohesive concoction. Barney shuffled about, occasionally 'lifting' an ingredient from the bench, and thus making the task nigh impossible till we contrived, by aid of a fresher piece of meat than we had allowance in our reserves to sacrifice, to drive him out into the corridor.

We all ate in the room where we had hung the banner, having dragged in some tables. Unfortunately, it proved impossible to keep Barney out, and once in, he would not submit to being removed. This final breach had about it the stamp of irreversible defeat, since it amounted to a penetration to the very head, or seat, of our network.

At first he condescended to bask by the window, but, by degrees, inched forward on his belly till his head leaned grotesquely against the one unoccupied chair (left in hope of Henri's attendance), and at last succeeded in toppling it.

At the next meal, in the pretty, flushing light of morning, Barney begged at table. The confronting presence of a dog that does not present its nose to the lip of the table but, due to consideration of size, holds its very skull as a drooping chandelier *over* it, could be expected to have elicited the very protestations that were indeed its result. His dogged insistence, to pun perniciously, at last necessitated action, so Mabel coaxed Barney downstairs with the soccer ball and, I assume, to the atrium.

By mid-morning, Cooder wandered down to again check our only exit.

'Yeah, farken hell, the truck's still there,' he said, on his return.

With access denied to the world without, I saw the need to regulate communication between the rooms within. The drawn-up boundaries placed upon the dog's wanderings were guarded by one or other of us, but often breached, whereupon we were always presented with a choice between his two dominating concerns: *our* food or *his* ball.

We locked doors upon him, to be spared the sound of his whimpering, which progressed to scratching, which soon left the doors more resembling plastic slatted entrances than solid surfaces.

Amid our plans and meetings to discuss means of escape, we were always getting up to let him in or out of his allotted spaces. *Our* allotted spaces excluded the Barkly's flat – Barney would allow none of us anywhere near it, so we had no means of ascertaining Mrs Barkly's fate. We assumed the worst, however, when J.D. reported a most unpleasant odour from that direction.

'Fucken awful,' I believe was his precise description after he had approached as close as he dared.

Amongst us all, we were also continually reflecting on Henri's whereabouts. At last, the possibility of his somehow having been rendered incommunicado stirred the others so overwhelmingly that I could only surrender to their whim to at once make our way downstairs and again check his flat and restore him, if indeed he was still there, to our company.

J.D. knocked on Henri's door; Cooder barged it in; Mabel inspected the flat. Henri's ancient backpack was missing (which amounted to his entire possessions) – as was Henri's own person. Cooder, however, found a welcome slab of beer in the fridge. We ascended the stairs and resumed our discussions over drinks.

If, by the evidence of a few torn sheets, Henri had escaped by a window, he had clearly done so before the bars were fitted to his. We had long since ascertained that all windows up to and including the fourth now had bars. Even the balcony Henri so loved was now inaccessible. The fifth and highest level had unbarred windows. (It seemed these had been deemed safe as none had a balcony or other means of ingress/egress.)

'If only we could get onto the roof,' said Mabel.

Mabel had many times stated her belief that if she could access the roof she might get network coverage on her mobile, but the door to the roof had been padlocked since Henri's foray.

Our musings on the subject ceased upon initiation of a loud and peremptory thumping at the door, accompanied by Barney's whimper. So fearful had we become, we were all instantly immobile in our disquietude. Eventually, however, Cooder leapt from the windowsill, which had become his favourite perch, and staccato-stepped to the door. He was within metres of it when it crashed down. Barney had risen on hind legs, pressed the full weight of his bulk against the door, and pushed it in. There was little doubt that, had Cooder been quicker, he would have been dead.

It was now impossible to keep in the warmth. Once Barney knew he could knock down doors, he would not suffer another to stand for very long, no matter the times we re-hinged them by various make-do means.

'If only he would knock the farken exit down!' shouted Cooder.

Cooder told us, on the morrow, that he had crept during the night to the conference room for warmth, there laying pillow and doona by the heater. Some time later, he said, Barney entered, and circled him continually for some time, evidently coveting the space. It seems that Cooder, having grown intemperate, at last shouted at the mutt. Barney growled in response so fearsomely that Cooder fled with neither doona nor pillow to spend the remainder of the night in his room. If the heater was our sun, then the dog occupied Earth's orbit, whilst the rest of us were frozen Mars.

Disquieted by this turn of events, we all together ascended the stairs, passing through the empty doorways, to arrive en masse at the empty conference room and found Barney laid out there luxuriantly against the heater. My acquaintance with such invasions being limited, at all events to the few occasions of my consenting to the affront, Barney had impressed me both with his full assault and seizure of our territories.

No longer could we hold possession of even our meeting space.

In succeeding days, the continual frustration of any and all enterprises brought about a gradual determination in the others to avoid the meetings which I saw as our one light, almost the ongoing celebration of our first coming together in cohesion and hanging the banner, which had but lately fallen.

It became necessary to accept the possibility of a far longer stay than any of us had supposed possible, and with that understanding came the need to ration our food.

'Yeah, well, it's not going to last long with that farken dog eatin' it,' shouted Cooder, not without good reason.

We wondered too how long we would continue to have water and electricity.

If the apartment block had been bigger, J.D. posited the hypothetical of turning on selected lights to illuminate the word 'HELP'. It was purely speculative, 'HE' being the most we could have managed given the windows available.

At one of our meetings, we discussed the all-but-forgotten presence on the inaccessible landing of Bertrand M. Pale. Could a man stand so long and be 'right'? None of us knew the answer.

Then, one afternoon, I was in the conference room typing up the minutes from our last meeting when a most abject scream emanated from J.D.'s quarters. I hurried down as fast as health and safety permitted, and arrived at the same time as Barney was departing.

That is when I got the horror of it hot.

J.D. had been sitting on his couch, watching TV, when Barney announced his presence by dropping the soccer ball on the threshold, demanding J.D. play. It seems J.D. was about to rise when the indignity of it all arrested him. If he was forced to play ball, at least Barney could bring it to him. J.D. kept yelling, 'Here, here, closer' and Barney would drop the ball incrementally nearer, barking as if to say, 'Isn't that close enough?' Finally, he dropped it in J.D.'s very lap, and the assurance J.D. gained by this victory hatched in his mind a desire for even greater mastery over the dog. He lifted the ball, waving it languidly in his right arm, as Barney barked with agitation and impatience, his backside wriggling so much as to dislodge bookshelves and cupboards. Enjoying the act of drawing out the moment under the showers of pages, J.D. turned to see the final credits of the show he had been watching, the ball still held teasingly in his right hand.

Barney – it seems – finally lost patience.

'Fark. Faarrrk, mate,' were Cooder's consoling

words. We had wrapped, as best we could, a sheet around the gushing stump. 'Geez,' said Cooder, shaking his head. 'Ya poor cunt, that's the lowest, man, gettin' ya poor fuckin' arm bit. Should'na held that ball so long.'

An inhuman gargle issued from J.D. 'Oh God, my hand.'

'You're all right, mate. But shit, I farken admire that dog. Farken raise me beer to the farker. Ha, J.D., hear that? I raise me farken beer to a dog. That's priceless, mate. Hee hee hee, three cheers for Barney.'

'Please ... my hand ...'

'She'll be right, mate. Stay in there.'

'It hurts ...'

Cooder tucked into some dog food he had found in J.D.'s room.

'Don't mind this *Meaty Bites* shit.'

'It's revolting,' cried Mabel, hot tears of disbelief coursing down her cheeks.

'What's revoltin', princess, is the way it makes you fart for the next forty hours. Nah, Barney, I admire him. But farken hate yappy dogs. Guess it's not their fault, but; they're bred that way. J.D. ...? Oi, J.D.! Youse lis'ning?'

'He's dead!' screamed Mabel.

'Not surprised with the shit you've bin talkin'.'

He was not dead. The three of us remaining were too weak to do much more than move J.D. to the room opposite. Mabel hinted that his body went missing soon thereafter, but I did not corroborate the claim. With only Barney's dry food left to sustain us, we were failing fast. Despite our weakness, or perchance because of it, he still insisted on his exercise. Mabel happened upon an easier solution than joining him in the atrium: we threw the ball down the stairs.

'Sweetie, we could maybe climb onto the roof from the window,' whispered Mabel during one of the dog's retrievals.

'But the need, the necessity, for a meeting, even if amongst the surviving members?' I remonstrated with her.

'Yes, honey, we *will* have a meeting but … after.'

In the glimmering light, Mabel projected herself through the open conference room window, my arms about her, as she reached with her tiny digits for the lip of the roof. Her hands made contact and, with my own cupped hands as a stirrup for her foot, she attempted to hoist herself up. My grip did not hold. Cooder hurried forward, only just preventing my withered self from joining Mabel in her soundless plummet.

Cooder and I stood enfolded in each other's misery and arms alike. I'm not sure which of us first saw the truck that had for so long barred our exit being driven towards the gate. I do recall Barney almost simultaneously appeared behind us. We looked below again to see a man who we believed was Memphis, standing with a familiar girl by a limo. Memphis put his fingers in his mouth and appeared to whistle, although there was no sound we could hear. Barney, however, stood tall, ears pointed, then about-faced and bounded downstairs. Without a word, Cooder let go of my waist, and ran after him. I swayed precipitously by the empty window frame as I heard Cooder's scream. He had tripped on the first step and landed on the last.

From the window, I spied Barney exit the garage and leap into the back of the truck. I saw two men and, even from my elevated position, I recognised them immediately as Brad and Scooter. They climbed into the truck cabin and soon it was driven away, disappearing among the buildings and factories.

Particles flamed in the air like fireflies, and I saw how little, in the dust of afternoons, those specks should be illuminated.

It was all I could legitimately do to say 'meeting adjourned'.

Phew! Now we must shuffle back in time to the day after Henri escaped the apartment block. It is in Rena's words, once more, that our tale continues.

Chapter Six

Tell Me About It.

Sunday 24th July.

Turned up at those awful flats today, looking for Henri. Called his mobile first but it kept saying no network coverage. Thought the bugger might need me if things weren't going the way he wanted with his new man.

Did I say he might *need* me? Rena, like when has he ever needed you?

When I got to his place, there was this great big bloody limo parked out front. Reckon it would need just about a six-lane highway for its turning circle. There was also a truck, *Memphis Chips* painted on the side, with two uni-looking lads standing next to it. You know the type: tall, unwashed, no abs.

At least I got there quicker than last time. Ask me, the traffic's a nightmare more or less everywhere in

Melbourne, even Sundays, but today out near Henri's place it was a dream.

Looking for the gate in the front wall, I met the most peculiar fellow I've ever seen. A cross between a used-car salesman and an Elvis impersonator. He looked my way and smiled, kind of like a cat smiles at birds.

'Hello, honey,' I replied in answer to the teeth. 'You look like you could be on the endangered species list but I won't mark that against you. You're an eye-stopper; just don't know if I can say the same re the heart.'

To give the leprechaun his due, he laughed, if you could call it that. Imagine if an elephant could laugh, with all its wisdom and memory, crossed with the grin of a baboon, with all its effrontery.

I'd interrupted him talking to the severest-looking woman you ever saw. Her expression could chop wood. Dark dress, dark features, hair pulled back in a pigtail so tight she didn't have a single wrinkle, though she must've been pushing forty. (I know, I know, I'm not far off that mark myself.)

The uni lads (I heard one call the other 'Scooter' – odd name) were hanging by ropes, welding bars over the fourth floor windows. Hmm, security-conscious mania, anyone?

'My dear sir,' said the lady to the leprechaun apologetically (like *she* was the interruption, not little ol' me), 'had not the flattery of your trust in my judgment brought confusion to conceit, I might have wondered at what had precipitated these decisions. Instead, to whatever in me is most excitable, can I add the adrenalin of decidedness to marvel …'

Thankfully, the leprechaun cut her off. Don't know about you, but that wasn't making much sense to *me*. And I'm not *that* dumb!

'Excuse me, Miss Pratchett,' he said, turning from the lady to me. 'May I help you, Madam?'

I told him I was here to see Henri and did he know him because I couldn't seem to get him on the mobile. He probably wasn't even there anymore. Trust him to pack off somewhere again without warning.

'May I be so nosy as to inquire your connection?'

'Friend. Strictly friend. I wish, but he doesn't. The name's Rena.'

He took my hand. *His* was gym-bunny-strong.

'Memphis.'

'Original. Come to think of it, you look like a prairie dog.'

Oops. Silence. From both parties. Gotta watch that routine, Rena. What works on stage doesn't always work off. The Pratchett woman blew herself up to ten times her natural size.

'Dear lady,' she said, talking to me (first time I was ever called a lady), 'from my viewpoint at the top of these steps, I cannot but marvel at the way in which my inestimable landlord, Memphis, has responded (he in his excellence of bearing and breeding) to such a pert deliverance, with all its deficiency of taste and manner, from a vulgar, wretched thing such as you.'

Me, vulgar? Give her that. But wretched? Memphis' mouth grew an instant set of teeth. And so pointy!

'Again, thank you, Miss Pratchett,' he soothed. 'It's not often that my skills are appreciated,' and he gave the longest drawn-out sigh you ever heard.

Next thing I know, he's offering me a ride in his limo to see if we could find Henri. I tell you, I just seem to attract them. Yeah, freaks. I pointed out I had a car of my own.

'Scooter, here, will drive it behind us,' and he pointed to one of the uni types, just finishing welding the last bar and abseiling down beside me.

They barred Henri's windows. His flat's one of only a few that have a balcony and it looked as if there were even bars on the access door to that. Couldn't imagine flighty Henri being too pleased.

Memphis took my synaptic delay as consent to the suggested limo ride. He disappeared to show Miss Pratchet inside via the garage door and past the dog, Barney, who could apparently get excitable. I could believe it by the titanic barks emanating from within. If the beast's bulk was as big as his bark, he was some monster.

I hate to say it, but when Memphis returned, Henri was forgotten.

Look, I'd never ridden in a limo before.

With Rena enjoying the novelty of a limo ride, we should return to Cassius, and witness how he is faring.

This Constant Forgetting.

Sunday 24th July, Melbourne 2005.

Well, he's back! Like an old cat, fond of its ease, Henri has returned to my life and my home, making straight for my lounge, with its bay windows, and retired exhausted upon the floor. After the maddening end to his first visit, I kept putting off calling him rather than risk more of the same, but in the end, I gave in and I'd barely hung up the phone before he was at the door. What most surprised and also gladdened me on his arrival, was the addition to his person of his traveller's backpack, though I scarcely dared ask if his bringing it constituted a desire to cohabit. In fact, I comprehended precious little of anything he said at first the way he was babbling on and on about his flat and his odd neighbours and odd happenings.

At first I took this talk of a security-mad landlord as lamentable in its silliness, but then he mentioned the landlord's name: Memphis.

I stared at Henri with considerable astonishment.

'That abominable blaggard!' I muttered.

The Memphis *I* know (and with a name like that, surely both are one and the same) seems always to have hindered my researches at every opportunity, in both my present and past lives. 'Seems we've both had dealings with this Memphis,' I told Henri. 'I'm glad you've escaped him.'

I fell onto my Chesterfield and Henri stood looking at me, his orbs wide, moist and glistening.

'Is it dangerous to know you?' he asked. 'I mean, jealous ex-boyfriends are one thing but what's the story with this Memphis?'

To my mind, with Memphis we were talking of the personification of darkness itself, but with Henri already so jumpy, I was reluctant to add more cause.

It appeared Henri had 'escaped' from his flat in the wee hours of the morning by tying sheets together to form a rope. The rope cut on the windowsill as he dangled and it tore through altogether when he was still two metres from the ground. He still displayed the resultant injury in a limp. I could hardly credit that such dramatics had been necessary.

'If I'd waited till daylight,' said Henri, 'my window would have been barred.' Then he smiled. 'That reminds me, gorgeous, when are we doing the same?'

I was slow to get his meaning. Barred up! How he could go from a brush with imprisonment (and worse?) to lusty sentiments. Same old Henri!

'Work first for me,' I told him, and he gave me one of his saucy looks.

Pandora strolled in on silent feet, and immediately leapt upon Henri's lap. Henri hugged her, at the same time asking the inevitable question.

'What *is* your work?'

Whereupon I explained, from the comfort of my Chesterfield.

'Henri, I am in the privileged position of remembering some of my past lives. Just as we have laws to explain the volume of a cube by multiplying its height by its length by its width, so too do we have rules for determining the 3D landscape of history. I have intuited those rules, allowing me to formulate an algorithm of any past moment. But that is as useful as knowing a cube's statistics in one place. What if you could factor in time? You would have a four-dimensional model which you could extrapolate to encompass, not just the past, but future events.'

'What's the point in that?'

I groaned. 'Henri, be so good as to be attentive.'

Quite to the contrary, he chose to be vastly affronted and signalled as much by plonking his feet on my beautiful Tasmanian oak coffee table.

'My friend, you needn't imagine I shall let your ridiculous pretence at being offended keep me from completing my dissertation.'

'Just a little more nicely, please,' he purred.

'If I consent, will you promise, faithfully, to listen?' Henri nodded.

'To know the outcomes of one's choices is to be

provided with a plenitude of bad decisions and a minority of good ones. Humans are infamous for not learning from their mistakes. Unfortunately, if you avoid history you won't avoid history.'

'In what way do humans not learn?' Henri asked lazily.

'In what ways? Why, in every possible way! For so much of history, people were born to rule and rank. Though the reign of kings ended in France with King Louis Fourteenth's execution in the French revolution, in some countries, the folly of hereditary rule continues as you know. In many others, it has gone only to be replaced with a new kind of royalty, the uber rich! And what of the modern fallacy that opportunities for leadership are open to all? Just think of the billions of dollars spent electing a U.S. president. Billionaires only need apply. And is the excess of follies and wealth of the Houses of Bush and Kennedy so very different from the House of Tudor?' (Henri feigned confusion). 'I ask you, Henri, does humankind progress? Or what we gain in one age, do we lose in the next? For every achievement in one field of human affairs, it seems something is lost in another.'

'Give me more examples.'

'Examples! Henri, you need only look to when we first met, two millennia past. The Republic of Rome reneged for Caesar, the liberty of sexual mores outdone by the licentiousness of the arena! The time freed from labour given over to the pursuit of the arts, but at the cost of the criminality of slavery!'

Henri endeavoured to interrupt but I spoke over him.

'The empire-building mania of Rome mirrored in the colonial expansion of the British. (Need I go on?) Did the Brits know better by being themselves a conquered nation? Not on your life! Now look to the new superpower in our present day: is the US the new Rome and is it to suffer the same end? The cycle repeats itself. I ask you, as I ask myself, is nothing ever learnt for good? Is all forgotten, only for mistakes to be made over and over by succeeding generations? Damn this execrable race! And damn this constant forgetting!'

With that, I own I made a melodramatic show of slapping my palm on my padded armrest. The action smacked so obviously of amateur dramatics that it only served to make Henri forget the meat of my speech by making him laugh at its consumption.

I continued. 'Tome upon tome of historical text – and to what purpose? We record our mistakes in letters, not integers. With a calculus for determining our future, we could put these figures into equations, substituting the results for written results on the other side. Then our ancestor's additions would not be cancelled by our own generation's subtractions, or our present positives brought back to zeros by our descendants' negatives. No, at last the human race can reduce in disasters and multiply in successes for *all* time!

'You mean,' he said, 'that we will have a collective consciousness and conscience?'

'Of a type.'

'Cassius,' he chuckled, 'think back to your parents. All those things we go through as kids – they're new to us even if old to our folks. Imagine if we *did* have a collective consciousness: no one would ever experience first love again.'

He gave me an exquisite smile but I was too focused to be distracted. His scepticism was still plainly evident. Everything I said, he believed only as a bagatelle! If only he could begin to recall.

'Please tell me, Henri, that you remember at least *one* of your past lives?'

'I forget.'

'You forget if you remember?'

'I don't recall.'

'Then you've forgotten?'

'What?'

'Oh, forget it!'

A spasm of pain passed through me and arrested my flow of words. I'm sure I must have paled to a brilliant white. In any case, thus interrupting myself, I stood, breathing deeply. At last removing his feet from my coffee table, Henri inquired after my health.

'I certainly esteem myself a robust constitution,' I assured him. 'However, the exertions of entering the mindscape are almost … well, don't fret too much upon it.'

'Mindscape?' asked Henri.

I retired to my room, choosing to ignore his plaintive look. Perhaps I could have delayed my work this one night ... But I still would have had to re-enter the mindscape sooner or later.

I have detected another presence. From his algorithm, it appears his name is Edgar Bumpton. Just as a cylinder or pyramid has a mathematical formula describing its properties, so too do humans, but in formulations many times more complex. Some have called that algorithm our soul.

Edgar Bumpton's algorithm is the perfect shape and expression of his name. He is singularly important to me, not so much for who he is, but what he carries. He has an object, which my maths has hypothesized as existing much as physicists hypothesized the existence of black holes before actually viewing one and confirming the fact of them. The object in question is a supersolid, which, by being a model of the universe, becomes a key to it. To find that supersolid would prove an inestimable boon since, in going outside the limits of one's world, it is difficult to then locate that world when returning.

And at times in the mindscape (to paraphrase the poets) 'I can connect nothing with nothing'.

I turned to my calculations to determine where Edgar Bumpton might be, leaving Henri in my lounge room, at last sight rhythmically patting my cat.

Oh My, Oh My.

Siin Sevada, 3003.

Oh my, oh me again, Edgar Bumpton. Yes, me of the supersolid fame. Such things I have to tell since that moment when I fell through the gate. The most extraordinary feeling. I rather fear I might have cried out; I certainly fainted. Frightfully horrible, but the next thing I knew I found myself on what I thought was a creature but it turned out be some sort of living bed that emanated heat as though it were alive! Its hairs bristled under me. At first I believed myself naked but then I saw that I was certainly clothed, yet in the lightest fabric I have known.

I went to get off the bed but noticed that its legs were as tall as I! Looking around, I realised everything was proportioned for people three times my height! The walls of the room opened.

'Good morning,' said many voices at once. The room's inhabitants revealed themselves. I have never seen more lovely creatures.

When they understood that I could only listen to them one at a time, they settled down. And so began my time on Siin Sevada, third planet of the Karkansas Star in the Ranch System, and member of the Free Worlds.

To describe a Siin Sevidian, one must first begin with his big head, which would all but crush his spineless neck, were it not for the saving grace of Siin Sevada's low gravity and thin atmosphere. (As a consequence of this latter, I have struggled with a shortness of breath since my arrival, much as a coastal inhabitant of our own world would on relocating to the high altitude of the Andes.) They are very tall, the Siin Sevidians, and so naturally look down on all other races. In appearance, they resemble opals, but opals possessed of plasticity wherein one may see, in its transparency, a shifting panoply of colours.

The Siin Sevidians told me I was lucky to have entered a gate into the freest of the Free Worlds since many worlds, as was pointed out to me, admit of degree in this respect: some are more free than others.

In this observation lies the genius and foundation of the Siin Sevidians' system. They have turned freedom into a commodity. Their currency is freedom, and their commerce the exercise of this freedom.

The wealthiest Siin Sevidians, and hence the freest by application of this most wonderful equation, may purchase for themselves greater freedom by buying it through the courts. Thus a Siin Sevidian, by degrees incremental or fast, depending on that individual's resources of freedom, may become exempt from taxes, rules of business conduct, and even civil law, including those relating to murder. Since each law that governs the conduct of the majority must of necessity curtail the rights of the individual, freedom from these restrictions has become the most sought-after commodity. And this is where the true foundation of their politics lies: on the primacy of the individual and that individual's right to freedom above the responsibilities and communal obligations of the collective.

Indeed, this latter aberrant wish was once so shunned, there was a time when people interested in community over individuality were tried and found to be un-Sevidian.

The Siin Sevidians have carried this freedom contrivance most excellently far by granting – no, granting is not the correct term, for this right is an inalienable one – by recognising the individual's responsibility to bear arms in order to protect himself from all the other individuals bearing arms.

This duty has extended to the planet as a whole and, of all the Free Worlds, Siin Sevada has the greatest arsenal. But to protect that freedom further, it is necessary to watch that neighbouring planets do not likewise stock weaponry. In their effort to disarm other worlds, and hence make the galaxy a safer place, Siin Sevidians sometimes arm some of these worlds to disarm the others and, occasionally, disarm the worlds they have armed.

The Siin Sevidians are engaged in a great many wars to bring peace to the galaxy.

To give a brief history, Siin Sevada was once a colony of the Dawn Empire. But the Siin Sevidians soon grew impatient of being answerable to a planet many parsecs away, and resenting the resultant limitations to their freedom, they waged war on the Dawn Empire. The Dawn Empire (though now much dwindled till it comprises of the original outpost, Bellerophon) is ruled by Kings and Queens. As a consequence, the Siin Sevidian has an aversion to monarchy, with its hereditary title and privilege. The system of politics enjoyed by the Siin Sevidians, accumulism, is essentially monarchy's antithesis, for it is hereditary privilege *without* the titles.

Nonetheless, the Siin Sevidians have something of a quaint and benign form of royalty in the form of their holo-film and interactive 'stars'. Despite the amorphous nature of these stars, some of whom are not even people but digital constructs, they may nonetheless be attended by a train of ten stylists, publicists, managers and suchlike attendants. By contrast, in the rogue worlds a single mother can struggle to feed her ten children, such is her wanton disregard, not just for her own freedom but – and this is where true culpability comes into play – also for her children's right to freedom.

The one criticism I have heard levelled at the Siin Sevidians (by their imported cleaning staff) is that they could instead channel their resources into bringing the rest of the galaxy up to half their level of comfort and well-being by lowering their own fifty percent. However, as they point out, many worlds simply do not wish to be free. If they did, they would immediately sign over their sovereignty to jurisdiction of Siin Sevada, or at the very least their primary industries, until such time as they appreciated freedom enough to buy it back.

As evidenced by these examples, the Siin Sevidians are the most honest and forthright people, even in the way they conduct war. They will openly and bravely fire their superabundance of plasma missiles into the military targets of their opponent's planets, whereas the enemy will, in paltry numbers, secretly and cowardly hijack space shuttles, which they fly into Siin Sevidian business sectors. The difference, I think you will agree, is obvious. However, I believe I can account for this tactic on the part of the rogue planets. Mistakenly, they confuse the way intergalactic corporations take over worlds with the way the Siin Sevidian military takes over planets: two very separate spheres of conduct.

On this last point, it appears that nations as we know them simply do not exist in this quadrant of the galaxy. Instead, companies have taken the place of countries, and Siin Sevada is no exception, since the appellation 'Siin Sevada' is itself merely a brand name – which shows you just how far this corporation has succeeded in promoting private ambition over public consciousness. The relationship that thus exists between employer and employee must not be confused with feudalism's power imbalance between lord and serf. As stated, the Siin Sevidian has an aversion to all such ancient forms of government, which limited freedom.

Even warfare is no longer a matter of nationalism, but more a matter of business, with many of the institutions of war contracted to private companies. The fact that Siin Sevada has more often than not found moral fault with worlds bearing abundant resources is a coincidence only the churlish would recognise.

As for religion, they allow a plurality, though the main god is Louanna, and the afterlife (which is very real for all Siin Sevidians) is Hennesota. Hennesota, as in the Christian concept of Heaven and Hell, comprises two levels: one where the good exist in perpetual bliss; the other where the bad suffer perpetual torment. Thus the Siin Sevidians are a people so enamoured of pain they have invented a place that is its absolute, which strikes me as a cheerful conceit, since it compels the motivation to right and goodness.

Religion is separate from politics and yet every politician is religious. Their God, Louanna, is the only authority any Siin Sevidian will recognise as operating above himself, and even then it is within the individual's domain to interpret the deity's will. That the deity's edicts more or less correspond with the Siin Sevidian's own illustrates the efficacy of the tacit arrangement.

Oh my, yes, it is a beautiful philosophy. And to think, *Gulliver's Travels* has been interpreted as satire! I can absolutely assure sceptics of the reality of the Siin Sevidian world. I am certain that the Lilliputians and Yahoos are equally real.

For the moment, I have been placed in a detention centre on Siin Sevada's fifth moon Debraska, in Kilwarren County – while my application for citizenship is being processed. In no way am I to confuse my quarters for a cellblock or the detention centre for a prison. I have been told to keep in mind that a prison is designed to keep people from getting out, whereas any detention centre is to protect people's freedom for their own good. Nor is the science of interrogation, to which I am soon to be subjected, to be confused with the inhumanity of torture.

I interrupt my first impressions of this singular world of Siin Sevada, since I can hear the slither of the anti-terrorist officials as they approach my cell. Although assured that this is a standard caution against any illegal immigrants to their planet, I cannot help but wonder at the low squeal that sounded continually in my cell last night, and how my resultant sleeplessness should help their cause today ...

Meanwhile, in another time and another galaxy, our delightful Rena was getting just as little sleep, although due to a somewhat different stimulant ...

Tell Me About It.

Wednesday 10th August, Melbourne 2005.

Okay, darl', this was the limit. I get all the freaks. Tell me about it. And Memphis was no exception.

How's this for his idea of chitchat? We were at his house (more like the entire top floor of a city skyscraper!) and he'd sent Brad and Scooter home (they'd been reading philosophy on the sofas), and we were lolling about on Linoleum crush – like that ever went with purple (the colour of his carpet). I'm sure you can picture us there drinking champagne glasses filled with Don Perignon and feasting from caviar side plates. Okay, very James Bond, but whoever said that wasn't a good thing? And this is what Memphis said (I'd just made some remark about IQs): 'Rena, the worst thing about dumb people is the fact they don't know it.'

'But that *we* do?' I asked, half-sunk in my end of the couch.

'Yes, if only they kept it to themselves!' and he fired off one of his bursts of laughter that begins low in his chest and ends in a squeal. Glad he was keeping *someone* amused. Couldn't find more freaks if I was trying. And believe me, I stopped long ago.

'Ah, what did our friend Jesus say?' asked Memphis.

Our friend? Memphis searched the air and came up with the answer.

'Bléssed are the stupid, for they run the earth!'

Again the laughter. A regular one-man-party, this guy. Spilt half his champagne on my Christian Lacroix (oh so low-cut!) top. Like *that* was an accident.

'Wouldn't have picked you for a believer,' I quipped, getting some purchase by kneeling on the pillows. See if that wouldn't get his goat! Actually, not a bad description, goat. But not the kiddie-zoo type. More your –

'My lady, I'm referring to Jesus the man, not the projection.'

'S'pose you're on speaking terms with God as well?'

'More than that, my dear. God is my paedophile.'

'Your ...! My ...! What?'

'Though He says I led *Him* on to do *me* wrong.'

I may be a lapsed Catholic, but I'm still uncomfortable with blasphemy. I know, I'm a contradiction. What Catholic isn't? Tell me about it.

Memphis leaned in closer, a briar of chest hair sprouting out the top of his purple velvet jacket.

'Rena, can I ask, have you ever done the forty-hour famine? Please, you must know it. The practice whereby well-off people go without food for forty hours to feel empathy for the homeless from the comfort of their own homes.'

Of course I had, and I'm sure Memphis could tell I had. (Catholic guilt: you can read it in our faces.) I took a nip of caviar. Ouch! Bet the irony wouldn't be lost on him.

'Rena, God did much the same in the guise of Jesus. You know, from the safety of immortality pretended to be mortal. Only, God's monstrous vanity meant he had to go better than forty *hours* in the desert; he went forty *days*.'

Shouldn't have told him I was a stand-up comic. Soon as people know, they try to out-joke you. Not sure about his routine. Here's another of his quips: 'Wealth doesn't make you happy.' Pause. 'Neither does poverty – ha!' Not sure about the laughing at your own jokes bit, either. Funny in a sick way, I guess.

'God is my bitch,' crooned Memphis. 'He stands by and lets people die!'

More profanity and more laughter. Soon I shut out the words altogether. The guy was possessed.

It's been an age since my last conquest. Can you tell? This Memphis – longest relation I've had in years. Does *that* tell?

We took a turn on the shagpile. Still, quite nice for a man to take charge for once.

'I hope you're not gay,' I said, conscious we hadn't got down to the act.

'Madam, I am omni-sexual.'

'Fine, but do you like girls?'

'Girls …?' His smile was sardonic. 'Oh, yes, quite; a subset of the species human.'

We're hardly a subset. More a majority by a slim margin. Memphis licked his lips. (Very long tongue. All right, another mark in his favour). 'As a species, my lady, I can't stand humans! And yet, of all the people I detest, so far you're the one I dislike least.'

'I'll take that as a yes to liking women.'

We danced with his head between my bazoomers. I gave something of a titty fuck to his tongue. He pressed himself against one of my legs, and what I felt there got me freshly interested.

'Baby, baby, seems like it's difficult to keep a hard man down.'

It was the kind of sex you should go to jail for. Absolutely bloody fantastic! But … (yes, there's always a but and this time it wasn't just my lard-arse waving in the air) the *problem* was … well, there's no other way of putting it – let me get to the point! – the whole thing was incredibly *sarcastic*.

Yeah, swallow that as a concept: sarcastic sex.

And … what's the word … *unnerving*.

He talks in his sleep, if you can call it sleeping, to toss all night long. And it's not ordinary sleep-talk either.

He's a total sicko.

Whatever the state of Memphis' mental health, we now leave Rena and hear again from Henri.

Going Mad In Melbourne.

Wednesday 10th August, Melbourne 2005.

Rena called today and when I told her where I am, she went right off.

'Henri, you bitch! So you're out of those awful flats and haven't told me?'

'Sorry.'

'Yeah, well, I must admit you haven't been on my mind as much as you should have been,' she said, then told me she's been seeing 'this guy' for two and a half weeks now. Said she didn't want to say who he is because I probably know him. Sounds rich but kooky. She forwarded me one of the text messages he sent her.

```
You, kero, match — you
do the math.
```

Cute. Some guy.

She said we'd catch up soon.

I've been – wait for it – *living* with Cassius for the same amount of time Rena's been seeing her guy: getting on to three weeks. That makes it long-term in my books. But what's most scary are the dreams I've been having. What they're about isn't so bad. *This* is the bad bit: they don't feel like they're *mine*. See what influence Cassius has on me!

The dreams have been of Pompeii – days of hanging out under pine plantations, sunshine and farming. Very straightforward, of course, where it's all come from. Just me churning over Cassius' tale in my sleep.

No, the really scary bit is that I've been dreaming about what went on *after* – after I'm supposed to have left Cassius on his own to get buried alive in ash while I hopped on a boat at Mycenae. A whole lifetime of memories, that entails! Cassius has told me *nothing* of what is supposed to have happened to *me* after the eruption. So I suppose that part of my dreaming can't be reconstituting his tale. It could be my subconscious extrapolating, though …

And what a life post-Cassius I live through in my dreams! Not whole lives, just the meaningful moments, or the moments after the moments, really. Like, say, sitting on a beach, after someone has just said something – I can tell that there's just been this important personal revelation – but I simply don't get it. I'm immediately transported into the next moment before I can. Most frustrating. All completely the influence of Cassius' ravings, of course. Don't suspect for a minute that I believe all this nonsense about past lives but, one thing's for certain; these dreams are by far the cheapest, most vivid trips I've ever had.

The last moment – I even remember that. The last moment of that other life I'm supposed to have lived. There's a huge wound in my side but I feel it only as a dull ache. I know I've fallen somehow, but in what battle and with whom? Couldn't tell you. Anyhow, this fellow soldier has just said something to me, something quite touching. Yet I don't know the significance of it. Then I fade into death and out of sleep.

Actually, that was a couple of nights ago, and last night was dream-free. Guess I'd got to the end of that life, although shouldn't I now be dreaming the important moments of the next? I asked Cassius this morning.

'No,' he replied sternly. He was sitting on his Chesterfield (as usual), with his sums and figures (as usual). I was sitting on the couch opposite, a leg over one arm because I know that annoys him. (And what annoys me is, he won't say it!)

'See, then, your story doesn't add up.'

'Confound you, man, it isn't a fabrication!

'The logic, then; it doesn't fit.'

'It accords perfectly with what I have told you, Henri. Recall what I said. Only if a person dies in surroundings to which he is deeply attached will his spirit hang about in that place, rather than immediately entering the body of a newborn and thus drastically reducing the likelihood of remembering the previous life.'

'So what happened to you, to make you remember?' I asked, and that set him off on a long tale.

Henri, my friend, whilst others fled Pompeii, I stayed. I shut myself up in my room, coughing, but soon comprehended that I had retreated into my very own tomb, for the soot and ash piled up behind my door, and made me a prisoner. I fainted — whether from exhaustion or the fumes, I cannot say. When I awoke, it was to death, not life (though I did not know it). I pressed my weight against the door but was surprised to find it moved so easily; nothing opposed the entrance. Outside, the fields seemed untouched, but everything was cast in a decidedly grey pall. I sat down to contemplate the absorbing subject of my peculiar situation, eventually lying on my back upon the equally grey grass. The low-hung dust clouds — for that's what I supposed them to be — formed a topography resembling the inverse of landscape. Yet unlike clouds they did not rise or, like mist, settle, but hung motionless — cloth over a topography of fruit. The meaning of what I was seeing eluded me.

Returning to my room, I would have stumbled upon a corpse but for the surprise of my legs passing through its mass as easily as through smoke. In agitation (and, I will admit, momentary terror) I leapt back. After restoring myself to my means and momentum, I examined the body. It was unmistakably mine.

Oh the horror of that discovery!

What I meant to do then in consequence, I cannot tell. What I *did* do, was roar, and to my own ears it was an inhuman sound of astonishment, rage, defeat – for the corpse on the floor was not the ghost of the situation; *I* was the ghost whose legs had passed through *it*!

I wrung my hands and cried out for you, Henri, but of course no answer came. Separated from you not just by your leaving, but also now by my death, I was inconsolable. Difficult as it was to rouse myself to action, I nonetheless commanded myself to do so, and ventured outside again, the better which to appraise my predicament.

Stumbling a short space, the roots of my sanity groped for tenure in that uncertain earth. They sought purchase and held. The greyness that permeated open space and recesses alike, I now understood to be the ash, which had fallen and buried the mountain and my property with it. Hades was on earth, and the ground had been raised to heaven, upon which (somewhere!) you, Henri, walked, talked, feasted and slept.

Day and night came with their usual intervals, but the difference in light was not marked. I lit candles for the evening – candles that did not diminish in height with the burning of their wicks but stayed as they were the moment I died. Soon I left them burning continually.

As with the near uniformity of light, so with the mildly varying temperature. Just the fluctuations of the grave. A warm wind occasionally wheedled through: heat currents through the earth.

I would frequently walk out amongst my fields but not, obstinately, through yours or those of other neighbours, since they resembled nothing so much as smudges and were just as impenetrable.

It was a sad and dull existence, at once seemingly endless and as brief as joy. My own company was the only society I kept, except for the farm animals, since I suppose the servants who died with me lacked my enchantment with the place, and so were quickly sucked up into the next life.

I stirred little, and heard as much, for days, weeks on end. I ate meals still on their tables but it was a mechanical custom, and it was the same meals that awaited me the following morn.

Strangely, I began to cheer up under the prospect of retaining my home. The so-called 'cloud sky', or layer above, was actually the new elevation of ground from where the soot and ash had fallen and compacted. One day I spied a lonely figure walking on this surface. I tried to communicate with the ghost but failed, since the figure was not, I eventually realised, a ghost but a living peasant. Days, months, weeks, centuries passed, till I felt myself liquefy and melt into every reach and corner of my property, becoming one with the earth – almost.

I observed the world above the way a fish must observe insects walking upon the surface of the water. The fish can poke its head into this surface world, but leave the water altogether, and it will die. The same is true of the ghost and its relation to the world beyond its territories.

One day, that very habitat I speak of, my *own* ghostly home, was threatened when, with the passing of the centuries, some earth fell away, revealing a wall of my bedroom. It was the wall you painted yourself, Henri. In an act of unforgivable vandalism, a farmer began to remove the stones to build fences to keep in his oxen.

The transplanted wall would keep in his oxen, but would let my consciousness disperse.

I retreated to my room, fearing I could no longer live in this grey world. Almost immediately, I felt myself being drawn into the next life, in Fifteenth Century France.

And that's where Cassius 'finished his tale', or more accurately, 'ended his rant', I'd say. Home, a hill of goats! I can just see the pastoral joy of life ahead with him.

'So you were entombed for thirteen centuries?' I humoured him.

'As I said, it felt both ephemeral and timeless. I can vaguely recall even longer incarcerations, in Egyptian tombs.'

Really? That was stretching credibility *too* far. I rose impatiently from the Chesterfield.

'And when this peasant dug up your house,' I interrogated Cassius, 'to use the stones to keep in his oxen – what then?'

Cassius, seeing that I was impatient to leave, spoke quickly. 'Henri, do you not comprehend the nature of eternal recurrence? My world dissolved and I was drawn into the body of a newborn. That babe was in France in 1404. My youthful occupations in that incarnation are not much to mention, but my adult profession was as treasurer, and I served many institutions and masters. In time, I came into the services of one very high, very powerful, very illustrious Seigneur Gilles de Laval, Sire de Retz, Chamberlain of King Charles VII, and Marshal of France! And again, my life was not of the ordinary kind – and nor was the one you lived alongside me there!'

Slowly, I sat back down on the Chesterfield.

Guess who narrates the next bit? Come now, guess! Seigneur Gilles de Laval, Sire de Retz himself? Yes! You are catching on. Oh, yes, you are catching on. Do you now see that it is unnecessary to go to sleep as one person and wake up as that same individual?

Chapter Seven

Don't You Know Who I Am?

Thursday 15th September, Nantes, France 1440.

The drawbridge was lowered upon my order and I offered my sword to Jean Labbé. Cassius lightly touched my shoulder before pointing to a parchment in the man's hands. It was sealed with the seal of Brittany, but I could guess its contents. The gallant sergeant was flush with the embarrassment of his duty. He approached, knelt, and unrolled before me the scroll.

'Tell me the tenor of this parchment,' I asked of him, keeping my voice even.

'Our good Sire of Brittany enjoins you, my lord Sire de Retz, Marshal of France, by these salutations, to follow me to the good town of Nantes, there to ...'

and the sergeant hosed his throat, 'clear yourself of certain criminal charges brought against you.'

Henri tugged at my side, put his face at my ear, and whispered. 'My Lord, Roger de Briqueville and the others have fled. It's still not too late for us.'

I pushed my faithful Henri away, and addressed the sergeant.

'I will follow immediately, my friend, glad to obey the will of my lord of Brittany; but, that it may not be said that Seigneur de Retz has received a message without largesse, I order my treasurer, Cassius – '

'My lord – '

'My treasurer, Cassius,' I repeated, 'to hand over to you and your followers twenty gold crowns.'

The sergeant stood and bowed.

'Un grand-merci, Messire! I pray God that he may give you good and long life!'

'Pray God only to have mercy upon me, and to pardon my sins,' I answered, reminding the sergeant of where true longevity resided.

While my horses were being saddled, André Barbier, the shoemaker, approached the sergeant. Cassius half-drew his sword but I stayed his hand. We knew well of this troublemaker.

Barbier regaled the sergeant with a tale that neighbour's son had but two days since gone missing, being last seen gathering plums behind the hotel Rondeau.

'And your imputation?' growled the sergeant.

Barbier hesitated a moment but regained his courage. 'Him!' he said, with a look in my direction.

'Hold your tongue, you libellous dog!' shouted the sergeant, and twice struck Barbier with the hilt of his sword.

Barbier reddened at the slur on his honesty, and also from the blood issuing copiously from his crown. With a handkerchief pressed to his wound, he retorted that disappearances such as the boy's surprised no one in Machecoul: it was but the latest instance in a litany numbering in the hundreds.

'Scandal and lies!' barked the sergeant. 'Still your voice unless you wish to be cast into a dungeon by your lord, against whom you appear to wish to depose. Remember, he has supreme power over your village.'

'Then what is the explanation of all these disappearances? Fairies spirit off our little ones?' cried Barbier.

The shoemaker's courage amazed me, even as he wilted under the injuries received at the hands of the sergeant's men-at-arms. I drew breath, the easing of immediate danger restoring me to the use of my faculties. Affecting a jauntiness I did not entirely possess, I laughed, the sergeant joining me only once Cassius and Henri had also begun. Yet I could see that to continue would be unwise. Despite his swift suppression of the man's charges, the sergeant was not entirely sceptical of their truth — how far had the rumours about me flown?

'Jean Labbé, on what charge were you sent to collect me?' I asked the sergeant once our laughter had died away.

'The … *alleged* crime *was* made known to me, Messires,' (as I suspected!) and he glanced at Barbier's puddle-shaped figure on the ground. 'Yet I refused to believe it of a man of noble rank.'

'And I pray you still refuse.'

Upon this the sergeant was silent. I could not restrain my shiver. His stiffness of manner alarmed me more than the overweening politeness he had hitherto shown me. Before, he had been embarrassed in his duties, as though a great mistake had been made; now he was nervous and irresolute. Was he now wondering if the abominable allegations were true, from just the word of one rumour-monger, though a proud and imperious one at that? The sergeant ordered his men to their steeds. I mounted mine, and left Machecoul with Henri and Cassius in train, and with soldiers before and after.

Our sombre cavalcade proceeded in silence but, on reaching the road, it was with lively emotion that the people in the villages ran alongside. I could not subdue a titter for they must have wondered at the redoubtable Gilles de Laval, surrounded as I was by soldiers in the livery of the Duke of Brittany, and unaccompanied by a single soldier of my own.

Peasants left the fields, women their kitchens, labourers deserted their cattle at the plough, all to throng the road to Nantes.

'See how the people love me!' I shouted to the sergeant who, like a true soldier, was leading the cavalcade from the front. Cassius shot me a quick look then glanced even more meaningfully at Henri. The two had always been 'thick' with each other, and in a manner to offend God.

'My lord, why provoke him?' whispered Cassius. 'He is already suspicious that the charge is true.'

The sergeant scoped the ruddy faces of the villagers.

'See, sergeant,' I said hoarsely, prescient of what was coming. 'My people truly do love me.'

The sergeant turned from the throng to regard me with raised eyebrow. He set his smile, and his face grew grim.

'Yes … but they are so silent, my Lord,' he answered over his shoulder.

For the first time, my stomach lost its equanimity, and plashed with the motion of my horse.

The villagers crowded closer. The sergeant glanced from me to them. For the first time, I marked the *true* expression on the peasants' jaundiced faces. It was anything but love for their lord.

Several of the women jostled closer.

'Look sharp about you,' hissed the sergeant to his men.

The soldiers nervously fingered the pommels of their swords. Cassius and Henri bookended my horse with their own, keeping me upright in the saddle, for I had begun to sway.

'Do not receive their stares, my lord,' grated Cassius, his black eyebrows joining together.

What was this new state of affairs? Treated like any common cock of the hackle – even by my own servants!

'Why, the people love me,' I answered jovially. 'I am the Sire De Retz, Marshal of France.'

The soldiers mimicked their sergeant by turning in their saddles to regard me, their faces glimmering white in the dusk. They too must have known the nature of the charges against me – loose tongues! Their expressions, too, had changed. I saw things might go ill with me, and regretted the twenty gold coins. I should have doubled that number.

A cry rang out from the crowd.

A woman's voice, shrill.

'My child! Restore my child!'

With that, a wild and wrathful howl broke from the lips of the throng. I'm sure it rang the length of the road to Nantes.

'Our children, where are our children?'

Hands – dirty, lined – reached out to scratch at flank and stirrup. The men-at-arms looked from the folk to me with a darkening change in emotion. My true circumstances, for the first time, became apparent to me.

I was their prisoner.

Behind me I heard a pitiful lament from Henri, 'What have we done, Cassius? What have we done?'

Cassius quickly silenced him, but not before the sergeant had observed the exchange. He turned his attentions from Cassius and Henri to me, the steely glitter of his southern eyes flaying me to the bone. He had permitted me to be free with him before; perhaps I could be free with him now. I opened my lips to speak, but before the insistent chant of the crowd and his stare (Oh his iron will! His cold heart! His unerring craft!) my words decomposed on the wind, unspoken. It was all too much!

'The edict may be death,' he said, his keen, pale face shining.

'I am no unbirched schoolboy,' I spat at him. 'Address me properly.'

'Messire.'

'This may have to be answered with a dual, Sergeant.'

'To the death?' he asked, his face whitening, for my skill with the sword is legendary.

'Bah!' I answered scornfully. 'When I kill a man, I kill him.'

The sergeant reined his horse in closer, till his steed and mine were chafing at the bit.

'Yes, but these were children, my lord.'

'I put myself to pains,' I answered coolly, 'to see that it was done right.'

Immediately, I realised my mistake. Betrayed by my own words! The sergeant sat straight in his saddle. His men listened to the villagers chant for their children with new and horrifying knowledge. Worry beaded on Cassius and Henri's brows.

'A confession!'

The sergeant gleefully told me that he would see me hanged, and that he could not have made a better catch; that he regretted the beating of the informant, Barbier, and would seek him out for restitution and a statement.

'Begone!' cried Henri, steering his horse alongside mine once more.

The sergeant gave us space but no respect. This was not reassuring. Was worse to come? I saw that henceforth I would be treated with none of the obsequiousness due my station.

The crying of the peasants died away only as the great gates of the Chateau de Bouffay closed around me, and the sergeant handed me over to the watch to be confined like any common jailbird. As though I had been caught cutting a purse!

I was allowed to choose my mode of confinement: irons, along with Cassius and Henri, or one of the cells below the level.

In the moment given me to make my decision, I

thought I could still hear the villagers' chant and my ears (some say pointed) pricked with the keenness of a cur's.

'Can you still hear them crying for their … their children?' I asked the sergeant.

'No, my lord,' answered Henri when the sergeant hesitated.

The sergeant cuffed Henri sorely.

'Are you sure?' I asked again, still vainly addressing the sergeant. 'For … for I think *I* can.'

The sergeant merely waited stolidly for my choice. I watched Cassius and Henri being roughly manacled and then withdrawn from my company. I asked that the soldiers confine me to the deepest part of the keep. The sergeant smiled contemptuously.

Angered by such discourteous behaviour, I was quick to respond.

'A lord cannot be shut up with his servants.'

The sergeant made nod to two of his soldiers, and together the four of us made our way down the stone steps. In my cell, the sergeant looked at me balefully.

'To think that royalty – '

'How thick is this stone?' I asked him.

'The thickness of several men laid together.'

'Then it must be your men chanting for children,' I barked at him, 'aping the plaint of the villagers.'

'I assure you, Messire, my men are involved in no such jest.'

'Then begone – please. And fasten this door.'

He did so, without further word. I heard his footsteps and those of his two men-at-arms, echoing in spirals upon the stairwell, then fading. I surveyed my dim surrounds, within walls that wept mildew. All was silence save the beat of my own heart and those awful, awful cries!

'Where are our children! What have you done with our children?'

When I awoke on the morrow, the twenty gold crowns were at the base of my straw bed. I should have tripled their number!

Friday 7th October.

The charges have become even graver, Cassius and Henri even more implicated. I shall not list the depositions made against me. Suffice to say, three hundred witnesses have so far come forth, but with only testimonies, not evidence. The commissioners have closed the inquiry. The duke – friend that he is! – is hesitating in bringing his verdict. Will he judge and sentence a kinsman? The most powerful of his vassals? The bravest of his captains? A councillor of the king? And, need I add, Marshal of France?

I have composed a letter to him.

MONSIEUR MY COUSIN AND HONOURED SIRE –

It is quite true that I am perhaps the most detestable of all sinners, having sinned horribly again and again, yet I have never failed in my religious duties. Since I have been languishing in prison, awaiting your honoured justice, I have been heartily overwhelmed with repentance for my crimes, which I am happy to acknowledge and expiate as is suitable. Wherefore I supplicate you, M. my cousin, to give me licence to retire into a monastery (but not too far south), and there lead a good and exemplary life. Awaiting your glorious clemency, I pray God our Lord to protect you and your kingdom.

He who addresses you is already in all earthly humility,

FRIAR GILLES, "Carmelite in Intention."

Most humble and humorous in one!

Tuesday 11th October.

Pierre de l'Hospital, the rat, and the Bishop of Nantes, have seen my letter! Why would the duke show it them? Those two have been the most resolute in pressing this trial. They claim to be horrified at the tone of my communication. As if it were an impious device of escape to become a monk! I shall find it most taxing.

I receive these intelligences from the lieutenant du procureur, M. Bumpton, who, on behalf of the duke, has been given the cue to do all that is possible to save me. He has visited me at night to say how it goes with my fate.

'Oh my, this is too horrible! Messire, your predicament grows worse. The bishop and the grand-seneschal have set on foot an investigation inside the very castle of Machecoul itself!'

My heart was ice. They would find their abundance of evidence.

Thursday 20th October.

Nicholas Chateau, notary of the duke, visited my cell to read the summons for me to appear in person on the morrow before Pierre de l'Hospital, President of Brittany, Seneschal of Rennes, and Chief Justice of the Duchy of Brittany.

The notary had come at an opportune time. Feeling myself already a novice in the Carmelite order, that morning I had dressed in white. He found me engaged in singing litanies. A profound effect it induced! I ordered a page to give the notary wine and cake before returning to my prayers with compunction and piety.

Friday 21st October.

This morning, the sergeant and four soldiers conducted me to the hall of justice. I asked for Cassius and Henri to accompany me but the sergeant refused. Such an air of distinction that man has!

I made quite an appearance in court, adorned with all my military insignia – Cassius' idea, as though to impose on the judges. (Cassius and I have had secret meetings, orchestrated by M. Bumpton on behalf of the Duke.) Cassius did not, however, approve of the rest of my outfit. Never mind! I wore round my neck massive chains of gold, and several collars of knightly orders. My costume, with the exception of the purpoint, was white, in token of my repentance. Cassius was wrong – I cut quite a figure!

Perhaps a little provocatively, my cuffs, the edging of my purpoint, and the belt surrounding my little round cap, were all of ermine, a fur that only the great feudal lords of Brittany have a right to wear. But am I not of that class?

'Messires,' said I, saluting my judges. 'I pray you to expedite the matter, and despatch as speedily as possible my unfortunate case; for I am peculiarly anxious to consecrate myself to the service of God, who has pardoned my great sins. I shall not fail, I assure you, to endow several of the churches of Nantes, and I shall distribute the greater portion of my goods among the poor, to secure the salvation of my soul.'

'Monseigneur,' replied Pierre de l'Hospital gravely, 'it is always well to think of the salvation of one's soul; if you please, think now that we are concerned with the salvation of your body.'

The man hoped to ruffle me. But I am the Sire de Retz, Marshal of France. I would disappoint.

'I have confessed to the Father Superior of the Carmelites,' I replied tranquilly, 'and through his absolution I have been able to communicate. I am therefore guiltless and purified.'

Pierre de l'Hospital raised his sallow face.

'Men's justice is not in common with that of God, Monseigneur, and I cannot tell you what will be your sentence. Be ready to make your defence, and listen to the charges brought against you, which M. le Lieutenant du Procureur de Nantes will read.'

I hate that horrid face of de l'Hospital's, like a baby mouse, all fat and pink and pinched! But I was not alarmed. As I had been forewarned, the crime of homicide was alleged, with aggravating circumstances, whilst the crimes of felony and rebellion were brought into exaggerated prominence. The intent was to avoid my being charged with a capital offence, so that I could be let off with the forfeit of some lands.

I had to contain my delight at the astonishment on Pierre de l'Hospital's face when he heard the form the requisition had taken. He could not contain his wrath. The poor man blurted at me, 'I demand you take an oath on the gospels to declare the truth!'

The duke stamped his foot at the disrespect to rank.

I took time adjusting my purpoint which – have I related? – was of a pearl-grey silk, studded with gold stars, and girded round my waist by a scarlet belt, from which dangled a poignard in its scarlet velvet sheath. I was quite the best-dressed and most dashing figure in that sombre courtroom of brown tunics and ruddy faces.

Meanwhile, the ridiculous de l'Hospital was boiling with indignation. I finally answered him.

'No, Messire,' I intoned, as if to a child. 'The witnesses are bound to declare what they know upon oath, but the accused is never put on oath.'

Pierre de l'Hospital shot a look at the judge. The judge turned to me.

'Quite so,' he rumbled between prominent jowls, 'because the accused may be put on a rack and constrained to speak the truth, an' please you.'

The Duke — my friend? — did not overrule this threat. I bit my lip. The rack? I have instituted that torture myself. I could not bear it upon my own person! Giddy with fright, I half conceded the first charges but claimed the charge of homicide to be false.

'Indeed!' retorted Pierre de l'Hospital. 'All these witnesses who complain of having lost their children — they lied under oath?'

'What am I to know of them?' I mumbled. 'Am I their keeper?'

'The answer of Cain!'

The rat! To invoke the Holy Book against me — that holy tome which has become so comforting to me in my incarceration!

'Hola!' I shouted, gripping the podium, 'I appeal to His Grace the Duke of Brittany, and ask an adjournment, that I may take advice on the charges brought against me.'

The duke — dear friend indeed! — nodded to the judge that the request would be granted. The judge conceded, though de l'Hospital got in the last word.

'Very well, then. However, as you deny these charges, and as we are obliged to save you from the rack (at least for the present), then we must question Cassius and Henri.'

Cassius and Henri! Of all my crimes, those two were the most intimately acquainted with them. They accused me of nothing, surely? And what of the indignity? A master is above his servants and should not have such brought forth as witnesses against him. I was not given the luxury of raising these objections for I was led from the court by Jean Labbé. As we passed the windows, I noted how Labbé stared at my beard (which always bristles blue in the light), and recoiled from me a little. The bluish tinge to my hair and beard is a blight of which I do not need to be made conscious. We passed Cassius and Henri as they were escorted from whence I was headed (the prison), to the court, from whence I came.

'Remember what I have done for you, and be faithful servants!' I called over my shoulder.

Cassius looked at me long enough to survey the outfit I was already regretting, and then he did not look again. Henri, meanwhile, shuddered at sight of me.

'I shall speak, my Lord,' whispered Henri, 'for we have another master besides our poor master of Retz, and we shall soon be with the heavenly one.'

My stomach heaved at this intelligence – Henri would testify against me?

Jean Labbé and his men pushed me to my prison, but with a detour past the rack. I amended my opinion of the sergeant.

Tuesday 25th October.

Last night, the procureur, M. Bumpton, visited my cell. The poor man was wringing his effeminate hands; his large nose drooped and dripped. His air was no longer one of solidarity but, it can only be said, of fear.

'Well?' I asked.

His weak voice cracked: 'Oh my, my lord, Henri has spoken out.'

'The traitor!'

'He only did so after pointing, trembling, to a large crucifix above the seat of the judge. He said that he was too afraid to speak of the horrors he had witnessed, and eventually been party to, before the image of his Lord Christ. Pierre de l'Hospital rose and veiled the figure of our Redeemer.'

'Yes, yes. Go on.' (If only men could do without God.)

'Cassius spoke up for you, my lord.'

'Ah, my trusted retainer.'

'He clutched at Henri and urged him to remember that he would condemn himself with his testimony, along with his master, but Henri was resolute.

'He turned from his friend, and related how, as a youth, he was brought to your castle and ...'

'Yes, continue, Man!'

'And ... raped, my lord.'

'Raped! Why, he positively begged for it!'

The procureur's answering expression told me my response had best been veiled. I had admitted to the very charges he and the duke were endeavouring to shield me from.

'I mean to say, what else does my ungrateful servant allege of me?' I amended.

The procureur wiped his abominable nose, but from his expressive brow I saw that he, too, was leaning towards the prosecution's opinion of my innocence.

'Henri was passionate in his denouncement, Sire. Perhaps if I quote him faithfully?'

'Perhaps you should.'

And the procureur reproduced my ungrateful servant's words.

Henri: The sire was then about to cut my throat, when his cousin, Gilles de Sille, pointed out that as I was such a ... such a handsome boy, my lord, I would make an admirable page. I was thrown in with Cassius, who warned me thenceforth to hold my tongue, as *he* had done, and to be grateful for my deliverance from the fate of the other children. Of this fate, he would not elaborate.

Not long after, I found in the oubliettes of a tower in the castle of Chantoncé a number of children's skeletons, some headless, others frightfully shattered. The horror of this overtook me and I swooned on the flagstones. When I revived, it was to ask whether *this* was the fate I was delivered from? I told Cassius of the existence of the remains and he informed our lord. The sire was discomposed by what he referred to as 'the great oversight', since the castle was to be ceded to the Duke of Brittany the next day, the Marshal being in great debt. That moonless night, myself and Cassius were summoned to the sire's room and made to swear a solemn oath to say nothing of what was to ensue. On the morrow, an officer of the duke was to take possession of the castle and, before that took place, it was necessary to empty a certain well.

Furnished with hooks and ropes, I went with Cassius to the tower in which the well was located. There, watched by the master, we began our task of removing the blockage. When we succeeded in raising the first obstacle, I almost swooned for, captive to our hook, was a child's half-decayed corpse. Such was my consternation, I nearly let go the rope, but Cassius commanded me to fortify myself and continue to haul the burden. With the surfacing of the lost soul, we were assailed by an insupportable stench, which caused Cassius and myself to retch, but which the master inhaled in ecstasy … Yes, in ecstasy, my lord. I could barely behold him any more than I could the corpse. Yet, despite my horror, I remarked the sire's nervous quivering of the mouth, spasmodic twitching of the brow, sinister expression of the eyes and contraction of the lips, which were drawn in and glued, as it were, to his teeth. Cassius abjured me to turn away, lest I be drawn in further, and so I did, before continuing to attend to the task. We filled three large cases, which were sent by boat down the Loire to Machecoul, where they were reduced to ashes by the sire's cousins. I counted thirty-six different children's heads, but there were more bodies than heads.

With dawn drawing near, the master panicked, and we saved time by dropping the bodies and heads down the privy, but one of the few intact corpses caught on a nail in the outer wall, so that it would be visible the next day to all. The sire and Cassius turned to me, since I was the lightest. They let me down by rope and I disengaged the wretch with great difficulty, its bloated eyes all the while staring at me.

And the horror continued on our return to the sire's castle, where we aided the sire's cousins and servants in burning the last of the remains.

I cannot tell you, my lords, just how profoundly that night's work affected me. Ever since, I have been haunted with a vision of heads, rolling as in a game of skittles, and crashing together with mournful wails.

'Of course I interjected at that point,' said the lieutenant du procureur, M. Bumpton. 'I told the court it was impossible that bodies could be burned in a chamber fireplace.'

'Very admirable of you,' I sneered. 'Go on with your account.'

Henri: It was done, for all that. The fireplace was very large at Machecoul; we piled up great logs, and laid the dead children among them. They burned, and then we afterwards threw the ashes out the window into the moat.

But there was worse to come, my lords.

I distinctly remember one occasion when two children were procured, and the one was made to watch the torments of the other before himself being raped, tortured and disembowelled. The sire then severed both their heads with a braquemard, procured for that purpose alone.

But the sire was often not sated by killing his victims, and would continue to sexually abuse the dead body, sometimes sitting in the entrails and ...

'Continue!' gasped the judge. 'You have sworn an oath.'

... and masturbating. Whereupon, having reached climax, he would faint, and be carried off to bed, where he would weep and pray for hours in abject contrition for his crimes.

'How many victims do you estimate, my poor man?' de l'Hospital asked.

Not more than three hundred, said Henri.

'Not more!' expostulated the judge.

The procureur, M. Bumpton, paused in reciting all this to me, his face cadaverous, his brow moist with sweat. For the first time, he raised his eyes to mine.

'Lies!' I denounced and then, recalling the salvation of confession, 'Well, at any rate, wild exaggerations.'

'Should I continue narrating Henri's confession, my Lord?'

'At once!'

Henri: Boys, and sometimes girls, were lured to the castle on some pretext by the sire's servants and, once inside, were raped and tortured. Soon I was involved directly in these acts, for very fear of them again being perpetrated upon myself. I remember the case of the two sons of Hamelin; whilst one child was being tortured, the other was on its knees sobbing and praying to God, till its own turn came.

Messire, the whole surpassed even Caesar, whom my lord clearly desired to imitate. Cassius and I used to read to the sire from the chronicles of Seutonius, and Tacitus, who recorded the cruelties. It was nightmarish bedtime reading.

'Of course, I again interjected,' said Bumpton, 'to remind all present that Henri was a peasant's son, a mongrel. It was impossible that he could read Latin. But even that, Henri negated. He simply turned to me and said calmly:

Cave canem[1]*,* lieutenant du procureur, M. Bumpton.

'A sigh of astonishment came from the more learned members of the court. "The Devil has him!" they cried.

'Cassius began to shout that his friend was touched in the head, and that Henri's words were the ravings of insanity. Silence was imposed and then Henri again reminded Cassius that only by confessing their crimes would the two prevent, if not their deaths, then the graver threat of eternal damnation.

'Pierre de l'Hospital bade him to continue his tale.'

Henri: Cassius and I both know Latin and he even remembers when we both spoke it as our native tongue in Pompeii, before the eruption of Mount Vesuvius. I was a slave in that life and Cassius my master. One day he was summoned to Jerusalem where he ... (No, Cassius, we must confess all, my friend, the truth will liberate ...) He was called away to Jerusalem where he ... tortured Christians to make them renounce their beliefs.

---

[1] Latin: Beware of the dog.

'The judge's owlish face tu-whit tu-whooed in astonishment, but Henri continued his tale, saying Cassius had told him how alarmed he had been to find, in his present life, Christianity now a full-blown religion, and his cherished gods of Olympus denounced as pagan.

'A sigh of horror ran the length of the court.

'"Heresy!" some shouted. And still Henri pressed on with the telling of his tale, saying that there was another man he had known in Pompeii, who had also been reborn in this time. A person by the name of Memphis.

'At that, Pierre de l'Hospital looked enquiringly at his secretary. "Perhaps he refers to the magician, my lord?' said the secretary. "We have oft tried to catch him and his familiar, the dog Barnabus, in the performance of witchcraft and heresy for which Memphis is infamous in these parts."'

'Pierre de l'Hospital then turned once more to Henri and somewhat impatiently demanded he tell the rest of what he knew, and so he did. Shall I tell you what I remember of his accusations?'

'Yes, yes,' I barked. 'Go on.'

'As I recall, his reply was essentially as follows.

Henri: The master sent a priest, Eustache Blanchett, to Italy to search for a skilled magician, and Blanchett returned with a clerk in minor orders. That 'clerk' was Memphis who brought with him the hound Barnabus. It was clear to all that the master found Memphis immensely attractive and before long trusted him completely.

Then one day, great thumping noises emanated from the room set aside for Memphis' activities, and out he rushed, terribly dishevelled. He told the master he had conjured great chests of gold crowns, but warned that a great serpent, a league long, had inadvertently also been summoned and was guarding the treasure.

This frightened the master so badly, he had the door barred, and so it remained. When the castle was sold, neither gold nor serpent was found inside the room – only the corpses of a hundred children. It was these that led to the first investigations of my master and the none-too-pretty pass we are all in today.

'Henri bowed his head in great shame as he ended his confession. Cassius took Henri's hand. Oh my, it was almost touching.

'Naturally enough, my lord, sentence was quickly passed. Cassius and Henri are both to be burned to death for witchcraft, without proper Christian rites, and thus condemned to eternal damnation.

'Fanciful ravings of an ungrateful servant, my lord.'

And so finished M. Bumpton's history. I sent him from my cell. The fool! Henri has spoken the truth. God had loosened his tongue!

I myself, as M. Bumpton assures me, will this night be sent a priest to make my last confession.

So here I sit in my cell, drinking wine and partaking of a hearty last meal. Surely there is no sin in the world, however great, which God, in his grace and loving kindness, will not forgive, provided one is not cut down before one has a chance to ask of him that forgiveness.

Ah, where would we be without forgiveness? And from so high a personage as the deity?

Someone less onanistic is up next in our musical chair of confession: Cassius ...

Chapter Eight

What We May Do.

Wednesday 10th August, Melbourne 2005.

Henri was aghast at the tale.

'Cassius, it can't be true.'

'Confound you, Henri, of course it's true!'

'In history books?'

'In history books.'

'What happened next?'

I leant back into my chesterfield. Poor Pandora, whom Henri had half hugged to death, took the opportunity to escape his embrace and decamp to her favourite spot near the heater, to lie luxuriating upon the floor, the heat emblazoning her belly.

'We were all three executed upon the morrow,' I continued. 'But not before De Retz took off his cap, knelt, kissed a crucifix, and made this pious oration to the crowd: "Remember that the Lord God is always more ready to receive the sinner than is the sinner to ask of Him pardon. Therefore let us conceive such a love of God, and such repentance, that we shall not fear death, which is only a little pang, without which we could not see God in his glory. For although – " glancing at us two " – we have sinned grievously here below, yet we shall be united in Paradise, our souls being parted from our bodies, and we shall be together forever and ever."'

What I did not tell Henri, was that the prospect of our imminent separation was even more horrid to me than any posturing on the sire's part. On that stark stretch of land, we would be hanged till death, then our bodies burnt to dust. There would be nothing to bind me to that anonymous spot. No covering to keep my soul compacted. It would be dispersed along with the wind that would strew my ashes.

I would not remember Henri in the next life, even though I did not doubt our paths would cross. How would I thrust myself into his remembrance when I would not myself remember? Can you imagine my turmoil as I struggled to free my hands of the restraining cord?

I fixed Henri with my eyes and resumed my narration.

'The stool was cast down, and the Sire de Retz dropped. The fire roared and enveloped him as he swung. The cord was cut and the sire fell into the iron cradle prepared to receive him. That is all we two saw on that day, since we were promptly executed thereafter. But I have learnt since that de Retz's body was removed before the fire gained mastery of it, and was placed in a coffin. The monks and the women present (Madame de Retz herself and other members of the most illustrious houses of Brittany) then transported it to the Carmelite monastery of Nantes, where it was buried with all the rites 'due' his station. A high and mighty end for a low and despicable monster!

'And what of us? We too were hanged but our bodies were then burned to dust, and our ashes cast to the winds. No hope for us of retaining any memory of that life before being whisked into the next. Even more of a travesty was what followed in the Carmelite Church of Our Lady. Celebrated there with pomp – oh such pomp! – the obsequies of the very high, very powerful, illustrious Seigneur Gilles de Laval, Sire de Retz, late Chamberlain of King Charles VII, and Marshal of France!'

At that infamous point in history, I ended my narration, conscious of Henri's horror and some new emotion produced in him – a sudden design to leave. Gone was the astonishment; in its place were revulsion and disbelief.

He berated me soundly, vowing that though *I* might fantasise about being implicated in such grisly deeds, he would never harm, much less rape and kill, a child. Ah but what we are capable of when we don't know ourselves!

When Henri recollected himself enough to notice my pleading eyes, he quit the room but, much to my relief, not to snatch up his trusty backpack and leave altogether. Instead, he simply removed himself to the outdoors.

I remained on my Chesterfield, as if stamped there by an elephant's foot. Could I have mended my speech a little? I should at least have told how, before Henri and I were hanged, the procureur threw my notebook into the pyre prepared for our bodies. Yes, my precious notebook, burned with our bodies, along with all the new equations I had formulated since those last in Pompeii, for my new life had given a new perspective on the conundrums of humankind. In earnest I had lived my life of nobility as a Roman soldier, but it was an unearned distinction. I supposed then that a mathematics of human thought and action could eradicate the mistakes of the mighty to make them mightier still. But *then* I had been one of those ruling elite, lording it over slave and foreigner alike. As a member of De Retz's household, my fortunes had turned: *I* was now the servant and outsider who squirmed under another's iron hand. Only by being a victim of injustice did I discern the central tenet of justice: that the accident of birth (where, when, of what parentage) should not determine the stature of the individual. Not only I, but others too in my newfound class, thought a great deal more than do the generality of servants. However, quite the obverse seemed true in the ranks of the nobility: few who were born to power were worthy of the accident.

Doubtless the contrast in my lives was further brought home to me by the intolerance I now discerned in religion. As proconsul in Jerusalem, I abominably tortured and killed members of a minority sect, the Christians, believing my acts to be perfectly proper. In that life in France, that sect was now the ascendant religion, and I, the pagan, in the fearful minority.

And, yes, I had committed crimes – unthinkable crimes – in that life as in the one before it. As a soldier of Rome, I had believed them logical, necessary; under the sire's rule, I considered them horrid, pointless; but they were no less barbarous because I saw them as such. If anything, they were the more so: I knew better.

I would not, could not, relinquish my striving, and so laboured long after the chores of the day on the undone chore of humanity: finding a way to end the historical cycle of error. Unlike in Pompeii, I saw in France that a mathematics that would improve the lot of humankind, must (to attain muscular effect) indeed do just that: improve the lot of the *whole* of humankind. Given this advance in my thinking during my life in France, imagine my despair at the prospect of my death on that featureless tundra and the erasure of my memory, written and temporal. The anticipation of pain was as nothing to the knowledge that soon all my thoughts would go up in flames. And my notebook would help fuel that very immolation.

I rose from the Chesterfield with a new determination to venture again into the mindscape. My anguish had exhausted itself; Henri's unease, it seemed, was growing. He rapped on the bay windows, his phone to his ear.

'What is wrong with mobile reception in Melbourne these days?' he asked. 'I can't get through to my friend Rena. Can I use your landline?'

Tell Me About It.

Monday 15th August, Melbourne 2005.

How'd I get into this? Memphis is a freak! When I told him Henri had tried calling several times but the phone kept cutting out, he insisted we go to Henri's flat. Memphis was quite dogged, even worried, which is an expression I can't say I'd ever associated with him before. I was still shaking from the all-night sex: the snide cup, the cutting nibble, the rude lick, the mocking thrust, all finished off with the acerbic slap. I don't remember much kissing, or at any rate enough to shut me up. Tell me about it.

Again, we drove the limo. Or I should say, Brad drove us in it, with Scooter next to him in the front, Memphis and I laid out in the back.

One of the many great things about limos, I had discovered, is that they have TVs. I asked Memphis to turn it on.

'Memphis Media? You own Memphis Media?' I asked him. 'Why, if you've been gallivanting around the world for thousands of years, do you only now decide to take it over?'

'Global communications, my dear,' he said. 'Humans have never been more alone.'

I could vouch for that.

The program was clearly a rehash of old news stories. When an item came on about walled neighbourhoods in Johannesburg, Brad and Scooter started on about it, though they couldn't even see the TV from where they sat.

BRAD These people, Scooter. Here they are, wealthy as. But can they enjoy it? Standing apart from the world of want and envy, they wall up their neighbourhood ...

SCOOTER ... yes, while outside is a wasteland of poverty and resentment.

BRAD What's the point of wealth if you've got to spend it protecting it?

A line came back to me from Blake 101. That's William Blake and 101's the code of the subject I took on him at uni. Yeah, I'm an Arts girl. English major. Tell me about it.

> Pity would be no more,
> If we did not make somebody Poor.

Memphis farted laughter. It nearly blew me off the seat. Scooter seemed thoughtful; Brad nodded. Memphis kept on laughing. He pulled a clown handkerchief out of his sleeve – it just kept coming – and wiped his eyes.

'Oh, that's priceless. "Pity would be no more / If we did not make somebody Poor." So obvious and yet who gets it?'

Memphis wailed into more hysterics of laughter, but I was far from laughing. I was pretty damned sure I'd said that quote in my head, hadn't I?

'Such a sad creature, Blake,' said Memphis, his eyes still streaming. 'I remember him well. Not even the poverty I forced upon him could hold him back. Really, though, I don't know why I bother. I gave Swift a beastly time as well but there's his *Gulliver's Travels* abridged and read as a children's book! Oh the white trash tragedy of it all! You humans, you really do make it too easy for me, though Cassius I'm not so sure of: people might really take heed of *his* history lessons because he, at least, can show them it's in their interests to change.'

Cassius? Not *the* Cassius Henri was seeing, surely; though heaven knows it's not a common name. Before I could ask, a news clip of the US President, declaring war on some small country, caught my attention.

'Those who are not with us are against us.'

And hot on its heels, another, with a reporter pressing the embattled president on rumours of US sanctioned torture.

'I don't know,' the president kept saying. 'I don't know.'

'Oh yes,' smiled Memphis. 'What you don't know could start a war.' And for a moment I almost thought the president faltered in his delivery, looking around as if to determine the source of impertinence.

I was cold with dread. The limo arrived at the flats – a soot-covered, oversized gravestone if ever I've seen one.

'Come, dear,' said Memphis, and pulled me with him.

What was I doing here? Okay, being alone is one thing. But alone with a creep?

Memphis smiled at me, 'Come now, Rena, you are not alone in your loneliness. You have the whole world with you!'

Again, reading my thoughts!

Memphis started to laugh but stopped almost

immediately. 'What is it you are thinking now? About Henri. What of Henri?'

'Just that I hope he … he …'

'He what?' Memphis purred, his eyes firing red. 'That he is with Cassius as we speak? And do you know what it is that this Cassius is working on?'

'He's working on a … I think Henri said it was … a Final Theory, I think he called it.'

Memphis' smile was impossible to read. He told Brad they might as well collect Barney, that the dog's role as guard for the flats was now superfluous. We all four got out, with me having to open my own door. Brad and Scooter got in a truck that barred the entrance to the flats and drove it forward a few metres.

'*Now* what am I sensing, Rena? An … envy of Henri …? Envy …? Because unlike with you and I …'

Memphis saw the connection.

'Ah yes, he's in love! Henri's in love with Cassius and you envy him that. How touching.'

He took my hands in his, so powerful, so hard. I pulled away, but he would not let go.

'I don't think Henri has told Cassius he loves him,' I said. 'Well, not in so many words, but I'm sure he does.'

Memphis let go of my hands.

'Then there is still time.'

Memphis' eyebrows rippled like a million tiny serpents. His eyes were black holes. Then, as though at the flick of a switch, his mood changed.

'There is still time,' he said, his voice utterly expressionless. He let go of my hands, pursing his lips as you would to whistle, though I couldn't hear a sound. He gave me one of his odd little smiles.

'For a dog's ears only,' he murmured.

Then Barney appeared – the most obscenely large dog you can imagine. The size of a bull, perhaps bigger.

My heart faltered and in my mind it was as if all the pieces of a puzzle clicked together at once.

Again, there was that smile.

Scooter hopped out of the truck and opened the back for the dog to jump in.

'Tell me, Rena, have you ever woken from one dream only to find yourself in another?'

'You want Cassius and Henri separated, don't you, so how about telling me why?'

But Memphis continued on his own path.

'Always so easy. So easy. Henri loves but still has his wanderlust, no? And he has concerns so he tries to call you? We shall ring him, won't we, Rena?'

'If you're who I think you are,' I trembled, 'then why can't you simply achieve whatever you want with a spell?'

'For the same reason God does not intervene directly in your lives: freewill. You humans have the right to choose as you please. God appeals to your kinder instincts for influence. I have something more reliable to draw on.'

I asked the inevitable.

'Stupidity.'

'Who are you really?' I asked, my tongue tripping on teeth.

Brad and Scooter drove out of the carpark and onto the highway.

'Your phone, Rena.'

'It doesn't work. No … network coverage.'

Memphis handed me his.

'And now, my dear, with playtime over, I need you to call our dear friend Henri.'

Escape at Last?

Monday 15th August, Melbourne 2005.

Guess what? I'm to totally escape at last! Rena called, the dear. She's won two tickets to Paris! Asked her why she didn't want to take her man friend and she didn't sound too happy. Can't be working out between them. Oh well, I'll do what I can with a good dose of platonic love. I'm pretty good at that, though I'm not altogether comfortable leaving Cassius on his own just now, poor thing.

He's not well at all and looking worse every day. All this indoor activity at his sums and figures. I got him out for a bit. Finally. Fresh air. So we went to *Settee*, though Cassius' mood soon spoiled things.

I'd just finished a very nice chicken and tarragon burger with mustard yoghurt; he'd barely touched his plain risotto.

'Cassius, you never initiate conversation,' I huffed. 'I feel like I'm always talking, but you never say how you're feeling. I'm getting grumpy now. Is that noise annoying you?' I asked, gesturing to a very loud menagerie of boys at a nearby table.

Cassius nodded and started talking about going home to work on the 'formulation' of his 'Final Theory'. It was certainly doing nothing for his peace of mind. These people who can't relax!

I still hadn't told him about those tickets and I didn't want us parting in a bad way, so I tried to segue into the topic with as much subtlety as I could manage, which isn't that subtle.

'I don't have a hobby, do I, Cassius? Every time I go to a country, my hobby is to learn the language for the next one. What do I do when I get to Spain? Learn Japanese? With all these lives I'm supposed to have, perhaps I should be swotting up on what I'll need for the next. Hmm, I think my next life's in Rome – perhaps I should go there now to get a head start.'

'Rome's arenas of antiquity, Spain's bullrings of today,' said Cassius matter-of-factly. 'Merely the replacement of cattle for cattle.'

I shot up at that.

'Cassius, I can't take all this make-believe any more.'

'It is not make-believe.'

'I think I should leave.'

Cassius was half on a reply, but to a different answer, and stopped.

'You're leaving?'

I told him about Rena winning the airfares. But it doesn't have to be forever, I kept thinking in the back of my mind, even as I put it to Cassius that our separation was inevitable and probably permanent given our different lifestyles and outlook. I like him, yes, but such a stay-at-home! No, I'm about to go mad in Melbourne and he isn't helping! I certainly didn't tell him how Rena won those airfares – that's the bit I left out. The prize was in a Memphis Chips' packet!

'Do you love me?' he asked.

'Do I …? I was a bit startled, just finishing my latte. Eventually I said, 'I had a childhood friend, very smitten with me, but I had to tell him, if I didn't know you, we could fall in love. I think we know each other now.'

Cassius pleaded with me to stay out the week. It became quite embarrassing and I felt rather mean, but the feeling passed. In fact, shambling home, with me half supporting Cassius, I realised my mind was already gone from him.

Rena's posting me my ticket (I gave her Cassius' address) and it should arrive in a couple of days. Then, only another two before the flight. Rena's meeting me at the airport on the day of the flight. She sounds as if she's busy right up until then, so rules out staying with her in the interim.

Okay, a working week with Cassius. I can handle that, just.

But can *he*?

The Imperfect Present.

Siin Sevada, 3003.

Oh me, oh my. Edgar Bumpton again. Well, I *had* been pondering in which tense to write my memoirs. Before, I was tempted to write of the imperfect present in the past perfect. But not now!

Things have turned out for the worse! Interrogations — they have quite unnerved me. Conducted over days with no sleep between, and (embarrassing to say) with me naked, in the cold. And there is nothing more I can tell them!

These are not ordinary interrogations but, rather, trials of a sort, conducted in the myriad testing rooms, or 'reality postulate' chambers.

In one such confine, I was presented with a continuous mirror: above, below and to every side. I saw myself in it, not as myself staring at my reflection, but as my reflection staring at me! Oh the horror of dislocation, compounded when (though not usually a violent soul) I punched the glass with my left hand – I have always swung with the right! The glass shattered, or so I thought, until I saw it still unbroken. Am I now only a reflection?

In another chamber, I saw myself from the viewpoint of the entire galaxy, losing myself amid its vastness. Screaming, I overcompensated by somehow mentally 'zooming in' till I was now looking up at my colossal self, and feeling all the horror of a mouse about to be stepped upon.

Still other chambers opened up existences that I have never lived. I found mirrors, looked into them, but never saw myself. I encountered friends and family to whom I was neither friend nor family nor even a thought!

I came upon rooms where I could tell the history of things by the objects that furnished them. In others, I scarcely knew which way was up.

I stumbled upon an isometric landscape. There was no perspective and hence no diminishing in size of the appearance of things over distance. As miniature creatures walked away they became giants. As giants approached, they shrank to midgets, whilst always appearing to remain the same size.

In yet another chamber, I saw hell was forgetting the meaning to things; heaven was the comfort of knowing no connection had been missed. I mistook dead people for the living. I saw the same person walk opposite ways at once.

What is the point of these torments?

My, my, it is terrible!

There is another human here. One. He acts as interpreter between myself and the Siin Sevidians. Such a funny man. How to describe him? Quite simply, he is dressed absurdly like a comic book villain! He walks as if he were eight feet tall when, in truth, he is quite short. The sheen of his exaggeratedly tilted hat serves to add to the impression that he sees himself as a giant. As for his face, it is adorned with an impossibly pointy goatee and razor sharp sideburns. In all, the confluence of styles, landing somewhere between eighteenth century English gent and American cowboy (he has mock spurs on his pointy boots, for heaven's sake!) is odious in its trashiness.

To top it all off, he swings an ivory cane that is too short to touch the ground!

Oh my, but the thing that really hit me was the revelation of his name: Memphis.

'Sir, are you the same Memphis who is landlord of my flat?'

'The same.'

'The coincidence!'

'Edgar Bumpton, there is no coincidence in life, only accidents.'

He was sitting opposite me in my cell, which is wondrously dome-shaped. I have measured it out in steps and it is five metres in diameter. The ceiling and floor are by turns a milky translucency and a perfect transparency. This second state is most scary of all, since my room seems to perch above a lava flow, so that when the floor becomes see-through, I feel as if I am plummeting to a scalding death. Sometimes I see stars above, sometimes the Siin Sevidians. Entry is by walking through the wall! I can do this myself, but only when the Siin Sevidians deem it meet.

I touched Memphis on the shoulder, intending to ask if he would help hurry my petition for freedom. He flicked my hand away and the force threw me half across the room. I stared at him in horror where I lay.

Was he one of those giants the video store clerk spoke of? I put this to him.

'You are a giant,' I said, 'shrunk in size to appear as the most powerful superhero.'

'Something like that, Edgar,' said Memphis, beaming. 'And now, I have some questions for *you*.'

Memphis appears to be after two people. One is called Cassius. I know no one by that name. The other is Henri.

'Oh my, might that be the same Henri who is my neighbour?'

'The same, yes.'

I asked what reason he could possibly have to seek out that apparently benign fellow.

'Edgar, my chum, if Henri is to slip through my grasp, then I at least may be able to delay Cassius in

228

the mindscape till such time as Henri grows sick of him and departs.'

It didn't make much sense to me. 'Why would you want that to happen?' I asked. 'And, more pressingly, what *is* the mindscape?'

'Why, *this* is the mindscape, my friend. We are in it.'

And Memphis laughed.

Coping with Madness.

Tuesday 16th August, Melbourne 2005.

Counting down. Got my ticket in the post. Will be leaving Friday. Only three days to wait! Rena texted to say she'll meet me on the flight. Funny thing is, her messages have all been from someone else's phone: 1317 616 666, how's that for a number? Tried ringing it once and I just heard crackling. I hope we get on that plane okay.

Cassius is weary, weak, busy with seemingly pointless calculations for his 'Final Theory'.

And how's this for loopiness on *my* part? I asked him about his mad logic today. If you start arguing with a madman using his own logic – or illogic – that's the fastest way to end up insane yourself.

'So, Cassius,' I said (he was sitting – more like rotting – on that bloody Chesterfield of his. I was in the one opposite). 'After we were both supposedly hanged in France, we forgot all about that life because of our violent deaths and having no prompts for remembering them – is that right?'

'Correct.'

'Then how do you remember past lives in this life?'

Cassius made a peak with his hands. From the way he nestled further into his chair, I could tell I was in for a lengthy tale. He began his explanation with something of a précis, annoyingly, but eventually got to the point.

'Henri, when I died in Pompeii, my soul did not immediately fly into the body of a newborn for two reasons: firstly, I was attached emotionally to the surrounds in which I perished and, secondly, those surrounds were preserved in ash. Fourteen centuries later, a farmer dug up those surrounds and my 'life' of limbo ended. My soul found corporeal habitation in France in the Fifteenth Century, alongside you. In that time, memories of my old life in Rome came back to me in snatches. Unfortunately, the nature of our deaths, then, at the hands of the French authorities, meant that I was drawn immediately into the next life, with no time to dwell on the one before, as I had been afforded in Pompeii. You could say I forgot myself, and indeed did so for a further five centuries of lifetimes. I came to myself, again, in the life before this one I'm currently living now. During the Second World War, I was a ship's captain running guns to Crete in their fight against the Germans. My ship was my home, and when a U-boat sank the vessel, and I went down with her, there my soul resided among the fish and coral until in 1973 Spanish marine archaeologists found my boat, attached pontoons to it, and brought her to the surface. With the boat's internment, my soul was jettisoned into the physical housing you behold today. What became of you, Henri, a Cretan resistant fighter, I discovered in the death ledger of that isle. The day you died was also the exact day you were born into your present life, in 1976. Whilst I have been afforded three occasions for respite from the wheel of reincarnation, you seem always to have been drawn into your next existence upon the immediate termination of the last.'

It was loopy all right but, strange to say, I was following it.

'Okay, then,' I put to him. 'But how, in that case, have I been dreaming of that first life you've told me about, in Rome? If I've never served a sentence in limbo, that is.'

Cassius smiled. 'You're remembering that life because I *prompted* your memory. I have discovered it is possible to attain vague recollections even of lifetimes that were not 'rounded out with a little sleep' in limbo, to quote Shakespeare. What prompts those lives, have been my exhaustive readings of histories and first-hand accounts in particular. A reminiscence by a scholar I vaguely remember having known in some capacity or other. A transcript from a trial I can indistinctly recall as being contemporaneous with my own activities at the time. All kinds of things can and do set the memories rolling.'

I wasn't convinced there weren't still holes in his fabrication and pressed him further. 'How did your previous lives begin to come back to you in this present one?

'In early childhood, I remember seeing a painting of Pliny the Elder and feeling at once a sense of family. Then I read Pliny the Younger. As I read him, the same thing happened. I believe it is from them that my mathematical knowledge comes. Indeed, in this life, as a grade one student I possessed grade five maths, and was hailed as a prodigy. The point is, however, that my memory was prompted.'

'Which is what you're trying to do with me?'

But it wasn't working. At least not completely because luckily my Ancient Rome dreams have abruptly come to an end. Probably because I died in the last one I had.

Wednesday 17th August.

Two days to go!

Guess what I dreamed about last night? Paris. Yes, quite nice if it was today's Paris. But no, it was the Fifteenth Century, rat-infested, stinking version of the place! I can't handle these dreams! I can't handle Cassius. He scares me. His ... stories scare me. This world, this life will do for me, so I'd hate to think it didn't end with death. Just imagine starting over again. Shitting your pants, crying in your cot, the warzone of kindergarten playgrounds. Who wants to go through that again and again? And the teen years are no better – in fact, worse! Perhaps if you had some maturity in them from a previous life ... No, that would be worst of all! Ugh, ugh!

Anyway, all this brainwashing could almost have me thinking Cassius is a cult leader, except he doesn't seem to have one follower apart from stupid ol' me. After all, it's what cults do – make you concentrate on the past, on failures, till you forget the present with its goals. Very clever. Or maybe it's just a way to make me stay longer because Cassius knows the days are ticking down to my departure. Gay marriage? Forget it. Me and my backpack, we're moving on. It's the only way I know to live.

Cassius keeps harping on my call from Rena. It's obviously playing on his mind. See what I mean? He doesn't want me to have any friends apart from himself – another trait of the cult leader. Today, he said he's worried about the role Memphis might be playing in all our lives, and I must admit that one stopped me short.

'You mean he *made* Rena call?'

'Don't you see it's a possibility?' he asked almost pleadingly. 'Are you sure you've told me everything she said?'

Again, I neglected the little bit about the source of the two fabulous plane tickets. A small omission, surely.

He asked the question again.

I nodded yes. A white lie, but then a sudden thought: 'Is Rena going to be okay?'

'Probably none of us will be.'

My stomach slam-danced. But only for a beat. Of course she'll be okay. Cassius is the mad one, the cult leader. Usually they just try to tell you your loved ones never really cared for you, and things like that, as a way of separating you from the outside world. Cassius goes one better: he tells you they're dead. Or hints as much.

I know all about cults. For a time – yes, I admit it – I was in this happy clappy kind of church. But I got out of it. I woke up to the bullshit. Past lives, future lives, parallel lives. My friend, there's only *this* life, so make the most of it!

Thursday 18th August 2005.

One day left and Cassius looks awful. Seems he's bracing himself for a trip into the mindscape (yes, crazy!) and for my leaving, too, I guess. I'll try to repeat his logic here, now that I understand it. God, that's scary – that I'm understanding his logic.

There is the physical world and then the non-physical world of mathematics, with one equally describing the other. That is, every person is represented by both a physical body in the corporeal world and a non-physical algorithm in the mindscape. Cassius' hope is that the two are connected, and in a more substantial way than one is 'connected' to one's image in a mirror.

Now, we're mostly aware of just the corporeal world, and the meaning of this other world is beyond that, so Cassius means to get outside this world and into the mindscape.

To do this takes great mental energy, he says, and is dangerous. Let me see if I can explain why. The self is the limit of associations. Every association one has is connected with oneself. But by getting outside oneself, there is no limit to the number of potential associations, and this is where things can easily become overwhelming. It is also the greatest danger Cassius faces apart from Memphis. See, it is very easy to become lost in these associations to which one is not directly connected – the same as we can be overwhelmed by news of disasters and killings in faraway lands on TV. In being outside oneself, one has no personal or experiential link back to one's being. To hark back to our analogy: in the mindscape you might meet someone whose face was familiar to you even though you had never met!

There is, however, and very fortunately, a literal key, which also acts as a legend, to aid navigation within the mindscape. It is called a supersolid and Cassius hopes to steal one of these from a certain Edgar Bumpton.

A perfect model of the universe would be the universe itself. The supersolid is definitely not that, being about the size of a die, and its mathematical parallel reasonably small (at least for a mind like Cassius'). No, the supersolid is not a map *of* the universe but a metaphor *for* the universe.

Like a work of art, in being metaphorical the supersolid is both itself and something else. In this way, it can bridge both the physical and the intangible. The supersolid makes it easier to find one's way back since, by the strength of its glow, it alerts one to the proximity of the gates. These gates are direct doors between worlds and dimensions.

Cassius must see the future. Cassius needs to form a proposition whose meaning of the subject is contained in the predicate, and can be verified by comparing the subject *with* the predicate, as in 'eight minus five is three'. Thus if we know that eight is the present and three is the future, he can calculate how we reach that future: by subtracting three. The answer is the missing part of the equation. He has formulated a proposition that is only verifiable by observation. He has, so to speak, given today's world the numeral eight, and tomorrow's three. By examining the future he will work out the algorithm. From this, he will be able to apply his formula to all outcomes, and thus formulate a better outcome for humanity.

I can't believe I understand this stuff! It's like I've heard it all before, but in saying that I think I really must be infected with Cassius' madness ...

I just now went looking for Cassius to tell him what I have been thinking. When I found him in his room, he said he was readying himself to enter the mindscape to try to resolve a particularly troublesome aspect of his research. He said he would probably be unresponsive for some time, so I promised to tend to his body while he was in that state – how morbid this all is! – and refrain from calling the police.

Been looking out the window to distract me. Memphis Industries! I see their ads everywhere now. You wanna know the strange thing though? I haven't the least idea what Memphis Industries *does*, apart from making chips.

Poor old Cassius! He tells such tales. He reckons he has encountered this other human intelligence in the mindscape, the current holder of the supersolid: Edgar Bumpton. Edgar Bumpton! My neighbour in that ghastly concrete slab – the one who asked me to watch his place. Of course, I could very easily have caught Cassius out on that one but I didn't even try. It did, however, remind me of Mabel and the rest of them back there. I've tried calling Mabel but can't seem to get through, so I hope everything's okay. I mean, whoever heard of a guy having to escape his own place by tying sheets together? Damn near broke my neck.

Yes, I should ring Mabel. *Will*.

I've been checking on Cassius a lot and hearing his mutterings with growing alarm. While lying on his bed and completely 'out' of it, I suppose in his own mind he *has* entered the mindscape ...

The Collective Individual.

Siin Sevada, 3003.

Oh my, this is terrible. Memphis visited again, telling me of his schemes. He is persuading the Siin Sevidians of his plan to safeguard the primacy of the individual's rights once and for all. By what means? A mind-meld! With the Siin Sevidians becoming one individual, then that individual need never have its freedom restricted by taking into account another individual's rights. I must say, when I first found myself on this planet, I was impressed by the efficacy of its system. Now I am not so sure that when put to its absolute it is not madness!

'Whose personality would this collective individual take?' I asked.

Memphis smiled.

'Why, the strongest.'

Laughing, he passed through the spongy wall. Almost a second later, a shape emerged where Memphis had departed. At first, I figured Memphis had forgotten something. Then I saw it wasn't him at all but a tall, broad fellow with dark hair and features, and brows thick and furious.

'Edgar Bumpton?' he asked in a tone, which suggested he had no patience for delay.

'My ... yes ... yes, I am,' and, because I felt it appropriate, I put forward my hand. He stared at me as if I was stupid.

'Confound you, this isn't a social engagement. Time is scarce.'

Just by our staring at the wall, it parted for the two of us. On the other side, I asked him if he was intending to help me.

He didn't answer directly, but said his name was Cassius and then just looked at me as if waiting for me to say something monumentally important. So I said: 'There's this odd character here who's after you. Odd name too – Memphis.'

Cassius' face turned pale. Oh my, I had feared Memphis before but now that this man, who appeared so strong, evidently feared him also, I verily quivered. Cassius said our first necessity was to get ourselves to a place of safety. For this, he made recourse to the oldest trick: he retrieved from his satchel a cloak he had secreted in one of the chambers. I climbed on his shoulders and threw the ample cloak around mine. Thus, together, we were as tall as a Siin Sevidian, and could pass for one – from a distance. Reaching again into his satchel, Cassius then pulled out my supersolid – yes, *my* supersolid! – and waved away my every protest of ownership.

The corridors, courtyards, and colonnades we passed through resembled abstract compositions. Giant spheres, cuboids, impossible objects. Cassius claimed to have seen some of a dear friend's art amongst it all. Given our flimsy disguise, our path became ever more elliptical, skirting this gathering here, that gathering there. Occasionally we did a complete about face at the approach of a lone Siin Sevidian. Beneath our cape, the supersolid was glowing brightly.

'Is this how it indicates proximity to the gate – by the strength of its glow?' Cassius asked.

We had stopped in a paradoxical vortex to rest,

and there we shared our knowledge of the strange object and the even stranger place to which we had both come, each pursuing our own truth as we saw it.

Oh my, the things Cassius told me! This place is both a fiction and a possible future 'physical system'. Not the future as an actuality, but what it will be in our world if humankind continues on its present path.

'For some reason,' said Cassius, 'you have stumbled into the mindscape but, instead of seeing an abstract world of sums and figures, your mind is viewing it as its physical outcome. What is your normal vision like?'

'Here, pristine and perfect, but on earth my glasses are like deep-sea diving goggles. What do *you* see?'

'I am seeing, not with my eyes, but with my mind's eye, while my body remains at home in my bed. It is taking an incredible mental energy. Part of my mind here, the other part controlling my actual body as if by remote, making sure it breathes.'

We continued on our way and, with the aid of the supersolid at last reached the gate, though not without numerous alarms. We passed through its shimmering surface, to be transported to a different place and time.

Oh my, can this get more terrible! Just when escape seems assured, Cassius and I find ourselves in a fetid bog, with mud up to the knees on Cassius, and to the waist on me. It is a place of the most monstrous flora – bulbous, pendulous, stalky – high as skyscrapers above us. But worse are the buzzing insects – chitinous, slimy, huge as hands, sluicing through the mossy peat. The noise is primal, grubby and wet; the smell, earthy, fetid, rotting! Ugh!

'Here,' commands Cassius, offering a begrimed hand. He has mounted a rock, stained green and khaki with slime, and somehow manages to haul me up beside him.

'Oh my, where are we?' I ask. 'This place is prehistoric.'

Cassius doesn't answer as he painstakingly wipes mud off the supersolid.

'Is there a gate out of this world?' I ask.

I join him in staring at the wretched cube glowing faintly beneath its pall of mud. There is, but it must be some distance off.

A horrid clicking noise starts up behind us and we both turn to see a black and red mask of inscrutable expression, connected to a many-legged body. As the creature approaches, two mandibles, large as cleavers, and a mess of a mouth, mucous and saliva-strewn, expands before us. Oh my …

'Help, Cassius – please!'

Recovering my senses, I see the creature is dead, with a javelin-shaped weapon lodged in its head, and Cassius standing over it.

'What is it?' I whisper.

'A centipede.'

'A centipede! But it's two cars in length! So have we somehow entered one of the smaller cylindrical universes?' I pant.

'Yes.'

'But the spear …?'

Cassius stares at a slushy extrusion of plant matter above us: 'Someone or something threw it from there.'

I am staring in wonder at Cassius, so it is he who first sees the being that emerges from the foliage. It is the peculiar look on Cassius' face that makes me turn and see what he has seen: a being that stands upright … mammalian … and, like us, caked in mud. Nonetheless, it is unmistakably human. A woman ancient in years, her skin a canvas for the impasto mud.

Cassius' face flushes in pain – and some emotion that I can't quite decipher.

There is no mistaking what he yells. It should neither more nor less horrify than any of the other events, but it does both for its everydayness as well as its utter unusualness.

'Grandma!'

I turn to run, because I want to find the next gate. I see what looks like a giant green baseball glove, held half open, and with three black spines pointing inwards. I climb into it, brushing one of the spines, then the other, and wonder at Cassius' screams.

'Don't, man! Get out of there at once!'

I finally turn to him as the pitcher closes around me like I'm some sort of white, rubbery ball ...

A Real Story?

Friday 19th August 2005

Grandma?

Can you believe that? Of all the babble Cassius muttered in his trance while I was tending to him, nothing was so absurd as *Grandma*. It made me laugh. Not long after that, he came out of the mindscape.

'Water.'

I gave him water. The poor dear looked dreadful.

'That explains my Venus flytrap,' he rasped and for a moment I thought he was referring to my backpack, full and waiting almost expectantly by the door.

'What are you on about now?' I cried.

He told me that in the mindscape he and Edgar Bumpton had ended up in a pot of insect-eating plants, which Cassius had owned as a kid. Yeah, right. So now he doesn't just travel in space but also in time.

'Edgar would explain that particularly fat and noisome Venus flytrap,' said Cassius.

My staring brought out the explanation.

'Don't you understand! The poor man was trapped inside the Venus flytrap. I noted as a kid one its clubs became particularly bloated. It closed for ten years. I suppose that is how long it takes for a one centimetre wide vegetable stomach to digest an entire man.'

That was getting far too morbid and deranged. I turned to leave, wanting to give myself plenty of time to get to the airport.

'One more story,' he croaked.

I walked to the door and lifted my backpack to my shoulders.

'Please.'

I opened the door.

'It is real!' he yells, his voice shattering.

I walked back over to him.

'A real story?' I confirmed. 'About *your* life, this life, now?'

Cassius nodded.

I took off my backpack and sat down; I could spare him another hour.

'It is about my grandmother. I didn't just inherit these Chesterfield from her, but also many of her papers. It is from some of these papers – transcripts of my grandmother's final conversations – that I now wish to read to you. My reasons, I trust, will become evident   ...'

Chapter Nine

That Son of Theirs.

You wouldn't believe what happened, Lil. Yesterday Judy came to visit with that husband, Hugo, the doctor, and they brought that son of theirs. He didn't say hello or anything, and I know he hates to even call me Grandma... His hair? Dyed blue this time. Cassius – what a name. His parents gave him a perfectly good name, but that's what he wants to call himself.

I gave them all a cup of tea. Tea with a saucer, mind you – they don't seem to bother with them these days – and we all sat down on our Chesterfields. Got them from England, you know. Couldn't buy them these days. Too expensive.

Judy was looking at that *Yamaha* I got to fill out the room a bit, so I asked her to play. You know Judy is a concert pianist, don't you, Lil? She got that from her mother, of course. Garth doesn't have a poetic bone in his body.

Yes, I did everything I could for that child. Every Sunday I used to take Judy up to Mrs Ross's for lessons, paying out of the grocery money. And now she's made a career of it. But, like I said, I asked her to play a tune, something we could all sing along to. Of course she didn't want to at first and hid her face behind that long hair but I insisted. So did Garth and she said she would then.

'All right, Dad, for you.'

Isn't that lovely? She's a Plain-Jane, and we were always worried about her, but she *did* get a doctor. They've just bought a two-storey house together. Did you know that, Lil? It's the only one in the street... Which suburb? Oh, I can't remember off the top of my head, Dear, but one of the best ones. It's even got a brick fence and a gate where you have to say who you are before you can get in.

Sorry?

Oh, yes, Judy. She's very good, you know. I won't argue that. But those fancy pieces – up and down the keyboard.

'Do you think you could swing it, Dear?' I asked.

Garth gave me a look but he knows how sensitive I am to noises. He was falling asleep on his favourite couch and the others looked half asleep themselves, but it was impossible to talk over the racket.

'Maybe put the soft pedal on, dear.'

'Don't you like it, Mum?'

'No, it's lovely. Isn't it lovely, Garth?

'Yes, Edith,' he said crossly. I don't know why he was cross. He couldn't have been listening; he had his eyes closed. But she's such a lovely player. So much talent. They say she's one of the best in Melbourne, but it was late and I don't think any of us was up to it at that volume.

'Maybe later, Judy, when your father isn't so tired.'

'No, it's all right, Edith.'

'No, it's not, Garth. We don't want to worry them with your health now, do we?'

Garth looked around but I had to say that. You know what a chore it's been for me looking after him these past months. Oh, I don't complain, Lil; he *is* my husband, but did you know, and I'll just mouth this, he wets his bed? Yes, it's true! I've had to put plastic under the sheets! It's ruined all my linen. I've spoken to the doctors about it but they don't do a thing.

What was that, Lil? Oh, don't be silly: *he'll* never know.

Yes, and about that piece –

Sorry? Who was it by? Oh, something foreign. Very beautiful though, but a terrible ending. Lots of thumping and then the lid being slammed down.

I asked Judy if that was in it. She was very upset. That's musicians for you; they're terribly sensitive to the music. Her husband, Hugo, told me it was in the piece and took her outside. That son of theirs, Cassius, disappeared out back.

Later we had some of that delicious shortbread I make, and I got Garth to put on some Richard Clayderman. So soothing you'd hardly know it was there.

<u>Mrs Saffy's Account</u>   <u>Sunday 10th December 1989</u>

Something odd happened today, Lil. Do you know, I think I got smaller?

Yes, you've noticed? It happened this morning, when Judy and Hugo took Garth and I to church. That son of theirs didn't want to come, of course. Never was baptised, you know. Breaks Garth's heart to see his favourite daughter bringing up her son godless, but what can you do? Always had a mind of her own, that child. Takes after her father, you see: very wilful ... Sorry, Lil? Oh, well, yes, she gets her talent from me, that's understood.

We were in the church, Lil, in the front pew, like always. Out of necessity, of course ... Yes, Lil, out of necessity. There are a few weak voices in the congregation, as you well know, and I don't mind carrying the greater part of the hymns myself, that I don't. That's my contribution, Lil, and I've never wanted thanks for it. Never ... Sorry, but I get upset when I see my achievements go unnoticed.

The Reverend Memphis was sermonising about something – I never really listen – and ... Oh, no, Lil, I believe in God, but I've always liked the social part. Tea and cakes afterwards, and a chat with all my friends. Garth's the thinker, dear, that's why he likes a chinwag with you ... No, I meant someone to bounce ideas off, dear... Now, don't be silly, Lil ... Yes, knows his Bible back to front, my husband.

I was sitting thinking how Gargery's wife had let herself go since the pregnancy when Marcia Tate wheeled in that son of hers. Remember Jeremy? Contracted Meninga ... meninga ... Meningococcal disease six months back and none of us had seen anything of him since. Imagine, all that just starts from a headache! Well, this is how I could tell it was him, even before I could see. The singing softened in the back rows – they're always the laziest ones – but as they grew louder again, the middle rows got softer too. And I must say, when Marcia wheeled him into view, I even missed a bar or two myself. Such a shame, you know, and a lad of sixteen.

The hymn finished – the *Lord's My Shepherd* (Garth's favourite) – and we all sat down again. Wood shuffling on wood; quite a din it made. The Reverend Memphis closed his book last, with a little slap. I don't know why he drags everything on so – they last long enough as it is, his sermons. And then he had to feel that receding hairline of his – you won't find that in our family, Lil (Garth still has a full head of hair) – and talked about God's love for his people. Still, lovely deep voice that man has, like Rock Hudson … Yes, I know, Lil. You don't need to tell me. I can't ever watch a film of his again knowing that … Cary Grant, too? Oh, rubbish, Lil, I don't believe you. Not him. Not my Cary. It isn't possible.

Yes, the Reverend Memphis, he was talking about God's love for His people. Normally I switch off during the sermon but I was listening this time; I don't know why. My ears hurt. But all the time I was listening, I was taking a peek at that Jeremy, in that steel contraption of his. He looked very angry, Lil, and very sad. Garth saw me looking and squeezed my hand. He's always said we've been very lucky with our lot. No problems at birth and no Carys … Oh, all right, Lil, I did know about his "persuasion". But don't upset me with that right now.

So, Mrs Tate had squeezed in at the edge of a pew next to Halliday, with her son parked out there in the aisle. One on from Garth to my right, if you count that a seat. She was looking up at the Reverend and holding her son's hand. The Reverend said something about heaven being completeness and she squeezed Jeremy's hand hard. I saw her do it. *He* just looked at the floor, to his left. Didn't turn around or anything. Marcia shook his hand a bit and still no response.

Well, she's never been much of a looker, that Marcia Tate, but she grew worse then. All scrunched up and red, her face got. Then she put her hand on her son's shoulder but he still gazed at the floor. Marcia, her eyes like diamonds, finally put her hand on his neck, and he responded then.

And during all this time the Reverend kept rabbiting on.

'... and if you ever think you've been abandoned, you're wrong, for God loves us and never leaves us, and never does us any harm.'

'Rubbish!'

You can imagine what response that got! There I was, in front of all these people, shouting out 'rubbish'!

Garth turned on me sharply. He's never raised a fist to me yet and, God bless him, he didn't then, but he'd have been cross, I know. Very cross. He cherishes our upstanding position in the community, Lil, and didn't want me going and ruining it with nonsense. But something else about his silly wife seemed to surprise him even more because his hair fell out of place. I mean, here I was thinking the wind had glued it down – permanently! You wouldn't believe my embarrassment when I looked up and saw the Reverend looking at me. All my neighbours, too, with their eyes in my back. I felt Judy's hand on my shoulder, from behind where she sat with Hugo. She couldn't get a grip; only folds of tweed coat and a

252

blouse, all scrunched up in those pianist fingers of hers. Garth was looking down at me … Yes, Garth! Now, I know I've never allowed that he's shorter than me, Lil, but he always was. By a good two inches. But he's now like a man should be: taller than his wife. I might even take a turn with him on the dance floor in light of things.

And that, Lil, was how I shrank.

What does Hugo think? Being a doctor and working in one of those fancy hospitals and all, you'd think he'd know, wouldn't you? But he only said afterwards, when we were out in the gravel car park, that it's natural for people to shrink a little in their old age, as well as to stoop. Well, I never! Me, stoop? You know as well as I, Lil, that I always got deportment awards at our ladies college. Finest in my year, every year … Oh, you used to do your best, dear, but if you haven't got the carriage … It's nothing like that, Lil; it's how we're born.

Don't scratch the table, please, dear. I know you don't mean to. It's just those nails of yours … Fashionable, I'm sure. But at our age?

Yes, quite right, where were we? The car park, yes. Judy asked, with us all out there, she asked about my clothes.

'Yes, what about the clothes, Hugo? They're several sizes too big.'

253

'Well, dear,' said that know-it-all doctor to my daughter, 'maybe your mother put the wrong clothes on in the morning.'

Well, I never, Lil! And with me right there!

Judy pushed aside that silly fringe which she half curls over one ear, and stopped by the car door. Yes, the blue one, before you ask.

'But look at her shoes, Hugo. Look at them!' said Judy.

Garth and Hugo looked down at my shoes. The one shoe I still had on was slapping up and down as I walked.

'Feet don't shrink, do they?' she asked.

Mrs Saffy's Account   Monday 11th December 1989

I'm glad you could come again today, Lil. As you can see, I've shrunk even more.

Yes, you've spoken to Judy. Poor thing; she's terribly upset. Garth's beside himself. I even think that doctor's a little shaken … No, Lil, that's enough.

Well, then, how did it happen this time? … Sorry, Lil? … Yes, we're ahead of you there, dear. We've noticed that too. When it happens, it doesn't happen slowly, but all at once, and then I'm a few inches shorter.

All right, sit down, Lil. Yes, over there. At the head of the table, if you like. Good.

I feel trapped, Lil, like one of those flies there ... Oh, what, Lil ...? Yes, Judy's son, Cassius, got that today ... a flytrap. The things kids spend their money on ... Oh well, yes, I suppose you're right, Lil. All those petticoats we used to buy. Anyway, Judy says he's something of a haughty ... hoarder ... horticulturist, that's it.

Anyway, Lil, you've got me off track. What happened today? It got worse, as you can see. Oh, I'm not complaining. I've had a hard life, Lil. You know that better than anyone. A son that married a tart without my blessing... Yes, Lil, a tart. And then there's my sister: – a disgrace to the family. But I've kept them all together, Lil. All of them.

Yes, Lil, I haven't forgotten. About the shrinkage, yes. Here it is, then. You'll just have to bear with a little preamble first.

I managed a chat with Judy today. We sat over there, on my lovely Chesterfields by the gas fire, and –

What, why don't we sit on them now? Wear and tear, Lil. Wear and tear ... No, the dining table's fine.

Do you know what Judy said to me, Lil ...? What? No, no, she said:

'Can we really talk, Mum?'

Isn't that lovely? So I said, 'Of course, dear. What about?'

'Well,' she said, pushing that fringe over her ear (I'll have to get on to her about that at some point). 'Well,' she said, 'it's about this … about this …'

'Shrinking?'

'Yes, Mum, it's worrying.'

'Oh, it's nothing, dear. Hugo's probably right.'

'Are you sure?' she asked, putting her hand on mine, and do you know, Lil, I felt how my skin must have felt to her: like filo pastry. That's old age, I suppose. Anyway, she'd just asked if I was going to be okay and I'd said yes, and Judy leant back, smiling.

Yes, Lil, I'm selfless in that way. You've always known that.

'Well,' said Judy again, and she was gathering herself up. 'Hugo's got to get back to the hospital and, um, when you're …'

'Going? So soon?' I was alarmed, Lil, betrayed. Here I am, not long for the world. A daughter whisked away to the city. An upstart husband who never lets her visit. A son with blue hair, like Cary. I don't mind telling you, Lil, I was put out. Very put out. I jumped off that couch, there, that very one you're looking at now, an effort for me at my age, and do you know what I said?

'I won't be here next time, Judy,' is what I said. 'You'll be visiting an empty house,' I told her. 'Your father and I … well, Garth is already making arrangements.'

'Oh, Mum!'

She jumped up like a rabbit. She's quite thin, that girl, like me. Not like her brother. I don't know why anyone would run off with Hardy anyway ... Oh, no, Lil, I love my children. I don't know where you get that from.

Anyway, Judy sat at the piano instead of rushing off. Do you know she called someone out to tune it this morning? Said it sounded tinny. Always good for some ragtime, I thought. That's these musicians for you – perfectionists.

I could see Garth and Hugo out the window ... Yes, it is bright in here. That Cassius went around opening all the blinds this morning. All of them. The curtains, the lace ones, and even found the keys to unlock the windows. I'll have to shut them again directly before dark ... Oh, he's a terror, that kid. Says if we had a fire we'd never get out. But you can't be too careful, Lil, what with these perverts roaming the streets, and the darkies down the road. And I don't know about this cold park breeze, either. This room used to smell lovely of lavender.

Garth was boring Hugo, no doubt about the roses. I could see them owing to the windows being open, of course. Garth pottering about, Hugo with him, the light shining off his head. The two looked foolish. Really, my husband! Says he likes to watch something grow, hence the roses. He probably tires you with that too, does he, Lil ...? What ...? Oh, well, if you find it interesting. Bores me to tears, personally. But the point is, Lil, Garth should think more. I mean, doesn't he know? Hugo's an important doctor with better things to do. He works in one of those big hospitals. Prince-something, it is.

Anyway, Judy was playing something mournful. Nice but difficult … They never clear up after themselves, my kids. I was always running round after them. Day in, day out. But what a doleful tune it was. I can't abide mopiness, as you know, so I tried to get her to snap out of it by suggesting we do something. Shopping, I said. That always makes me happy.

'Why don't we buy a hat for Hugo, dear,' I said.

'Why?' asked Judy. She got up from the piano.

Now, I'd just said to Judy she should get a hat for Hugo. A nice one.

'But what for?' she asked.

Why these children can't just say yes, and listen to their elders, I don't know, Lil, so I had to say, 'Well, Judy, it might … – it might just keep the sun off a bit!'

She was at the window by this time … Yes, taking in the breeze. She was looking out at Hugo.

'But he works inside, Mum.'

She was simply refusing to get the point. I walked over to her but she returned to the piano.

'Yes, dear,' I said, 'you're right. And I suppose it's still not good manners to leave a hat on indoors.'

'Well, why would you want to, Mum?'

Streuth! For a fancy pianist, she's dense sometimes, my daughter. So I had to spell it out for her, word for word.

'Well,' I said, 'Hugo hasn't got Garth's full head of hair, dear. You'll just have to hope your son inherits that.'

Judy turned round and slammed the lid down on the piano. The whole thing rattled. And she'd just had it tuned!

'Don't you ever think about what you say, Mum?'

Yes, I know, Lil, it wasn't a nice thing to say ... What? That's the first time you've ever heard me apologise for anything? Oh, that's rubbish, Lil, and you know it. But, you see, I felt – I won't say sorry. I wasn't. Hugo's always lorded it over me – but bad – at the time – and I shrank ... Yes, shrank some more. And Judy turned round from the window and saw it straight away and yelled to Hugo to come in. Quite a commotion there was, and me at the centre of it all. Garth came in a minute later, pottering along. Yes, that's where it all happened. By *that* window. You know, it's quite a nice view out there. I might just leave the curtains open, after all ... Oh, I'm still going to lock the windows, Lil. Never mind that.

You look like you want to ask me something, Lil? Fire away.

Yes, Lil, I guess that started all this shrinking nonsense. But you know, now that you mention it, I don't know why, Lil. It's just that, when I saw that poor boy, Jeremy, struck down so early in life, and heard the Reverend Memphis going on about all that stuff, about everything being for a purpose, I thought, well, I thought, 'What purpose could that be? Being disfigured? Feeling miserable? None.'

You're sure it's for the best, are you, Lil? Very likely. I don't know anything about God's ways and – Why, Lil, you're white! … What's that …? I shrank …? Just before, when I was saying that stuff about Jeremy?

Here, let me stand … Yes, up against you. Oh no, I'm as short as you now, Lil! … Oh, no, Lil, I didn't mean … What …? Don't I think about what I say …? Imagine it in reverse? What, that now you're as short as me?

Yes, I see, I'm sorry. Oh, God, Lil, I felt it again!

Mrs Saffy's Account   Thursday 14th December 1989

I can't believe you've been recording what I've been saying, Lil. All this time! Just to make fun of me. I know I'm an old woman, with a lot of silly habits, but you're not much younger yourself … All right, I'm sorry, Lil. But what's old age anyway? Nothing to be ashamed of, surely …? What, Lil, you're sorry, too? Good, let's leave it there, then. Oh, and I guess you had better keep it up … Yes, I mean the recording, Lil.

Lay it out there on the table, where I can see it ... No, it's all right, Lil, I want you to.

Oh, can you hear that? Through the bay windows? Judy's playing that lovely piece again ... Yes, that's it, *Berceuse* by Chopin. To think people can feel that deeply, Lil, just takes my breath away. It's so sad, isn't it? I didn't know you could feel that sad. I feel like I've been an insect all my life, living on the skin of a lake, never diving in – never even knowing the surface could be broken! But then I suppose, who'd want to break it anyway? I never did like breaking things.

Oh, Lil, would you please go inside and tell Judy to take her foot off the soft pedal. I want to hear it! She's petting the keys like at elevator volume. Off you go; that's a good dear.

Ah, Lil, you're back. Thank you for that. You know, I wonder why I haven't used this courtyard more often. Being cooped up inside, with the soapies going – I don't know what I was thinking. Take a seat, and I'll tell you about yesterday.

Judy and Hugo were out – I don't know where. I think Hugo was trying to get someone to listen to my story. He phoned his colleagues in Melbourne and they just gave him time off. That's why they're still here, you see ... Oh, well yes, Lil, I suppose it's more than that. Anyway, Judy thought maybe they'd try and get the media in – that might wake them up – but I don't want that, Lil, that would be terrible. A whole lot of strangers, traipsing about my home. I haven't been able to clean it up so well lately, and I'm a house-proud woman, Lil. You know as much.

They were out, and it was just Garth and me, watching a film Judy bought us… *The Sound of Music*, that's right. Anyway, I could see Cassius out the front, through the windows. He's been weeding the garden for me, and has started composting the scraps … Yes, nice enough, I suppose, Lil, but the point is, he wasn't dressed fit to be outdoors. Not at all. Rings in both ears, holes in his jeans, Mrs Gerny looking over from next door. Goodness knows what she thinks of me. A tramp, probably, and all thanks to that son of Judy's. And what sort of name is 'Cassius' anyway? His parents gave him a perfectly good English name when he was born but as soon as he could talk he insisted on Cassius. He apparently does very well at school. Top of every class. Reads, reads, reads – everything! Has bad dreams, apparently… Oh, I don't know, volcanoes and things. But the way he dresses! I don't know how his mother can bear the shame of letting him get about like that. I know *I* wouldn't. Anyway, I took my eyes off him a minute (the glare outside was straining my eyes) and I told Garth to do something about it.

'Yes, Edith,' he said, whistling between his teeth. He knows I hate that habit. He had his eyes on the telly, but he couldn't have been interested: it was a show we'd watched a million times.

'Garth, you're not listening,' I said. He was flexing his elbow like he does. Says it helps. Lot of old wives' tales, I say. The things those doctors tell him. One even told him to have some time on his own for a while. As if that would help, with me not there to care for him. Really, Lil, the things people say. Which reminds me: he wet his bed again last night. But that's another story ... Oh, no, Lil, he can't hear.

Anyway. 'Garth,' I said, 'I want you to say something to Cassius, while his parents are out.'

'It's not my place, Edith,' said Garth, and started on that arm-waving thing again.

Isn't that always the way with my husband? Every crisis – *I've* had to deal with it. Hardy's running off – Garth would have let him crawl back if I hadn't insisted. And then there's my sister – you know more than anyone how I've suffered with her, Lil. He goes by the Bible but he doesn't live by it, my husband.

'Someone's got to straighten him out, Garth,' I said, 'and you're the one to do it.'

Garth turned to me quite slowly (you know that way he has). He turned off the TV with that whatsit thingummy ... oh, you know ... the remote control. Look, I don't understand anything about machines, Lil. Anyway, he turned to me, stopped that stupid waving, and said, with a full-length Reverend Memphis pause, that there was nothing he *could* do. The child had blue hair, like Cary. It could have been prevented if he'd been to Sunday School and a few other things Garth could mention …

Yes, I know, Lil. I don't want to hear about it. Anyway, I haven't finished yet. Do you know, he was in there, right next to us … Yes, Cassius! … Had he heard? *I* hadn't heard *him*. I nearly jumped up in fright when he clapped his hands behind us … Yes, clapped. I don't know what was so funny. Garth went white. How could he scare his grandfather like that? Doesn't he know just how –

What, Lil …? Well, he just waltzed over to the telly, took out the *The Sound of Music* and put in another movie … What was it? Oh, stupid rubbish. *The Incredible Shrinking Man* or something like that. And not very funny either. And then he left.

Garth and I just sat there, watching. It was a full hour in before one of us could get up and turn it off. Poor Garth, he hadn't moved. I knew his elbow was aching but he didn't even try that arm-waving thing. And now we can't use it at all … The arm? No, Lil, the video player … Yes, just won't work. Oh no, Lil, don't trouble yourself over it. I'll get a professional to look at it, dear … What, Lil? You noticed they put the child lock on it yesterday? The little brat!

How's he been since? Do you know, Lil, I felt terrible about it afterwards … Oh, Garth's right, I know that, dear, and if it's true – shocking. Just shocking. But I felt it all the same, Lil. I felt … Well, Lil, sometimes I'm a new person and sometimes I'm not.

And when I'm not that new person I don't know how she feels. But it isn't nice, Lil, it isn't.

Oh God, I'm shrinking again.

<u>Mrs Saffy's Account</u> <u>Saturday 16th December 1989</u>

Hello, Lil.

Lil!

Lil!

Yes, down here.

Don't cry, Lil, stop crying. That's it, sit down. You've spoken to Hugo, have you? He's had me down at the hospital, doing every test. He's rung up everyone he knows. You know, Lil, I think my daughter was quite lucky there … Oh, no, I mean, she could've done worse for herself. That's all.

No, *I'm* all right, Lil. Just sit down on the carpet … No, I'll stand, thank you. I don't want you looking down on me … Oh no, I know you wouldn't, dear. Anyway, that forgotten, how's Garth holding up? Good …? You know, Lil, I, I – I let him sleep in my bed last night. Well, what's a few more loads of washing …? Quite right. That's what *I* said. Do you know, he held my hand? Under the sheets. I think that's the first time in ages.

Now, no sympathy, Lil. I think I can get by so long as no one shows me any sympathy. I never had any truck with mopiness and I sure as eggs don't now.

All right, I'll tell you how it happened today. Oh, Lil, before I start, do you think you could give that plant a water? The one Cassius got … Yes, the Venus flytrap. I've grown quite fond of it lately. Oh, Lil, not there. You have to water it from the base. Don't you know anything about carnivorous plants?

I fed it an ant this morning. I found it crawling on me. And me my present size – it was as big as a rat! … No, Lil, it's all right. Just finish your tea. Oh, Lil, don't put it down there! That's French polish. I'll get Garth to give you a coaster.

Garth! Garth!

Oh, what …? You'll just hold it? Well, all right. Now, where was I? Yes, as I was saying, about the shrinkage. When we sat down to dinner – 6 o' clock, same as always – that's when it happened. We had our plates on our knees. Garth had the telly on. Takes his mind off the pain, he says. Judy was sitting with Hugo, on that couch there, where you are; and Cassius was stretched out there on the floor. You wouldn't believe what he was wearing … Oh, well, of course you saw him when you came in the door. Jeans with their knees out, a black shirt with all kinds of profanity written on it. I'm just glad Garth can't see so well these days.

This funny little item came on the news all about Bengals getting flooded … What, Lil …? Bang-la-desh? Yes, you saw it, too …? Five thousand dead … Well, five hundred, then. Dreadful stuff, anyway. They showed a little girl – lovely dark hair – holding on to a chimney pot. You couldn't see the rest of the house – just mud. Then suddenly the chimney sank beneath her and she let go. The cameraman must have tried to help, then, because we just saw the bottom of the boat. A dreadful picture, that. Shaking here, shaking there. Just a silver hull. But the sound was still on: liquid screaming. I thought these journalists weren't meant to get involved.

Cassius, closest to the TV all this time, rolled onto one side, head propped up on one arm, and do you know what he had the effrontery to say?

'Hey, Gramps, why does God get off on drowning people?'

Gramps! Garth hates that. He almost choked on his mashed potato. Hugo came out of his stupor and said, 'Cassius, that's enough.'

'But why?'

Judy kicked Cassius in the foot and Garth saw.

'It's all right, Judy,' said Garth, wiping potato off his vest, 'it's about time your son got some religious instruction.'

I saw Hugo blanch at that.

'Cassius, God moves in a mysterious way, his wonders to perform,' said Garth.

'Oh, come on, Gramps, that's a fob-off.'

Garth went perfectly still. Judy fairly growled at Cassius. Hugo put in his bit, too, telling his son not to question his grandfather. I don't know why, but

Garth's sitting there, like a stone statue, made me think about Jeremy ... You know him, dear ... Yes, I mentioned him the other day. The one who had that meningococcal disease.

Then the other three went at it, with Cassius getting redder and redder. My stomach bunched up, Lil. I didn't want that little unpleasantness coming out. You know, when Cassius surprised Garth and I.

I must've dozed off a bit (these Chesterfields are so comfortable) because when I came to, as it were, the room was slightly bigger and filled with noise. Judy and Hugo were telling Cassius to respect his elders. He was standing up, competing with the TV for noise (I saw Garth had his finger on the volume button).

'Cassius, please, will you shut up!' said Judy.

'Why should I, Mum? You've always said it behind their backs, how you don't know if you love or hate them! Well, I know, I know how *I* feel!'

Garth shot a glance at Judy. She couldn't look back at him. And Cassius was sobbing, Lil. It was terrible. His words trailed off. He was fighting for air. Judy was looking at Garth – she'd stopped trying to calm Cassius down by now – and Hugo was about as red as that mug ... Yes, in your hands, dear. Better put it down, now. That's a dear.

Anyway, what I was seeing was Jeremy ... Yes, right there, in the lounge, clear as the picture you get on telly. He was sitting in his chair, trying to move a toggle with his tongue. A great big man was standing behind him. Chap with a flowing beard ... yes, white. How did you know that? Anyway, this white-bearded man was filming. Had a great big camera in his hands and Jeremy's chair was slowly rolling towards a lake ... Yes, the local one, and Jeremy's mother was asking this white-bearded man to help. But the man refused to get involved, saying he had to be objective. He was just reporting the facts. The chair gathered speed, and in the boy went – splash! Right there in my lounge room.

Then it all cleared. TV off. Hugo standing over Cassius, palm raised.

'Cassius, that's enough.'

'But – '

'Enough!'

Hugo raised his arm. Cassius rolled away and stood up. He stopped gulping like a fish and found his tongue again.

'God is all powerful; God is all good; terrible things happen.'

'Hhnh!' And he made this awful face.

There was silence for a second. It felt so funny after all that noise. My ears were like when you're up in a plane. I wanted to pop them. What Cassius had said came back at me as though we were either side of a dam wall and I'd just heard the echo.

'God is all powerful; God is all good; terrible things happen.'

I could feel the words filling the room.

'Yes, Garth, why is that?' I asked.

I think Garth nearly fainted. He had a hand on my knee and was just about crushing it. Everyone was looking at me. Even Cassius was staring open-mouthed.

'Yes, Garth,' I said. 'Why's Jeremy – you know, Marcia Tate's son – a prisoner to a chair if God loves us so much? He's only sixteen. He couldn't have done much.'

Garth was furious with me later. He hates me to contradict him in front of people. Especially family, and especially a communist … Who's a communist, dear? Why, Hugo, of course. I thought you knew … What are you saying? Surely not with that two-storey house in Prahran? Oh, is that where it is? I wouldn't know a communist from a columnist anyway, dear.

The short of it is, Lil, when all this fuss was over, I was smaller. Again.

Mrs Saffy's Account   Tuesday 19th December 1989

Oh, I don't know what I'm trying to say, Lil. It's just, well, it's just that I'm having thoughts I didn't have before … I never really *thought* at all before … Oh, I thought *certain* things. How Jessie, my sister, had carried on. And Hardy and his fiancée. But that's only seeing as far as your nose. And, you know, when I think of myself, just a week ago – a child. That's all I was, a child.

What? Well, this is it: Why …? Yes, why …? I don't know how else to put it, Lil. Why the universe? Why like this? Why not, why not – oh, I don't know – why not pink elephants?

What's that, Lil …? You're sure this is making me smaller? Here, I'll stand up against the door. Mark the wall above the top of my head – your nail will do, dear (they're long enough) – oh, you've cut them? That paper knife, then, and we'll see if I'm smaller when I'm done with what I'm saying … which is what exactly? I can't put it well, Lil. It's just, 'Why?'

I'm like a teenager, you say …? Unhappy with the world …? Really, is that true, Lil? You started to question things as a young adult? I guess I didn't have time to. Straight into nursing, no time to be a girl. I've had a hard life, Lil, I don't mind –

Who says that?

Oh God, Lil, was that really how I talked? Why's this happening to me, Lil? Why me?

I asked Cassius that this morning. He looked at me like I was queer or something. He'd been avoiding Garth and I since … well, since that unpleasantness, and I caught him this morning while he was pruning the box hedge … Yes, that's right, a kookaburra. He's pruning it into the shape of a kookaburra. Says if it can't fly at least it can have a good laugh about things. He's a sensitive soul. Takes after his mother …

And who does Judy take after? I'm beginning to wonder about that just now, Lil. Perhaps she takes after what I might have been. Isn't it funny what history and circumstance can do? If Judy was born when I was, would she now be like me? Or if I was born when she was, would I now be like her?

I got Cassius to sit on the couch … Yes, the Chesterfield you're on. Usually I get him to lie on the rug, but what does it matter now? I said what I was feeling, offered for Garth to make him tea – which Cassius refused – and I kind of drew him out. We actually *talked*. Cassius said that he felt the same way as me. It took him a bit to believe I wasn't up to something, but put down those rusty secateurs (imagine bringing them into the house!) and gushed forth. Anyway, he said what he'd discovered was, the world isn't made for you. There's no reason why it should turn out the way you want. He was curling his fingers round his lovely locks … yes, even if they are blue (I think he prunes them too) … and I thought, yes, that's exactly right. There's no reason why things should turn out one way or the other, whatever we want …

Yes, but why *that*, Lil? Why the wanting? Either God could've made the world how we wanted it, or else made us so we didn't want it any way at all.

What, it's to test us? Oh, rubbish, Lil. You always had a weaker mind. Oh, you tried your best. But if you haven't the brain capac … Oh God, sorry, Lil. That was vintage Edith, wasn't it?

You know, I wonder where she's been of late?

Mrs Saffy's Account   Friday 22nd December 1989

Oh, hello, Lil, what do you think of my new home, this silly little doll's house? It's been stored away since Judy grew out of it and now I'm living in it! It's not so bad, Lil. Hugo put it up on this table so nothing can get to me … Oh, you know, the cat or something … Yes, Garth gave it to next door's to look after. Just until … For a little while, anyway.

And what's that thing? That's an amplifier, Lil. It's so you can still hear me. Looks like something out of a bonnet, but isn't Hugo a clever thing the way he's rigged it up … What? I am *not* softening to him, dear. I still don't forgive him for looking down on us, never letting Judy visit before. You know the rest.

What's Hugo doing about it? The shrinkage, you mean? He's tried, Lil. He really has. They've threatened to sack him at work if he doesn't 'stop with this illusion'. I think that's how he told me they put it. He wanted to film me, as a record of it all, but Garth wouldn't hear of it. Same as he won't let Hugo take me off to any doctors now. Says it would kill him to have all that publicity.

He doesn't want us all becoming some sideshow

attraction. And besides, it's not a doctor I need, he says. It's was a minister. So he called Reverend Memphis … Yes, about eight this morning he came. Quite a good chat we had. I'm starting to see …

What, Lil? You thought I hated him? I never *hated* him, Lil … And all that stuff I was saying yesterday about the world being unfair? In hindsight, I think I was overtired, Lil. That's all. No, the Reverend's put it all straight now.

How?

He came inside – it's getting too cold again to be out … What, you thought I liked it outdoors, now? I do, Lil, but I can't have Hugo carrying this doll's house around with him everywhere. He might drop it.

Anyway, the Reverend came in in his black suit and dog collar. Plus he's started slicking some of his hair over his crown. A much better look. I even told him so. He put a hat on after that. A hat inside! Well, dear, I let it pass. Anyway, I was still on that jalopy about God not caring and the Reverend Memphis simply nodded all the way through like he knew every word I was going to say. Garth was getting very upset, talking about exorcisms and all that rot, but the Reverend just sent him outside, then rested his big chin on the edge of the table and looked at me squarely. I was sitting on the balcony of this doll's house, right where I am now, so his eye looked at me through the railings.

'Edith Saffy,' he said. (I could feel his deep, silky voice rumbling through the front door, up the stairs, and blowing out behind me.)

'Edith Saffy,' he said. 'I do believe God is trying to teach you humility.'

'What?' Using big words on me. What was the Reverend up to?

'Yes, Mrs Saffy, humility. Have you seen a pattern in all this shrinking business?'

The Reverend turned his head to the side so that his ear was level with my face. It was hairy and waxy and not what I like to see before breakfast.

'I can't hear you, Mrs Saffy.'

'What?'

He turned his head so I could see his great big lips and his bad teeth and smell his bad breath.

'There is a pattern in all this. Preceding the moments when you shrink by degrees, there is always something you *do*.'

He waited a bit, then said, 'You question ...? You question ...?

'Life?'

'No, Mrs Saffy, you question *God*. And that's what does the damage.'

His face had a kind of bitter look to it, but you know, Lil, I saw he was right. It was true. That's how it all started – I looked at Marcia Tate's son and I thought, how could a caring God allow that? Being frozen in life.

And how can He, dear? Lil! I hope you're not starting to doubt, too. You should talk to the Reverend Memphis. He'll put you straight like he put me straight. How exactly? It was like this. He told me I doubted because I couldn't see the whole picture, what God's got in mind. We're just small – what did he say? – cogs in the universe's machinery. Something like that. He can explain it all better than – no, wait! No, I think I can do a good job of explaining it myself. See that flytrap over there, Lil? Yes, the Venus flytrap. I had Cassius raise it up so it was level with the table. Something of a garden for me … Morbid? There's nothing morbid in that. Anyway, Lil, I had a point to make. This morning I was fossicking, clearing away the weeds that get in all the peat moss. They ruin it completely, and I saw an ant in one of the … the whatsits. These things that the Venus flytrap traps things in. We'll call it a glove, then. Anyway, these gloves have got three spines in them – hairs, according to Cassius (he's a know-it-all for a fourteen-year-old). I saw this ant brush against one of the hairs and nothing happened. The gloves are meant to close when they're brushed but the ant kept licking the nectar with its funny mouth and everything was fine. But then, when it went to leave, it knocked the other hair and the glove closed. Isn't that clever?

What, you don't see quite how, Lil? Cassius explained it to me. These gloves are so well designed, Lil, that they only catch living things. See, if a pebble

or small stick falls on the leaf it won't close. But if –
how did Cassius put it – 'two of its hairs are touched
in succession or one hair is touched twice', it will.
Remarkable, isn't it? And that's what I've seen, Lil …
Oh Lil, catch on! *Design*. Everything's so well
designed. There's a reason for everything … Even for
Jeremy? Yes, Lil, there is. We're just too small to see
it. And with all that doubting, I don't think you're
small enough!

What's the matter, Lil? Sulking on me? Water the
Venus flytrap for me, would you, dear. With me down
here, it would be like doing a whole lawn. And you
know what my arthrit – oh no, Lil! Not like that! I've
told you only to water it from the base. You're meant
to fill up the tray. The water gets sucked up. Really,
Lil, you never caught on as quickly as I. Oh, I know
you've … What's wrong, Lil? You've gone silent on
me …

Mrs Saffy's Account   Monday 25th December 1989

It's all right, Lil. You didn't mean to, Lil. As a matter of
fact, I've had a wonderful time. Can you still see me,
Lil, if I don't move? That's a good girl. Just whisper
into that thing, dear. Hugo's rigged it up so I'm not
deafened.

I'll start my day from the beginning.

This morning I was sitting at the toy piano pretending to play that Chopin piece, trying to remember what I'd liked about it. You can't play the thing because the keys are painted on and the piano is wood right through (it's a toy after all!) and of course I can't play it anyway, but I couldn't even remember the way the piece made me feel.

Sad …? Yes, maybe. And I thought that then too, because suddenly Judy started playing it at the real piano. Isn't it an awful world, I thought, and shrank. I shrank so my feet couldn't touch the floor and I had to lower myself off the stool. I ran out the front door of my doll's house and tripped down the steps into that little pot-plant Cassius put at the front so I'd have a bit of a garden. I can't tell you the shock when I fell facedown in the peat moss. Terrible. All these horrid things crawling about, all actually bigger than me! I trudged through the mud to a little stick (a log to me) that was leaning against one of those – what did we decide to call them? – 'gloves' of the Venus flytrap.

I don't mind telling you, it had me puffed. I'm an old woman, Lil. So I sat down but then a great big black thing appeared above me. Yes, a spider.

Huge …

What's that, Lil? It must've been terrible for me? Yes, that's the obvious response, but it's wrong … Let me finish my story, Lil.

The spider landed right beside me and I screamed. It had abseiled down on a thread that looked to me like a chain leading to the anchor of an ocean liner. Anyway, it came down and just looked at me. Ever had twelves eyes all in the one head staring at you?

No, I expect not, but there I was with my back against the glove of the Venus flytrap, looking for somewhere to run, and it hit me that the flytrap was my best chance. So I crawled through the green turnstile bars, being careful not to knock the hairs inside, and when the spider edged round one of the green walls, I ran through to the other side. The spider then crawled right in (amazingly, didn't trigger the hairs) and a big hairy crane of an arm reached out at me. So I bumped against one hair, then threw myself at the next and the trap closed. The third hair impaled the spider and the walls started closing and it got crushed. Luckily it was fatter than me or I'd have been crushed too. And of course the walls had started oozing.

What ...? Blood ...? No, Lil, the digestive enzymes. My feet were stinging in the wet. My arms were aching too as I pulled myself up the arch of those green bars, looking for a gap to squeeze through, with the spider vaguely groping about below me. Once I was up, I actually watched as one by one its eyes winked out ...

A village dying ... I don't know where I get these fancies, Lil!

It was one of my … my moments of …

Sympathy! Yes, that's it, Lil (why are words getting harder to remember?) and it made me shrink, which was actually a good thing for once. It meant I could squeeze through the bars, and it was like emerging into another world. A world of sense.

What's that, Lil …? How so …?

I think people aren't big enough to see everything in overview or small enough to realise its complexity. In this micro … Yes, that's it, microscopic world I'm in now, I can see that everything has a purpose, a reason.

What about what happened to Jeremy …? How could that have a reason …? From down here it doesn't seem so bad … It is? Oh, you wouldn't understand, Lil. I always got things quicker at school. There's a point to everything. You just can't see it.

But I haven't finished my story yet, Lil.

I have to tell you what happened once I got out of the flytrap.

Obviously there'd been a bit of a downpour while I was in there … Yes, that was *your* fault, Lil, watering from the top rather than filling up the tray. Anyway, the pot was filled to the rim with water. A nearby insect was walking on the meniscus of this lake, and I found that I could do the same.

You Must Remember.

Friday 19th August 2005.

Henri rose, his eyes wide and wet.

'I … I thought for a minute,' he stammered, 'you were about to tell me a *real* story. A real one, Cassius! Not this – not some fiction about a shrinking relative!'

He made for his backpack, which was still resting by the front door.

'Don't go, Henri.'

He hoisted his backpack onto his shoulders.

'I must. The tickets are paid for.'

'My love, you will kill me, and yourself too. You must remember – you have glimpsed your former lives. But don't imagine it is for this alone I want you here; it is for *you* alone.'

Henri, his face awash with tears, regarded me across the dim room.

Chapter Ten

Not Here, Nor Now, Nor There.

Friday April 3rd 33 AD, Jerusalem.

> I went with smiles, with laughter too,
>   Prepared for endless fun,
> But met with only nastiness.
>   What had I done?
>
> I went with gifts and anecdotes,
>   But got an icy stare,
> Oh why oh why and when and where?
>   Not here, nor now, nor there.
>
> I went up to the mountain,
>   To dig myself a cave
> But were they ever known to give?
>   For no one gave.

I went out to the desert,
  To call the sand my home,
But all the grains were owned by them,
  And so I roam.

Lastly they took me in bondage,
  And nailed me upon a cross.
Why should the memory choke me still?
  It was their loss.

Chapter Eleven

Insufferable Gloating.

Friday 19th August 2005.

As I now sit here, my world films over in dread.

Henri has left.

As I make my way from bed, unable to eat or rest, my world films over in dread.

A knock?

A change of mind? I open my door only to behold the most hideous creature known to humankind apart from itself. The vile thing was oozing smugness from every pore. It was that abominable, rancid and third-rate creature that has harangued me all these millennia – Memphis himself.

'Why, good evening, Cassius.'

He knew instantly from my look that Henri was gone. The gloating could not have been more insufferable. Memphis produced a six-pack of beer from beneath his clichéd purple-lined cape. We ordered pizza because I could not cook, and he *would* not. When it arrived, the way he rapped and raved, scissoring the pizza with his teeth, vitamising it with his saliva, I could only watch with not a little nausea.

'Sure you don't want any?'

'You eat like the Sire De Retz,' I spat.

'Him!' Memphis wiped an impossibly soiled and darkly purple sleeve across his ample mouth. 'Oh my, remember that court case – delightfully amusing. The nobility banded together to do everything they could to protect one of their own from sentencing. And what of that little history lesson today? Graft, corruption, cronyism –still alive and well. And, meanwhile, what of the posterity of our friend, the general Gilles? Thanks to Perrault, today he is remembered benignly as a character in fairy tales, affectionately known as Bluebeard.' Memphis slapped his thigh. 'Oh you humans, you make it so easy for me.'

Laughing, he got up, examining my CD collection and picked a tune to his taste. Next, he was dancing grotesquely on my carpet.

'They that have the power to hurt, and none do hurt, tra la la … they rightly inherent heaven's graces.

Tom tiddly pom. Cassius, my dear friend, sweetest things turn sourest by their deeds ...'

'... Lillies that fester, smell far worse than weeds,' I finished for him.

'Shakespeare! He believed everything and nothing, and died forever.'

And with that, he pulled me to my feet. He mocked the music, dancing with me in the most sarcastic bent and sway of the hips, introducing offensive turns here, sardonic spins there. I disengaged, sickened by the sneering attitude of one who could – *can* – never create anything beautiful himself, but is always ready to denigrate another's efforts. I fell into the couch.

'Oh, Cassius, do you think I don't *want* to be stopped?' the creature sighed extravagantly. 'To only exist because you humans do? To count on your stupidity for my survival? Immortality is a hard thing to bear and I depend on you for its termination. But somehow I think the will to live is stronger even than the will to forget, and I will win out once more.'

He quit his dancing and fell noxiously close by my side.

'Ah, this beautiful music,' he bubbled, an arm jovially embracing my shoulders. 'Sometimes I almost admire this species. Cassius, what's that look?'

'It's just ...' I began, the tears escaping my lids.

'Go on.'

'It's just that Henri – '

'Ah, Henri, never far from our thoughts.'

'He always reminds me that for every World Trade Centre there is a Sagrada Familia. For every Nazi organisation, an Amnesty International. For each cuff, a kiss.'

'But never enough kissing, no? Our friend Catullus would lament that. Do you remember him?'

'No.'

Memphis patted my shoulder, the gesture curdling my innards.

'Even you, Cassius – *you* forget! Perhaps it is now time I told you of your lives between being burned at the stake with Henri in Brittany, and your life now, when you at last remembered.'

'There must be a great many lives in between,' I replied, endeavouring at the same time to shove him off.

'Indeed, and perhaps too many to delve into,' he laughed, pulling me in closer. 'Your wheel certainly turned, I should tell you, and you became less of a monster. No more torturing of Christians and children!'

'I am relieved of that. Did I know Henri in those lives?'

Memphis slapped my knee, transported as he was with raptures of gloating.

'You have always known Henri! In every incarnation! But let me tell you of the life you had before you were a gun-runner in the Aegean, providing Henri and his fellow Cretans with weapons with which to resist the Germans.'

I couldn't muster the interest to know. Memphis evidently could read the wanness in my face, for he shook me, trying to impart his excitement.

'You'll certainly want to know about this incarnation, my friend! It is the one in which you succeeded most wonderfully in your ambition.'

That got my attention. I succeeded in shaking off his disgusting embrace, and rose to my feet.

'I found the final theory?' I demanded.

Memphis leant back in the couch as if preparing to nap.

'Ah, but that would be telling the ending to your story before it was begun,' he said dozily.

'Did I know Henri then?'

He sat up, rigid. 'Yes, again, yes! You have known him in every incarnation, and it is from his reminiscences that we have our story.'

'*Our* story?'

'Why yes, Cassius, for *I* have always been involved in your lives as well.'

Henri takes over our tale – not the Henri of the turn of the twenty-first century, but the Henri of the turn of the twentieth. His following reminiscences were found in his effects after his death.

The Perfect Fit.

London, 1906.

I don't know why Cassius singled me out to hear his story but perhaps my pensiveness accorded with his own, and he recognized as much, drawing to the mood. We had just finished cards – have I told you I belong to a sort of club? – and I had seen that his heart wasn't in it. Normally unbeatable with that fantastic memory of his, on that night he was … still brilliant … but somehow less so. The others played meanly, Memphis the most, but I had never cared much for the competition; it was more the company that drew me, and Cassius was the biggest draw-card among the pile.

He got up from the card table and excused himself to the drawing room, where he hoped to smoke. The others wished to continue, thinking their game had improved, whereas it was actually Cassius' that had weakened. I excused myself also, a moment later, and joined him, not in the drawing room as he had indicated, but in the library where he now sat in the dark with only the reading lamp to cast his features in atmospheric shadow. He had retired on a Chesterfield, the table and lamp beside him, and for all the world seemed lost to both. I sat on the chair opposite and saw him open his eyes as if with great effort.

'That you, Henri?' he asked, pupils dilating in the dark. Although Cassius was of that school that addresses people by their surnames, minus the Mr or Mrs, only progressing to Christian titles after years of civility and formal pomp, he had never called me Sherard — always Henri — and neither had I (in some strange spirit of familiarity that didn't feel earned) ever called him Quintus — always Cassius.

'Yes, Cassius, Henri here. Had enough of cards.'

'Yes … yes.'

They were only two words, or the one uttered twice, and yet they conveyed a weight of meaning that served both to intrigue and compel me. Cassius possessed every quality of genius, and yet I had never observed them to come to the fore and unite. His powers were like a half-seen figure flitting along a heavily wooded slope. A forest of conifers, perhaps, with their architectural panache for shutting out the light and making of the ground an arid waste of pine needles, bristling cones, and roots to trip the unwary. None of us had bayed or brought down the prey. Neither myself in his present company nor the moths at the card table. We all suspected that Cassius had something great he concealed, and our biggest bet was on who could draw the magnificent confession. The others were scientists; I, as you know, an artist; they didn't even count me in the running.

I got up and went to the drinks table, returning a moment later with a bottle of port and two tumblers.

'Cassius?' I asked, proffering one.

'Yes … yes.'

He took the glass and drank as though he were consuming a revivifying draught rather than the mere liqueur that it was.

'What is the matter?' I asked. I had never been so personal before, but the inquiry did not appear to strike him as intrusive; at any rate, he gave no sign. I saw his moustache twitch in the denuded and focused lamplight. The hair was shot through with grey, but the light was kind and transformed the bristles into a sparkling silver.

'Oh, it's something mathematical, Henri.'

Defeated! At the outset! Cassius is a mathematical genius. I was − still am − a painter, untutored in the sciences save art, if that be a science also. I saw Cassius's brow crinkle. His grey, hooded lids began to shut. I noted two thumbprints of blue beneath his eyes and knew that the man was tired, deathly so. I was losing him once more, letting him be taken up in an unceasing tide of dream and thought. Without further ado, I leant forward, flicking shadows out behind me like ostentatious coattails, and at the same time sending one before me, which rose up the row of shelves and butted its head upon the ceiling.

'You know,' I began, seeing his eyes strain open courteously, 'they always say that if you can explain your specialty to a layman, then you must really know your subject.'

Cassius lifted his hands to his temples and regarded me meditatively. 'I don't know that I do, these days,' he answered paradoxically.

I looked through the double doors, through the drawing room beyond and spotted, like a candlelit Punch and Judy show in a starless night, the vision of the card players two rooms away. They seemed small now, shut off; figurines in a doll's house. They were leaning forward. Each had his feet tucked under his chair, toes scrunching the carpet. It was a good sign: they were concentrating; they had money on the outcome; they would be there all night.

I turned back to Cassius. 'You know,' I tried once more, 'if you explain your problem to me, you'll be forced to leave out the details. Otherwise, I won't understand it. It might just be that you're getting bogged down in the minutiae. That can happen, if you're too close to a problem.'

Cassius smiled an amused smile and motioned to the double doors. I got up and fastened the one with the ceiling latch, closing the free-swinging door upon that. The card players were now in argument. I sat back in my seat, feeling the leather puff out beneath me. The leather was no longer cool as when I had first sat down; but now supple and warm.

'You believe in higher things, don't you, Henri?' he asked.

'I'm not sure what you mean.'

'Being an artist: the Muse, divine inspiration, that sort of thing?'

'Well,' I hedged, not wishing to stall him so early, 'I'm not so sure.'

I could see him frown at this. Four black notches were instantly axed in his forehead. With the chiaroscuro lighting, facial expressions were heightened, even caricatured. Quickly, I put in, 'But sometimes …' and faltered. 'Well, what I mean to say is, Cassius, most of the time it just seems like hard work. Painting, I mean. Very hard work. But just occasionally it does come all at once, like a thunderbolt, and then you wonder …' Cassius was grinning '… and then you wonder if you thought of it at all.'

He slapped his thigh and almost yelped. It was the most animated I had ever seen him.

'Henri, my friend, it might just be you *are* the one to understand!'

And so, having poured us another glass of port each, and having downed the contents, I, Henri, awaited Cassius's magnificent confession.

'The same thing happens with me, except that it is in the realm of pure mathematics that I get my thunderbolts. When I feel I've discovered something really important, it's not like I've discovered it at all, but … well … rather, that I've intuited it.' The broad smile on his face all but lit up the shadows.

'You mean …?' It was hopeless; I was losing his meaning already.

'Perhaps I should explain,' said Cassius and he unnecessarily adjusted his cufflinks, a mannerism I had seen him affect when giving lectures.

'There are two schools of thought,' he went on, 'regarding mathematics, harking right back to Plato. There are those who think that we *invent* mathematical laws to describe the way physical systems work' (Cassius saw me die a little here ['the motion of the planets, displacement, that sort of thing'] – I visibly revived), 'and then there are those, like the Platonists, who think we *discover* them.'

'You mean – ' I was catching on now ' – that actual laws may underlie the structure of the universe, determining how it all works?'

'Yes, yes,' said Cassius, 'and we intuit parts of it when we come upon a great equation.'

'Such as?'

'Surface Area of a Cylinder = 2 *pi* r ^{2} + 2 *pi* r h.'

I pushed my faculties to the edge. 'You mean,' I asked Cassius, extrapolating, 'that great works of art might be the physical manifestations of timeless equations?'

'Yes, why not?'

At once the notion arrested me. It appealed to my experience and fancy. I told Cassius of my obsession with perfect works of art; how I'd read Henri James' *The Turn of the Screw*, published just that summer,

294

an exhaustive five times, just to see if I could find a distracting passage, an inferior line, or an out-of-place word. I could find none. Everything related to and harked back to the theme. James had told his story and told it in as many words as were necessary, no more, no less.

Our mutual friend H.G. wasn't so sure, but then his and James' writing styles differed.

Cassius once more carried a boyish grin. He was alive.

'Henri,' he said, 'it might sound like the height of insularity to say so, but there must be no greater pleasure than to know that someone has felt as one feels oneself. You've hit on it, boy. Yes, simplicity.'

'Simplicity.' I'd regressed to echoing him now but he did not seem to heed it.

'Saying the most number of things in the least number of words' – now he was echoing me! – 'that's the beauty of it. That's simplicity.'

'You're losing me now, Cassius,' I was brave enough to say.

He craned forward on the lounge, gripping the armrests.

'The same's true of mathematical algorithms. Ockham's Razor: if ever a mathematician comes up with an algorithm to describe a physical system, one of its tests is simplicity. It might sound strange in this field, but it's the aestheticist's test. Does it look nice? If the equation, to use literary parlance, is long-winded, cumbersome, circular, inept, then there will be some doubt as to its … well … its correctness. Or, dare I say, its truth.'

Cassius leaned back in the lounge again, seeming to ache from the previous exertions. I pushed on.

'There's more to this than all that, though, isn't there?'

Already, I felt I could press him. Our relations had proceeded so far.

'Yes, yes, Henri, there is. And, believe it or not – I don't know if I do – I'm going to tell you. You might be the one to understand.'

Again that phrase, 'the one to understand'. My heart drum-rolled at the thought of the amazing confession.

But his conversation seemed to falter, then. His face came over pale. His lips twitched wryly and he added, 'And I'd always thought you were a dunderhead!'

I sat up straight. I looked about. The room was dark and empty. There were only the two of us. The conclusion must be drawn: he was referring to me! Cassius leant forward and touched my arm. 'Naturally, Henri, impressions are often wrong. No doubt you've heard that, for all my talent, I've never really achieved anything major.'

I coloured at this, and in the limited light range of black and white, I went darker. Yes, I *had* heard it. The imputation had been made; from our fellow card players, Memphis the most. 'For all his supposed genius, he's no Newton,' Memphis would say with that pinched-nose inflection of his. 'If a mathematician's going to discover something great, it will be in his youth. After that, he's just filling in time. Besides, Cassius's card playing is all memory, no method.'

'Yes, yes,' said Cassius, sighing, 'I see you *have* heard it. But it's not true. I've made the greatest discovery in mathematics yet, and that's to prove that it isn't invented; that it actually underlies the fabric of the universe.'

'And how have you discovered that?' I asked a little tartly. There is nothing so intimidating as being faced with genuine as opposed to blustering arrogance.

Cassius retorted: 'Because I've been there!'

'Been where?'

Cassius let the challenge soften, to deaden in the wood a little, before responding.

'Yes, I've been there, Henri, only I can't prove it. I don't really care to, now. I just want someone to know before … before …'

I could see Cassius's lips quivering and wondered at such emotion.

'Yes?' I asked.

'Well, it's just hard getting back, that's all.'

Cassius stiffened with the memory of some great labour. I wondered what. He is a strong, sturdy, wide-shoulder man, but even this conversation was taking its toll on him.

'Getting back?' I asked. 'How does one get "there"? Is there a door?'

Cassius laughed, for the second time showing a friendly disdain for my ignorance. 'There's no door, Henri. As it's intuited, one gets there through pure reason. The intellect, if you like.'

'Then perhaps you had better start at the beginning.'

Cassius lit a pipe and puffed on it. He leaned back in his lounge, his body all shapes and curves once more.

'I was born in Bromley, Kent, to a shopkeeper and a seamstress. Two uncomplicated parents, but with a working-class ethic founded upon hard work and honesty. In short, they were not prepared for a son destined for the field of the abstract. Yes, no doubt you have heard that as a boy I was hailed as a prodigy. I learnt maths before I learnt English. At six, one could ask me to do any sum, the square root of six thousand and fifty-seven, say, and I'd have the answer faster than it took to figure the equation on an abacus. My parents were worried that I was impeded mentally. Mathematicians dismissed me as such. But it soon grew evident that in every other way I was a normal boy. A little sombre and withdrawn, perhaps, but, in the main, normal. My computational skills were an extra gift. When I was nine, I was interviewed in the Pall Mall. A young reporter, your friend H.G. incidentally, asked me how I managed to tabulate such large sums in my head, and I replied, "I just see it."

'That's the key, Henri. I see mathematical problems with as much crystal precision as you can visualize a painting in your head. The problem, as we both experience, is getting them out on paper or, in your case, onto canvas.'

I nodded as expansively as a stage actor who endeavours to communicate his every expression to the patrons in the furthest rows. Cassius continued.

'When I was doing my doctoral thesis – yes, it happened in my youth' – (Ye Gods, the man could read minds) – 'I took a cocktail of drugs to keep my mind running on track. I found I couldn't work in snatches, at intervals, but that my best thinking was done over long stretches. I'm a marathon runner, not a short distance sprinter.'

'I've a writer friend who's the opposite,' I put in irrelevantly. 'Mr Beerbohm. He can't quite pull off the novel.'

'But of course sleeping and eating interfered,' continued Cassius, quite as if I hadn't spoken. 'I was staying at one of the university colleges but of course I found that dreadful. Too intolerably noisy for a person with real brainwork to do, so I rented a house on my own. My scholarship bore the expense. There I set up keep, and planned sieges of a week in which, helped along by narcotics (intended to focus rather than dull the mind), I would concentrate on the mathematical problems concerning me.'

Cassius had been awarded numerous honorary degrees. 'One never thinks much of prizes till one receives them,' he is notoriously quoted as having opined.

'Well, one day – ' Cassius broke off suddenly, setting off on a different tack. 'You know about dimensions in mathematics, do you? Anyway, you can work in three, four, five dimensions – and so on. We only live in the third.'

The way he said that, that we only live in the third, startled me. I had a hard enough time rendering three-dimensional space on a flat, two-dimensional canvas.

'One day, when I seemed to be thinking along particularly fruitful lines, I suddenly found myself completely unaware of the outside world. Of the room. Of my body. I had my eyes open, but they could see nothing; instead, I was looking with my mind's eye, and it beheld a matrix of computations. A universe of figures. Literally. I remember I was in my study at the time. It had been – nay, *was* – a bright day. The blinds sliced the light into cut sandwiches on the petunia-pink wall opposite my desk. But I could no longer feel the warmth on my shoulders; could no longer smell the gardenias in the window boxes fanning their scent under the open windows. I was oblivious to my senses. I was oblivious to my body.

'It wasn't frightful, because I had a new body. But this new housing was wide, unbearably wide – wider even than my shoulders – but it had no height. It was flat. Absolutely flat. I could only move about in the one plane, but by what means of propulsion I knew not, and butt into similar pancake creatures. This went on and I grew alarmed. I tried to fight my way back to this body but was unable to do so. Panic set in, but to no avail. Finding a sort of impartial curiosity once more, I set about the logical extrication of myself from my predicament. I tried to communicate with my fellow pancakes but had no means of doing so. No mouth, no voice, and hence no words. Becoming panicked again, I fell back on my maths, and communicated that way.'

'How?' I interjected.

'Once more, by thought, but in a logical way, with each thought proceeding to the next like the steps in simple arithmetic. By this process I learnt the pancakes' names. And they weren't names as you or I use them; they were equations.'

'Equations?' (There I was, parroting again.)

'Yes, mostly they described a pancake in terms of its property. Surface area, basically, for the simple shapes. More complex equations for the others, but still your standard geometry. Anyway, these pancake creatures were called – in fact, came into action something like the way an abacus works – by processing these equations. To multiply, they simply added on; to divide, they subtracted. In such ways did they mimic families. For a while, my breakthrough was profound. Until I saw that their equations were for flat objects, with breadth and width but no height. That accounted for the peculiar compression of my vision, my sense of being forever the horizon, without being afforded a glimpse of the interceding distance. Immediately, I added my own height and factored it into the equation. Straightway, I found myself in my own body again, dirty and emasculated.'

I had to ask myself, did I believe Cassius's story, that one could journey to another place, to the mathematics of life, through thought alone?

'Just look at yourself,' said Cassius, reading my thoughts. 'Here you are, so engrossed in my tale, that I bet you've become insensitive to your surroundings.'

And so I had. I looked around and almost blinked, even though the light was poor and downcast. I felt my backside growing numb on the seat, whereas before I had felt that I was floating. I became aware of my body with all the cramps and irritations of the day. Perhaps one could... Ah, but it was so fanciful. The man was a charlatan. Or else ...?

He continued.

'For a while, I was too thrilled, and not a little scared, to enter this realm again, let us call it a "mindscape". My landlady threatened to call Scotland Yard, thinking I was on some 'pipe dream' although I suppose that was so. My studies at university faltered, my own lectures reached my ears as nothing but garbled and weak transmissions from a higher fidelity source, and I kept to myself in a sort of cowed temper. But the temptation grew, the desire inflamed, and once more I prepared for a siege. I re-entered the mindscape, but this time in three-dimensions where I engaged in computation with spheres and cuboids until even *their* company was not enough and I progressed into the fourth, fifth, sixth dimensions – on and on, still – until it became increasingly harder to get back to this world and my body.'

'Why so?'

'Because it is hard to look at you now and not feel deprived of senses when even in the fourth dimension I could view you from every side at once.'

I wanted to take this as evidence of a particular esteem Cassius held for my physical person, but knew he was just using me to illustrate a point. Nodding my understanding, he went on.

'I had a plan in all this. I wasn't just amusing myself on some wild trip. I had formulated a scheme for getting the most out of it. Here was a world of pure mathematics. One progressed from simple equations to more complex ones by working through them as you or I might figure a sum in our ...' Cassius looked at me speculatively. 'Well, in your case, on paper.'

Cassius stopped and tilted the lamp so that it lit my face. He scrutinised me closely. I only smiled and blinked. Satisfied, he let the lamp rest flat again.

'Sorry, what I meant was, well, to begin with, all the maths was pretty abstract, pretty unrelated to the real world. I think that's why so many kids are put off it at school: by bad teachers who just make them go through number-crunching exercises. They don't try to show them how it relates back to life.'

'That was my problem,' I admitted. 'Couldn't see what my seven-times-table had to do with anything, but thought Mr Verne's *Twenty Thousand Leagues Under the Sea* a jolly rum adventure.'

'Yes, yes, exactly,' said Cassius, thumping the chair and reminding himself of his corporeal body in the growing gloom, 'that's when maths gets exciting, when it has relevance to life. So, at last I managed to work my way through the maths every physics student knows. But then something came up. Remember earlier what I said about the great debate over whether mathematical laws are intuited or invented?'

'Yes, but you've proved they're discovered.'

'It's not so simple. You see, someone like Newton comes along and develops laws that describe the motion of the planets. They seem to fit. In other words, the model fits the matter. Someone wants to know where Pluto is at a given time of the year and he just needs to punch in the relevant data into Newton's equations and he'll know pretty accurately. But that's just it. Although very accurate, it's not one-hundred percent, and that's where doubt comes in.'

'Doubt of what?'

'Doubt over whether Newton hasn't managed merely to invent some pretty clever laws that can predict the motion of the planets – laws that one can superimpose over our solar system – but which don't actually underlie it.'

'But you've just said – '

'Wait a minute,' said Cassius, raising a finger, 'you'll see my point in a second.

'Two hundred years later and Einstein (you may not have heard of him yet but you will) comes up with *his* theories. They seem to fit the actual situation even better, and that's the key word, "fit", but are even they the final ones?'

I must have shown my confusion, for he elaborated.

'Listen, laws in physics are accepted if they fit the situation, but after a while anomalies and discrepancies surface. Newton's laws might have accounted for the general motion of the planets, but not for everything. So what do physicists do? They try to come up with new laws that still fit the situation but have even fewer discrepancies.'

His point dawned on me, and a question arose from my new understanding.

'I ... I thought physics built on itself in a steady way? One brick atop the other, so to speak. But you're saying, with each new theory, a whole wall's torn down?

'Yes.'

'So, in a way physics doesn't build on itself?'

'No.'

'It just fits the picture closer and closer each time?'

'Yes.'

'Well, now you've gone and confused me!'

Cassius smiled and reached for the bottle of port. I shook my head. Already my mind was spinning. He decided against it himself, and instead made a tent with his fingers.

'Henri, do you ever wonder what it's all about? Life, I mean?'

'Yes, sometimes.'

The tent collapsed to a prayer.

'So do I. *You* try to find out through your art, through literature, through music. *I* try to discover it through mathematics. I don't know if you can relate to this feeling, but sometimes the world seems so absurd, there must be a reason to it!'

'Yes ... Yes, I have felt that way.'

'Let me tell you this, then, Henri. In this mindscape of deductive reasoning, I resolved to work my way up every near-miss algorithm until I got to the final one, the last one, the one which described the whole universe, which fitted the universe perfectly, which explained away the purpose of it, the reason, and why we poor fools must be the ones to question why.'

'And have you done that?' I asked. I was leaning forward in my seat. Cassius leant back in his. Air puffed out from the leather in a sigh.

'Not yet. But I think I'm in a good position in which to do so.'

'Why do you say that?'

'It's funny, but do you know what physicists get up to? They look at physical systems, like the orbit of the planets, and they try to fit equations to them. *We've* got all the material stuff at hand; it's the maths we have to dig out. Well, in the mindscape, it's just the opposite. They've got all the algorithms; they've just got to decide what physical systems they might describe. So I'm in the best position, straddling both worlds. In other words, I can verify my data. I'm the first person to get outside the set.'

'Cassius, this is too good to be made up. You've told them, these mindscape creatures, that there are *actual* physical systems, haven't you?'

'Yes, but they don't believe me.'

'Ha!' I slapped my knee. Away in the distant card room, I heard the players break off their conversation, and immediately regretted being so demonstrative.

'That's torn it,' said Cassius. 'They'll be out here inquiring in a moment.'

And so they did. Memphis was terribly aggrieved when I gave him to understand that I had just heard the great revelation for which we had all been seeking. And me an artist! We went our separate ways soon after. It was nearly three in the morning.

For the next few days, I didn't manage to catch up with Cassius. No card nights had been scheduled and, besides, I didn't wish to renew the topic there. But with the daylight and the drudgery of painting – for it *was* work (nothing came to me in that interval) – divested of its book-lined dignity and ghost-story lighting, Cassius's story had already taken on the aspect of the absurd. I dreaded meeting with him, lest he laugh at me. A card night was eventually planned and I didn't go, lest the others were in on the jest also. Cassius left a wire, saying he had missed me at the club.

And then I had a dream. I suppose a few things had brought it on. One can always trace the threads in the day that have inspired the dream at night, but the two major influences were still the talk with Cassius and a growing faithlessness in my work. Nothing seemed to be going right. Every brushstroke had to be laboured for, nay, fought. And here was

Cassius, if his story were true, given free access to the fabric of existence. The dream was this:

I woke into a world that contained everything great in ours. The *Sagrada Familia* was there, finished, as if Gaudi had seen to the laying of the last stone. (At the time, I was frequently travelling propelled by a wanderlust I couldn't then or now explain.) There were other great buildings and artwork, too. Even that which had been made, and was great, but had been destroyed, exists in this dream world, as do those great works that are yet to be made. Gods wandered about these buildings, regarded these paintings, listened to this music, and watched these strange art forms that moved like windows, and experienced yet others not yet invented.

For some reason, I had been brought to this place, as a curio perhaps. I asked one of these tall slender gods what it all meant. He or she (it was impossible to decide the gender), said they had made earth so that earthlings could make art.

'Why,' I asked, 'if you can make a planet and set it in a universe, could you not make the art yourselves?' The god replied that only mortals living amid the imperfect could ever dream of the perfect, and thus make art. For art was always an improvement on reality, and found meaning and structure where there was none. I asked this god for one last favour.

'Could you tell me if any of my artwork has been decreed truly great and thus found a place on this world, the double and dream of ours?' The god said he/she would inquire, but to wait in the meantime till he/she returned. I had stood for only a few seconds when I awoke.

Devastated.

Nonetheless, I caught a motor car to Cassius's house, intent on forgetting my brief suspicions and relating the dream.

When I got there, I found him in bed in a shocking state. He had deteriorated severely since I had last seen him. He was incredibly weak from neglecting his body. I fed him a little – apparently he had just come out of a stay in the mindscape. He seemed pleased to see me, and his desert-dry lips parted a little.

'We're almost there, Henri.'

Is it …? Do you think it will …? I mean, is it going to be good news?'

Cassius smiled in understanding.

'Well, it's more amazing than any earthbound mind thought up.'

Cassius gripped my hand. I told him my dream. He appeared to like it greatly and grinned.

'D'you know, my friend, I've never had a representational dream.'

'What do you mean?' I asked, puffing up the pillows behind his back.

'That's your jargon, isn't it? Representational? What I mean is, they've all been abstract and they've all been much the same.'

I gave him water to lubricate his speech.

'Everything's crisp to begin with. I can't explain it better than that. There are all these white lines on black but they're neat. Drawn with a ruler, so to speak. Forming a pattern. But then the pattern starts becoming complicated. Solids form, and then multi-dimensional shapes. After a second, everything becomes a mess. White rules. Before, all was silent; now, a great unmusical clanging predominates. But it is completely arhythmical. A bang here, a clang there, and then a pause. Followed by a rapid thudding, say. It's all very nightmarish and ... well ... the mess is total. Then I wake up.'

I fixed us a drink. Given the man's dreams, I wondered how he could let his kitchen get into such a state.

I stayed with him for the next few days, nursing him back to health. But we both knew it was a patch-up job. He was going back into the mindscape. One final time. He believed he was only a step removed from the 'big one'; the algorithm that explained everything and tallied with the physical universe in a perfect fit. The mathematics in agreement with the reality.

I feared the answer. For one, Cassius was already unable to explain the discoveries he had made, but he had imparted the nature of them. For a while it looked like everything was predetermined, and I churned out paintings mechanically. Later, it seemed that we had free will after all, and I jumped on the ferry one day to France to celebrate that I could act on a whim. Cassius was understanding and, appreciating the artist's modest income, paid for my fare back.

But the real answer we both feared was the ultimate meaning of life. We had both, in our antithetical ways of thinking, seen life as absurd, sometimes sickening. At moments it looked up at us as if from a puddle, with a malicious and maleficent leer. I couldn't decide what might be worse: an indifferent universe, content to let us stand or fall; or a malevolent one, intent upon the latter. Or, perhaps, a benevolent universe, the option least likely to make sense. For why the random misfortune, the unpunished crimes? Perhaps that would constitute a schoolmaster universe, smugly teaching independence to kids through random punishments and rewards.

And why the present set-up, of worlds, moons and stars? Of solar systems, galaxies and universes? And why we, humans, alone in it all?

Whilst attending to my personal matters one afternoon, I ran into Memphis. He inquired, rather bluntly I thought, whether Cassius was dying. When I answered that it was a strong possibility, he seemed strangely pleased!

'Tell me, my pet, are you two growing *closely*?'

I didn't at all like the intonation.

'Ah, from the way you recoil, I see that you haven't. At least, not as far as I fear.'

Again, his horrid insinuations.

'What do you mean?' I demanded, not one to let myself be intimidated with scandal and libel of an Oscar Wilde nature.

'Tell me, Henri, you still nurse the belief that you fell in love with an engaged woman, Ms Rena Denori, in your late teens, and, even with the event of her marriage, have never been able to love another woman since?'

I was nearly speechless with anger.

'I hold Signora Denori in the highest regard, I'll have you know. And Signor Denori himself, if you don't mind.'

'Then I see that you do,' returned Memphis. 'In that case, I have nothing to fear from you.'

Fear? Again this talk of fearing me.

'Envy, more like,' I counted. '*I* am the one privy to the magnificent confession.'

'Oh, that,' and his laugh unpleasantly resembled a cat yawning.

I hurried back to Cassius.

After a long, languorous meal we both wished to stretch further, Cassius lay down to enter the mindscape. It was to be his last journey; we both knew that. It was therefore incumbent upon me to relay to the world his last finding, the one that would put paid to all further search and inquiry. I felt sick with the responsibility. Cassius managed a dry smile before closing his eyelids, and they fell with such heaviness that I wondered how he had kept them open for so long. After having gained in dimensions each time he travelled to the mindscape, he came back to our mere three more and more like a cripple each time. He said he couldn't move in our world. It was too … too messy. Where was the simplicity in it?

And that, I knew, was the horror. The world is jagged. I don't just mean at its edges, but in its make-up. I leaned back in my wicker-chair. Sleep crawled up from a well and took me in. When the bucket hit, I dreamt another dream to make me fear that I, too, was descending into a private hell.

The dream was this:

I owned a studio, the sort one expects an artist to have. There were great arches, pointing onto blackness, curtains suspended in illogical order from the rafters, and all manner of antiques and oddments scattered about. I stood at my easel, brush in one hand, palette in the other, and set about capturing my subject, the one and only inestimable Cassius. He sat, as he seemed always to do, in semi-darkness. But the blacks weren't solids; they were spaces. I tried to paint him but I failed. I searched for the reason. I conjectured several. The most believable concerned scale. I had only attempted a miniature portrait of Cassius. Obviously, this would not be enough. The man was bigger. I embarked on a full-length painting, no cropping of legs or arms, but on completion I realised that it, too, had somehow failed to capture the man I knew. Again I looked for a reason. I saw immediately that my portrait had only caught Cassius from one angle. That, too, was inadequate. The man was multi-faceted.

To solve the predicament, I settled on recreating him in a full-length sculpture. 2D effects were thrown over for three. I was ascending in worlds as Cassius had done. With the last piece of clay pushed into shape, I stood back from my work then compared it with its source, Cassius, still sitting in the dark, and realised, once again, my failure. I had only caught the surface of my subject. Pushing my sculpture to the floor, I yelled and cursed. Cassius looked on, amused. I had him pose naked so that nothing was concealed, but even that only went skin-deep.

Next I invented a contraption that could photograph people's innards, so that I could start, in some crazy occult way I barely understood, with the bare bones, and build up the identity from there, yet only succeeded in making a Russian doll. Finally, I began at the level of atoms as described by Democritus, finding a kind of key for the man's makeup, and from that, by some mystical process, was able to create a double. But even that didn't work. It still wasn't him. At last, in desperation, I took my brush and signed the original: Cassius himself. The next day he posed for someone else and I was left with a copy.

I awoke from this dream in fight. Cassius had risen, white as light, and grabbed my arms. I looked into his eyes, clouded with anguish. But then they cleared, and light shone through. Cassius breathed out. A room aired after stale months.

'Yes, yes, thank God,' he said.

I took his head. 'What is it?'

'There are more fundamental laws to come, Henri. Thank God they weren't it! This is the final theory now. I can see it.'

And with that, Cassius slipped back into his world of sums and figures. I sweated all over, even on my palms. Cassius was about to discover the scientific principles that could not be explained by deeper principles. In short, the final theory. I pulled from my breast pocket the notebook I had come to carry whenever in the man's presence.

Cassius's face twitched and tightened to unnatural pulses. His features comprised a study of concentration. Every muscle and nerve tightened till I thought his face would tear apart. And then a sudden slackening of tension. A release. Bliss, such as of the type one might experience on gaining ascendancy into heaven. Every fear drained out of me with the ecstasy and relief on Cassius's face. I felt, for the first time in my life, what I could only suppose to be a religious rapture. Cassius's smiling lips, though inflamed like a cut that hasn't yet bled, gave me to hope – to believe – that I was loved, that the universe, perhaps even a god, cared with many times more, and much less self-interested passion, in *me*. Me, Henri! Whatever the final theory, it lit up Cassius's face, not from any external source (the room had grown strangely dark), but with an internal light, shone from deep within.

And then, just as suddenly, it was switched off.

'You did it!' I howled.

Cassius nodded, slowly, painfully. The effort seemed to break bones in his neck. I could see he was near death. Was there an afterlife? Even that would be answered. But there was something more important I had to confirm first. He said he had seen the final theory coming, his expression of victory seemed to confirm as much. But he had been mistaken before. So far none of the mathematics had ever quite fitted with the universe. Though each successive one had drawn closer, so far none was the perfect fit. Was this the one?

'Is it right? Is it right?' I cried. 'Is it the whole answer, the complete, simplest mathematical description of absolute existence? The final theory?'

'Yes, yes,' he rasped, 'the mathematics is faultless and so … so beautiful.'

For a moment his face came over in the most heavenly radiance but then it darkened. I could see there was a qualification. It was written in his brow.

'What's the problem, then?'

'The mathematics tallies perfectly …' he moaned, the deepest grief in his voice.

I was nearly mad with suspense. 'Well, what then? Why that horrid look?'

'The physics are beautiful beyond imagining, Henri.'

'Yes? But?'

Cassius breathed out his last words. 'It's the world that doesn't fit.'

Ho hum, never mind. It's time we returned to the Henri of the present-day, the above considerate and levelheaded incarnation being quite anathema to his modern Melbourne character. It's okay to be narrow-minded. The self is the only person who counts.

Grip your pillow tight. My day is your long, dark night!

Chapter Twelve

Home, a backpack!

Henri's travels in November, 2005.

Went to a do in Leipzig today. Just can't get away from these East German parties. Some man was eyeing me up, very cute, but ...

East Germany! Been here a week now ... Where was I before that? Prague. Prague's beautiful, the so-called 'Paris of the East'. The old part has been faithfully restored to exacting Disneyland standards (with EU money) and, exactly like Disneyland, it's overflowing with tourists. By my last day there, I realised I was no better than any of the other three million who go there every year. The equivalent of $20 for a taxi from the airport to my hostel, 60 cents on public transport for the same journey back. That is the difference between the visitor and the local's experience of a place.

Unfortunately, being in Prague was no better than watching a documentary on the city, since there was no one to share it with …

Shame Rena ended up not coming — especially with it being her tickets and all. I gather her new man put the hard word on her, judging from the text message she sent me.

So here I am in East Germany alone! A tourist still, a tourist perpetually! Wouldn't mind getting some skiing in, though it's not really the season for it here.

Caught a train out of the land of wieners today — might as well see this trip through to the end. Never thought I'd hear myself say that.

A quick dip across to France.

France? Why did I choose there?

Paris is as beautiful as Prague, though the French would swap that sentence around, if they conceded the comparison at all.

I stayed in the Moroccan section, and had a quick squiz at Oscar Wilde's grave. The visit felt strangely personal, as if I'd once known him, or at least shared some of the same troubles. Later that day, I was in a café, enjoying a much-too-rich patisserie, and someone had left a brochure with a picture of a ruined castle. It was actually the name of it that caught my eye: Machecoul. Where had I heard that before?

Ah yes! The place Cassius raved about. Home to Bluebeard, the Sire de Retz. A fantastic little story but apparently the place is real. I checked how far away it was.

Another train ride, this time not so fast, and overnight in a little B&B, then I headed out in the morning. Actually, it was as if my feet walked themselves to take me to a spot that was basically a crossroads with high green grass around it.

And there it hit me: either Cassius had finally got to me or I *had* actually been there before. The feeling of déjà vu, and of actually *remembering* was far too strong for any other explanation.

A flash of a woman in furs. A knight. A breastplate and toga. Roman soldiers. Swords flying. My father and mother fettered, myself tossed into a bag. A long journey to Pompeii. Then me as a present to him, Cassius.

The strongest smell of fire and burning flesh shot right up my nostrils, with not a whisper of smoke to be seen anywhere, nor any sign of recent fire. I looked up into the sky, unseeing, and a single image filled my head: me hanging from the left side of a scaffold, Cassius from the right, and the Sire de Retz between us! The hangman cut the cords round our necks and we fell into the burning cauldrons built to receive our doomed bodies.

The vomit rose in my throat. I turned from the crossroads, not to see, not to feel, and suddenly it was all I could do not to roll myself on the ground to quench the flames that were burning me up.

Cassius wasn't lying.

I *have* had past lives!

Three days and nights now of reliving remembered moments, each of them becoming more painfully personal. At last, in hope of an exorcism, I returned to the crossroads and sat myself down in the long green grass and, there, opened myself to every memory that stirred. After sitting some time, the thought came to me: in all my lives till now I have been travelling to find where I came from, and it was here. This was the home I had been searching for, and the reason I constantly left Cassius.

I was wrong because even there at Machecoul, I could almost recall a life before that one.

Now as I sit alone in a café in Venice (I've moved on again!), I have at last reached the heart of the matter: places aren't significant in themselves. Places only come alive through the people in your life. Melbourne is a great city. Great because it contains Cassius, and Cassius means something to me. Everything.

I've decided. I'm going home.

There was an oddly familiar man on the train who kept staring at me. He looked like a used-car

322

salesman. But I'd actually been listening to him talk to other passengers and I was impressed by how he could switch in an instant from French to Italian to German to English. And there was *something* about him that made me answer very readily when he spoke.

'Ah, excuse me, you are … let me see if I can pinpoint the accent; it is quite mixed … Australian!'

'Yes.'

I was very impressed. I told him my name.

'And yours?'

'Mephisto.'

I took him for an eccentric.

We got talking, as you do on trains. A bit about his life, a bit about mine. He told me he was heading to the Alps for some skiing. I told him I'd be flying Paris to Melbourne in two days' time. That I'd tried (with no luck) to change to an earlier flight, so was now at a loose end for a couple of days. He insisted he would take me skiing – I'd mentioned it was a passion of mine, when I could afford it. He even offered to lend me skis.

Oh well, he did seem to be rolling in money and he was oddly cute, so I said yes, and gladly.

I flew across the slope, a great big cracked pavlova. Maybe the markers had been changed. And … I fell.

When I came to, it was either night or I was completely snowed under. I scrabbled at the snow till I could get myself on my feet and was glad when I saw my backpack in the dim light. I picked it up okay, only ... I could feel it already on my back!

It was like I'd found a copy.

I struggled down the slope, thinking to find Mephisto — or anyone. There was something in the snow. A body. No matter the times I grabbed it, I could not haul it up to the light. In trying to grab it, I seemed to end up hugging myself. Something was terribly, terribly wrong. I searched the poor guy's parka and pants pockets. His clothes were very like my own, his pockets filled with the same things as in mine. Same wallet, keys, mobile.

Part of the snow shelf fell. Not *next* to, or *on* me, but *through* me. The light got in, revealing the face of the corpse. It was mine.

Henri!

I don't know if you've ever seen a grown man cry, but cry I did. Whole oceans. And not just over my *death*, but over my *life*. Cassius was right. Cassius has always been right. If we die in surroundings to which we are intimately attached ... our home ... then we will not immediately fly into the body of a newborn but remain ... remain as ghosts to wander, perhaps for centuries. My backpack was my home. It contained my history. It bought me time before my next life would begin.

There, in the snow, I thought: how will I ever tell Cassius that in the next life I will wait for him? Yet there is *some* hope! I can take my home *with* me, or at least the phantom copy now on my shoulders.

I struggled on and soon was crawling out of what I only then realised was a large crevasse. Still I pressed on, but only moments later, heard a noise behind me and when I looked back I saw the crevasse had caved in, burying my physical self – at least till the start of summer. Good. Less likely anyone will find me just yet. But that doesn't give my ghost self long to get back to Cassius. When they find me, they'll surely separate me from my backpack and that will mean …

Next day, I caught the plane to Melbourne, taking an empty first class seat. Only time I'm ever gonna get that luxury. All the way, I was hoping I would be able to communicate with Cassius when I found him. After all, he could look in the mindscape, and what was I now, if not mind alone?

Then Cassius' house. Somehow, through some superhuman effort (and perhaps a good deal of medication) he had dragged himself outside and into his car. He was pulling away that very moment. I dived through the door to sit next to him. I called out, yelled, touched him – nothing. Left my head resting against his shoulder. He rubbed it once or twice – because of me? Cassius, at least, should have been attuned to the mindscape.

My despair was terrible. I shook off my sadness enough to discover his destination. The building where I'd lived – a cyclopean tombstone. He tottered in, finding his way to my door. It was unlocked, the place empty. He wandered about, having to rest often and throwing up once. No one anywhere – except poor old Bertrand Pale. And this was the hardest thing to believe: he was still standing at the landing. Cassius hauled himself up the steps. I walked with him, but I was no protection. He approached Bertrand, Bertrand in his coat.

Bertrand was dangling from a chain, the chain for his dog Winnie tied to the railing above. His toes floated a centimetre above the floor. He was dead – presumably had been dead that whole time. He wasn't standing; he was hanging, and no one noticed.

My relief when Cassius at last returned to his car was short lived. For he drove to a doctor's surgery. The man looked on deaths' door.

The receptionist blinked several times as if she had just awoken at the door opening. She told Cassius to enter the consulting room. I took a seat and waited. When Cassius emerged from the consulting room, he spoke sarcastically to a man who had been sitting across the room from me.

'Here to offer support, are you, Memphis?'

Memphis!

I looked and saw it was Mephisto, the man from the train, whose suggestion of skiing ultimately led me to my snowy demise. So *that's* Memphis. Hang on … Then he must've … that shortcut he told me, across the slope … he knew of the crevasse! Perhaps even removed the warning sign! Henri, you fool.

I belatedly realised I *had* seen him before, when he raced me from the train station to the flats those many months back.

'Is the prognosis not good, Cassius?' purred Memphis, rising to his feet. 'Months, weeks? Such a shame that the mindscape is so taxing on the health.'

Cassius feebly tried to leave but Memphis easily barred his way.

'You know, Cassius, all this time I haven't been trying to stop you from finding the final theory. That is only halfway to recognising the gap between the actual and the ideal. And *I*, Cassius, am that gap. That is all you have discovered. Me. But how to crush me – that is the real knowledge. And the only way, my friend, is to make the conception the reality.'

Cassius was swaying unsteadily on his feet.

'I don't understand. I was developing a physics to help humanity avoid its mistakes.'

'Yes, but your physics tolerated the stupidity of people. It was a repair-job. Now had you derived a mathematics from *perfection*, that would have been more worrisome. A calculus from not the physical world, but the conceptual world as it is imagined through perfect works of art – Henri's especially. Don't you see, you could have extrapolated from your equations to form a physics describing a whole, new, harmonious way of life? What is the use of describing and delineating how bad something is? How few can put forward an alternative!'

'I don't understand.'

'Cassius, my fear was never that you might find out how the world *works* …'

Cassius completed the sentence.

'… but how it *should*.'

'Bravo! Oh you humans, you make it so easy for me!'

Memphis turned and walked to the door, but … on the way he turned to … to *me*, and looked me in the eye. That meant …? He could see me! He'd known I was there the whole time!

He winked. And I knew exactly what that wink meant.

'I got you!'

On the news: Arab and Israeli negotiations at a standstill; the West relinquishing further freedoms to feel safe from terror; security tightened globally; skulduggery at the International Criminal Court.

Cassius turns off the TV and stares at the blank screen.

The phone rings.

He picks it up, listens and nods.

I lean in close and hear the caller's voice —
European-sounding: '... and I am sorry to tell you, but
he is passed on.'

'Thank you.'

Cassius puts down the phone.

So my body has been found. Probably thawing out
in the morgue now. Any minute, they'll separate me
and my backpack ... my home! And then ... then I'll be
sucked into a new life.

Cassius makes his way slowly to his study and I
follow. He walks purposefully to his sarcophagus,
opens it and runs one hand over the inside wall with
its photographic history of his life. How well I
remember him showing it to me and explaining how
the slow decomposition of his body in this tomb of
memories would allow him to gradually enter the
next life whilst still remembering the last. His hand
comes to rest for a moment on a picture of me.

Where is he dragging his sarcophagus? Outside.
He throws off the lid, wheezing in pain.

He's stumbled back inside.

Comes out again with papers and his laptop. Drops
them into the coffin, scrunching up the papers. I see
equations. Mathematical formulae. Cassius enters his
shed.

'What are you doing?' I ask, waving my hands at
him. My hands?

They are translucent! At this very moment, my body and backpack must be in the process of being separated.

I know what he is doing.

Cassius emerges, petrol tin in hand.

'Cassius, please!'

He pours out the tin's oil, which is now more solid than I.

'Cassius, no! Don't. Please don't.'

He throws in the match; a bath of fire.

As it burns I feel myself burn away.

For the first time, entering my new life, I would remember the previous one while Cassius would forget!

But *I* would remember.

Oh, how I would remember yet.

And so with that, my dear friends, we arrive at the end of our tale. Which isn't to say it is over, because there is still the beginning. But first you want to know who am I, that I am privy to so many journals, letters and thoughts?

A little biography, then.

Some say I was born in the Manichean desert, others remember a time when I slithered on my belly, or concur with Plato who saw me as shadow, or speak of the Council of Constantinople. I myself have memories of a superstition darting into the recesses of cave walls.

I have long since realised that I exist only because humans allow me to. To discover that one is not a creature of the flesh, but of the mind, is a most powerful stimulant to survival. Through the ages, I have waned in one country, only to wax in another, but never have I had my existence seriously threatened. I represent the gap between the ideal and the actual, between one soul and another.

Oh you humans, do you think I don't want to be stopped?

I have grown foppish and conceited for lack of real opposition, even allowing bodies and movements potentially harmful to my existence to flourish.

But the likes of Cassius and Henri ... well ... these unions of love that last through life and beyond – however imperfectly – these are what I most fear. There is nothing so shocking, so beastly, or hateful to the imagination than to encounter another's happiness, particularly when it is a happiness that you yourself cannot partake in.

And so we arrive at the beginning, which is also the end, for that is your history, you humans.

The Gospel According to Judas.

Jerusalem, 33 A.D.

Wednesday 18th February.

My name is Judas Iscariot, son of Simon Iscariot. I hail from Kerioth, which is in Moab, twelve leagues south of Hebron. Like my father I am – *was* – a moneylender until Jesus made me treasurer of his apostolic band.

It's been two days since I joined Jesus of Nazareth, becoming one of his disciples. Two days. Oh, I know he was not keen at first, I know that. I sought him out in the market when Peter informed me a great prophet had come. But I had heard of this prophet earlier. Much earlier.

From Cassius Azouly and Henri Besaïd.

When Cassius and Henri went to receive the teachings of Jesus, Jesus said unto them that the kingdom of heaven was on earth. The two puzzled on this, and wondered how such could be possible when the earth smacked of hell. Jesus replied, 'I tell you this: whatever you forbid on earth shall be forbidden in heaven, and whatever you allow on earth shall be allowed in heaven.' And so Henri painted such marvellous visions of heaven that Cassius took inspiration from Henri's art, and set about devising a way this utopia should come to pass.

I offered to lend money for their venture in the hope that it would succeed in my lifetime. But they would not trade, saying there was no place for money in the kingdom of heaven.

It rankled with me, aggrieved me, the way they shunned my offer. But I did not let on that I was offended. Until an enemy knows he has got to you, he hasn't won. My face was a mask. They hadn't got me yet.

And so – and so this is what I did: I asked them to take me to Jesus who, as the originator of this thought, would surely be the better person with whom to trade. I didn't let on that this was why I wanted to talk with him, and they didn't let on that they guessed.

Then I nearly ruined things straight away. I practised my speech in my head on the way but still nearly ruined it. He is an imposing-looking man, this Jesus. Very imposing. Neither over-tall nor short, but the eyes, intense, and the voice, firm.

We were standing by the water, his hungry followers and disciples goading the sea to surrender its fish.

'Are you the last prophet,' I asked, 'or is there still another to come?'

The look he gave me, oh the look! But it wasn't such an impertinent question, was it? I don't want to follow the penultimate messiah now, do I?

'What is the kingdom of heaven like?' I asked.

The others spoke up, 'Yes, tell us what it is like, Lord.'

'If you have ears, then hear,' Jesus said unto us all. 'The kingdom of heaven is like a treasure lying buried in a field. The man who found it buried it again; and for sheer joy went and sold everything he had, and bought that field.'

So today I have sold everything I have that I might buy this field when Jesus has shown it me. Because he's inspired me, he has. Inspired. I've always been afraid, you see. Afraid of death.

Saturday 21st February.

Five days since I joined Jesus' band of disciples. Five. And still no sign of this field of heaven. The Pharisees and Sadducees question him on scripture, trying to catch him out. But he is clever, and can't be captured. I can see that.

We have now left Galilee and come into the region of Judaea across Jordan. Great crowds follow and more gather along the way. They bring their children, and Jesus lays his healing hands on these, then goes his way. I am certain his way will lead to the field of heaven; and I hope soon, since my moneybags are heavy beneath my cloak, and my feet sore with walking.

The others, he clearly prefers — Matthew, Peter and Mark. That is obvious. But today I helped him up a slope and he gave me a smile, and I could see they were jealous. My heart is light with knowing I go toward the light.

Sunday 22nd February.

Six days since I sold all I owned and took up with Jesus and his eleven. Six days. I am being worn down, and not just with money and walking. Jesus is holding out on me. On us! His twelve disciples. But *they* can't see it; only *I* can.

Imagine this, if you will. We were nearing Jerusalem when a richly dressed man intercepted Jesus on the road and asked, 'Master, I have heard of your teachings. What must I do to attain eternal life?'

'Keep the commandments.'

'I have kept the commandments,' answered the man.

That, I had also done, and was relieved.

But still the man asked, 'Shall I gain eternal life?'

I laughed, but the master was silent.

'Where have I fallen short?' cried the man.

Jesus pushed him aside, and continued to walk, yet he still addressed the man over his shoulder.

'If you wish to attain heaven, go, sell your possessions, and give to the poor, and then you will have riches in heaven.'

The heaviness of my heart, along with the heaviness of my moneybags, nearly dragged me to the ground. I have sold my possessions, but now I am to give that money to the poor!

Monday 23rd February.

Seven days now. Seven. But today has not gone so well. The others he likes: Peter with his amusing whining; Thomas with his gentle humour; Matthew and Mark especially for their lightness of demeanour. But me? I mentioned that joke, that Samaritan's joke. He did not laugh. He never laughs. He sees that nothing is funny.

He says things, but things no man can follow.

'A camel may sooner pass through the eye of a needle than a rich man enter heaven ...'

He said this today, knowing full well of my wealth. It was disguised as a generalisation but I knew it alluded to me. He knows he's getting to me. That is, neither one knows for certain that the other knows, but we certainly suspect. It's wearing me down.

Peter spoke up: 'We have left everything to become your followers, oh Lord. What will there be for us?'

Jesus answered, 'Only when you have nothing will you attain all.'

This seemed to satisfy Peter and the others, but not me; I'm not so sure. Jesus hooked me with his eyes.

'Judas, the walk will be easier if you are not weighed down.'

He knows! He must have seen the moneybags beneath my cloak. But I didn't let on that I knew he knew. I nodded solemnly, as if he had just voiced another of his weighty proverbs. I couldn't have the others knowing of my money. I couldn't sleep then, wouldn't, though I doubt that Jesus would ever take it from me in the night. He couldn't risk being caught with it on him, not when he talks of hypocrites so often.

Tuesday 24th February.

Today I gave away my money. All of it. It hurt me, it did. Hurt. But I did it. To the beggars and prostitutes Jesus likes so much. I told him of my deed, in front of the other disciples. They had given away all they owned long before, save the shirts on their backs, but theirs was a minor sacrifice. I had been the richest among them.

Jesus looked at me across our campfire.

'When you do an act of charity, do not announce it with a flurry of trumpets, as the hypocrites do to win the admiration of men. Your Father who sees what is done in secret will reward you.'

'I ... what ...?'

'You cannot serve God and Money.'

Wednesday 25th February.

Nine days. Nine! It is becoming very dangerous for me. Oh, I knew it would be so, but still I didn't really *know*. Not danger like this: real, in the pit of your stomach. The Pharisees are upset and will try to turn the Romans against us. So little I know but I do know this: the Romans do not interfere in religious matters of conquered lands. I should be safe on this, at least.

Today was the limit. The limit, I tell you! It was midday, and we had just completed a long trek – Sadducee, no food, none of us complaining – when we walked past a beggar. A measly beggar, whom we ignored (one has to; they are everywhere). I offered assistance to Jesus, boasting I could provide him with all he could want: food, a home, and an end to this ceaseless journeying, if he would but take me with him into the afterlife. I needed only to borrow some money from a moneylender and I would soon rebuild *my* 'kingdom'.

Jesus stopped, but it was not to respond to me. He was looking past – no, *through* – me. I turned to see at what. And standing there was the beggar, now accompanied by two men. I recognised them immediately, as the two charlatans who had started me on this fruitless quest: Cassius and Henri! They were giving the beggar some of their food and clothing, even though they did not look like they had much food to begin with, and were poorly clad. Well then, so be it. As birds flock together ... as Jesus himself says.

But then the impossible happened. While me, Peter, Adrian, each competed with the life we could offer him, Jesus separated from us and approached the motley three.

Cassius and Henri turned and listened, quite astounded, as were we disciples, as Jesus thanked them! Yes, *them*! They asked why he was thanking them when they had done nothing for him. And it was the same question I, too, would have asked had disbelief so effectively silenced me. Jesus disagreed with the two. 'When I was in trouble, you fed me; when I was hungry, you took me in; and when I needed protection, you offered me shelter.'

What was this? What new and twisted reasoning of the so-called prophet? Even clever Cassius and fey Henri were astounded.

Henri said to Jesus, confused, 'But when did we do these things for you?'

Jesus – the twist-in-the-tail ready – responded by pointing to the beggar, and saying, 'I tell you this: anything you did for my brother here, however humble' – such condescension! – 'you did for me.'

The viper! Again, it was to slight me; again, to mock me to my face! He turned to us, his so-called disciples, his 'hangers-on'.

The boldest among us (Mark, Luke – not I, for I was hurt to the core by the base betrayal) questioned why the prophet was not showing *them* the same favour he was evidently bestowing upon Cassius and Henri. Surely we (the disciples – his disciples) had actually helped *him* in all the ways mentioned? We! Not some beggar!

And oh to those deceitful ways, that pretence of innocence, add this: the gesture, child-like, but only child-seeming, to the beggar, when Jesus said, 'I tell you this: anything you did not do for your brother here, however humble, you did not do for me.'

The ungrateful, ungrateful wretch! Henceforth, he is my enemy. Cassius and Henri also, for all that smiling the 'prophet's' words induced. I have been reduced to penury – and for nothing.

The others bowed, evidently humbled by this schoolmaster teaching. Or was it that they were merely embarrassed?

They will keep on trying, I know it. Oh they will keep on trying to be good enough for him, but they never will be so. No not them, not me, not anyone but *he* whom the prophet chooses!

Thieves and prostitutes and rogues — such as Cassius and Henri — they will receive his favour because only the bad are good enough.

Thursday 26th March.

Nearly two months, now. Two months. I hold my tongue. Mostly. He won't get me again, won't humiliate me. I know his game now, and though I don't let on, he knows I know. He's too sage (let's say crafty) not to, but neither one of us lets on. It's our game. I almost believe he wants me to betray him.

You see, I have had dealings with a Roman general, Memphis. To escape the same fate that awaits Jesus, I am to explain the loss of my fortune other than by the truth (that I gave it away), since surely that would identify me as one of Jesus' flock. Memphis is smart, very smart. He suggested I say my money was stolen; and recommended two people as the culprits. The Romans, however, are unwilling to move on the religious matter of Jesus until the rabbis proceed first. I am to be instrumental in this process.

No accomplice aids me. The other disciples are drawn in completely by Jesus' self-aggrandisement. Jesus says we disciples may even have to suffer death though we followed him only because we believed he would bring peace. And yet it seems they will welcome their demise as a privilege. The charlatan! I see how he works. He revealed himself completely today. If *I* had given myself away before to *him*, *he* unmasked himself entirely to *me*.

This is how it went. I was niggling at him. Mildly, but niggling all the same. Oh how he prattles and twists words and twists them again! But I see through this 'son of man' to the man within. Oh yes I do. This is what happened. I was questioning him on the point of when a man marries a second wife whether he will then have two wives in heaven. He argued the matter initially but then grew impatient. He brooks no dissent.

'If you love me you will obey my commands,' he said at last, as if that ended debate. Oh yes he *would* say that, so everything is always someone else's fault, not his. 'And anyone who loves me will heed what I say.' Oh, I see, *that's* how it works. Against tyranny, bah! This son of man supports it! 'He who does not love me does not heed what I say!' Now now, careful, don't reveal too much! 'He who is not with me is against me.' There, finally, nakedly, he has revealed himself – utterly! 'He who is not with me is against me.' That's how it goes with the son of man. Despot!

At first I had no faith because I questioned, next I did not love him because I disagreed, and now I am outright against him because I am not with him, but that was his choice, never mine. I would have been his first disciple. But this is his doing, my turning against him. His choice. He wants this way; he shall get this way. I'll get him, not he, me.

Secreting myself away from our camp after dark, I went to the chief priests.

The agreement was thirty silver pieces.

Friday 3rd April.

On the route to execution they seized a man called Simon, from Cyrene, on his way to the country. They put the cross on his back and made him walk behind Jesus, carrying it. Cassius and Henri carried their own.

Great numbers followed, who mourned and lamented Jesus. And when they reached the place of The Skull, not far from the city gate, they crucified him, and the criminals with him – Cassius on his right, and Henri to his left. Cassius and Henri screamed with the pain and fear but Jesus, brow glazed with sweat, only said of the centurions, 'Father, forgive them; they know not what they do.'

'Father?' cried Cassius when his cross was upright and fixed. 'If you are the Messiah, the Chosen one, then save yourself – and *us*!'

Henri pleaded with his friend: 'Cassius, have you no fear of God? We are paying the price for our misdeeds. This man has done nothing wrong.'

By now it was midday and a darkness fell over the whole of the land, which lasted until three in the afternoon. Then Jesus gave a loud wail and said, 'Father, into thy hands I commit my spirit,' and with these words he died.

Cassius and Henri took another two days to expire.

Joseph of Arimathaea asked Pilate for permission to take away the body of Jesus, and Pilate granted the request. Whereupon Joseph wrapped the body, with spices of myrrh and aloes, in strips of linen cloth according to Jewish burial custom. Having so prepared, he then laid him in a tomb freshly carved into rock, with all the customary ritual.

The bodies of Cassius and Henri rotted on the cross till they fell away, their bones desiccated by the sun and broken amid the rocks.

Oh dear me, yes, my good man Judas Iscariot remembered all these happenings well, but not quite so well as all that. Cassius and Henri would indeed have lingered on another two days beyond Jesus' death but, being not so insensitive as people assume, I struck their legs below the knees with rocks, breaking the bones. It is not so well known now, but it was then, that the practice hastens death, since the victim can no longer rest on the sedile and so the blood rapidly pools to the lower half of the body. I did not, however, smash the knees of the man between them. Let him martyr himself, I averred. Martyrs, as I have always maintained, prove nothing.

Judas Iscariot, of course, hanged himself, as he would do in countless later incarnations – indeed, as he did in the life when he was known as Bertrand M. Pale.

As Cassius and Henri (legs broken and hanging from their nails) slipped into their final sleeps – or not so final sleeps as we now know! – their words were uncommonly touching despite their pathetic ring.

'Henri, will you love me in the next life?'

'Yes.'

'And if we were to die and be reborn again and again, would you go on loving me?'

'Forever, Cassius.'

'Forever and ever?'

FOREVER HUMAN

Author's Acknowledgement

Like I write in the preface, this book borrows from many long-dead writers in keeping with its main theme of humanity's past very much encumbering its present. I hoped to avoid naming those references so as to leave it to the keen reader to tease them out. However, since that might have left me open to the charge of failing to cite sources, I hereby reluctantly list them, thus dispelling part of the puzzle I intended with this tale.

Unsurprisingly, there are echoes, and sometimes direct quotes, from many writers throughout the book, and some affectionate homages of their styles, too. These writers principally include Edwin A. Abbott, Fyodor Dostoyevsky, Max Beerbohm, Emily Brontë, Mikhail Bulgakov, Henry James, Franz Kafka, Jonathon Swift, Jean-Paul Sartre, William Shakespeare, H. G. Wells and Ludwig Wittgenstein.

Certainly, three chapters borrow much more heavily. The Pompeii sections in Chapter Three owe considerably to my reading of the excellent Penguin Classics editions of the poetical works of Catullus, Horace, Martial, Ovid and the histories of Pliny the Elder and Pliny the Younger.

In Chapter Seven, much is freely adapted – and sometimes whole chunks directly lifted – from Sabine Baring-Gould's excellent abridgement of the Sire de Retz case (The Book of Werewolves, first published 1865). His work in turn owes a debt to M. Michelet's biography of de Retz, which was taken from M. Lacroix's sketch of the scandal, which in turn was taken from the abstract of the case ordered by Ann of Brittany. So it goes (to quote Vonnegut).

Frequent parlays aside, the final chapter borrows less heavily, but borrows nonetheless, from the New English Bible. 'The New Bible Dictionary' (organising editor, J. D. Douglass, London Inter-Varsity Press, 1962) was a helpful aid.

Equally, the wonderfully inventive supersolid concept belongs to the mathematician William P. Love, published 1989, a fact I also acknowledge within the body of the book.

Reference sources include 'Handbook of Magic & Witchcraft,' (Charles W Oliver, first published 1928, Rider & Co), 'The Origin of Popular Superstitions and Customs' (T Sharper Knowlson, first published 1930, Werner Laurie Ltd), and 'The Vampire' (Montague Summers, first published 1928 by Kegan Paul, Trench, Trubner & Co, Ltd). All three of these books, and the one by Sabine Baring-Gould, have been reissued by Senate, an imprint of Random House.

Even so, there may be a few omissions. Apologies in advance.

Rounding off, thanks must go to Ray Mooney who ran the novel writing course at Holmesglen TAFE, Melbourne, where this book first took shape in 2005; to Judie Litchfield's exacting edit, which was also something of an abridgement, with an unnecessary 12,000 words being excised; to Bryony Sutherland's follow up edit, which knocked the book into its present shape; and to my parents for their ongoing support and faith in my work.

Tom Conyers, 2013.